AMISH
LOVE LETTERS

Also by Shelley Shepard Gray, Charlotte Hubbard and Rosalind Lauer

An Amish Christmas Star

Also by Shelley Shepard Gray
Happily Ever Amish
Once Upon a Buggy
An Amish Cinderella

Also by Charlotte Hubbard
A Mother's Gift
A Mother's Love

Seasons of the Heart series
Summer of Secrets
Autumn Winds
Winter of Wishes
An Amish Country Christmas
Breath of Spring
Harvest of Blessings
The Christmas Cradle
An Amish Christmas Quilt

Promise Lodge series
Promise Lodge
Christmas at Promise Lodge
Weddings at Promise Lodge
New Beginnings at Promise Lodge

Light Shines on Promise Lodge
Family Gatherings at Promise Lodge

Simple Gifts series
A Simple Vow
A Simple Wish
A Simple Christmas

The Maidels of Morning Star series
Morning Star
First Light in Morning Star
Christmas Comes to Morning Star
Love Blooms in Morning Star

Also by Rosalind Lauer
Joyful River series
An Amish Homecoming
An Amish Bride
The Love of a Good Amish Woman

AMISH
LOVE LETTERS

SHELLEY SHEPARD GRAY
CHARLOTTE HUBBARD
ROSALIND LAUER

KENSINGTON
PUBLISHING CORP.

www.kensingtonbooks.com

KENSINGTON BOOKS are published by

Kensington Publishing Corp.
119 West 40th Street
New York, NY 10018

All Kensington titles, imprints, and distributed lines are available at special quantity discounts for bulk purchases for sales promotion, premiums, fund-raising, educational, or institutional use.

Special book excerpts or customized printings can also be created to fit specific needs. For details, write or phone the office of the Kensington Sales Manager: Kensington Publishing Corp., 119 West 40th Street, New York, NY 10018. Attn. Sales Department. Phone: 1-800-221-2647.

ISBN-13: 978-1-4967-4397-8 (ebook)

ISBN-13: 978-1-4967-4396-1

First Kensington Trade Paperback Printing: January 2024

10 9 8 7 6 5 4 3 2

Printed in the United States of America

Contents

A Love Letter Courtship

SHELLEY SHEPARD GRAY

I may speak in different languages of people or even angels. But if I do not have love, I am only a noisy bell or a crashing cymbal.

—1 Corinthians 13:1

The best time to do something worthwhile is between yesterday and tomorrow.

—Amish proverb

Chapter 1

January

"He's here, Jenni!" Mamm called out. "Where are you? We're all in the hearth room."

The announcement pulled Jenni from her musings with the force of a wrecking ball. Sitting on her bed, she struggled to feel even half as enthusiastic as her mother sounded about Matt's visit. "Okay."

"Okay?" Her mamm's incredulous tone drifted closer through the closed door. "Jenni, Matthew seems especially eager to see you tonight. Don't keep him waiting."

Jenni rolled her eyes. Heaven forbid she ever keep Matt Lapp waiting! Immediately embarrassed by her unkind thoughts, she got to her feet. "I'll be there in a minute, Mamm."

Her mother's footsteps paused right outside her door. "Hurry now. Kevin says Matt has some news to share."

News? Was tonight finally the special evening she'd been waiting for? The night her entire family had been waiting for? A burst of optimism filled her heart. Maybe Matt would say all the things she'd dreamed he would. Maybe, at long last, they could plan a future together.

"I'm hurrying. I'll be right out."

After opening her door, she realized she'd left her journal open on her bed. She closed it with a snap and returned it to its usual resting place—a pretty wooden box on the side of her bed.

She'd kept a journal for six years. Her parents had given her one when she'd turned fifteen. Mamm had said that all young women needed a place to store their secrets. And, since it was likely she'd be courted soon, she was surely going to have many.

Thinking back to those first months, Jenni sure did have a lot of secret thoughts. But most of them had been about how disappointed she'd been not to have a special beau.

Now that she'd just turned twenty-one, Jenni wished she could've given her younger self a talking-to. She should've spent more time concentrating on being grateful for her blessings instead of worrying why she wasn't the most popular girl at the Sunday singings. Everything happened in God's time. She knew that now.

Especially since she now had the perfect beau: Matt Lapp. Handsome, agreeable Matt. Her brother's best friend. He was blond and had dark green eyes. He worked at the lumberyard and made a fine living. Considering he'd never had too much in terms of guidance or parental support, they were all very proud of him. There had been a brief moment when everyone in her family had feared that he would jump the fence and none of them would ever see him again. Thankfully that had never happened.

Six months ago, seemingly out of the blue, he'd turned his attentions to her. It had been exhilarating and wonderful. She'd been so happy. Her whole family was happy.

But now . . . well, now she was kind of getting tired of his rather humdrum visits.

"Jenni, what are you doing?"

Startled to see her twin brother standing at her open bedroom door, she got to her feet. "Sorry. I was just putting something away."

Kevin looked as if he believed that about as much as he thought a hurricane was going to hit them in the middle of Ohio. But, like the caring brother he was, he didn't argue. "Oh. All right. Well, come on, then. We've all been waiting for you."

"Is everything all right?"

Kevin shrugged. "I think so. All Matt said was that he had something to talk to you about."

Her heart suddenly felt as if it was about to beat out of her chest. Maybe he really was going to propose. "Hmm," she said.

Kevin threw an arm around her shoulders. "Hmm?" he teased. "That's all you have to say?"

Looking up at him, Jenni felt her insides warm. Kevin Miller was the best brother. He was kind and caring and patient with her. He'd always made her feel good about herself, even when she was at times so awkward she wasn't sure there was very much that was good.

When they were twelve she'd wondered how his brown hair and hazel eyes could look so attractive on him while on her it just looked so . . . average. Why couldn't the Lord have given her the perfect features and Kevin the serviceable, sturdy version?

Because that, unfortunately, was what she was. She wasn't especially slim, and her face wasn't perfect. Instead, she was passably pretty and mildly interesting. She was the type of girl who preferred to blend into the crowd. In short, she was kind of, sort of forgettable.

"There's nothing to say," she said as they approached the

roomy back porch. "You and I know Matt could have news of any sort."

"He could also be getting ready to ask a certain someone something pretty important."

"Do you know something I don't know?"

"Nee," he said just as they walked into the room.

Matt immediately got to his feet. "Hiya, Jenni."

"Hello, Matt." Aware of her parents and Kevin both looking on, she smiled at him. "I hope you are doing well."

"I am. It's gut to see you," he said as he sat down on the love seat. Next to her brother. On either side of them were her parents. Each was relaxing in a chair.

The only other place to sit was in the last empty space: a rather uncomfortable rocking chair that her great-aunt had given her parents on their wedding day. She perched on the edge of it and tried not to feel irritated that everyone had left it for her.

As soon as she sat down, her father winked at her. As if he knew something she didn't.

Her nerves kicked in again as she, her brother, and her parents all turned to Matt.

"What is your news, Matt?" Mamm asked.

Matt looked directly at Jenni, took a deep breath, and smiled.

Jenni smiled back, but inside, her heart was hammering. The truth was, she'd always thought Matt was everything she'd ever wanted, but now she wasn't quite so sure. She wanted something more than what he was giving her. She wanted a man who felt she was worth courting. Not one who simply wanted to be part of a family he especially liked.

She'd sure never thought her future husband would ask her to marry him in front of her brother and parents.

"Matt, just tell us!" Kevin called out.

"Sorry. I am excited, but it ain't earth-shattering news."

Jenni felt her heart deflate. It wasn't a proposal. But that was a good thing, right? When she realized Kevin and her parents were waiting for her to respond, she cleared her throat. "What is it?"

"I got a kitten."

This was his news? "A kitten?"

He smiled at her. "It's adorable. It's pure black except for a spot on its tail that looks like a heart."

Her father frowned. "It sounds odd-looking."

"Is it a boy or a girl?" she asked.

"A girl kitten. She's tiny and cute. You're going to love her, Jenni."

Since she liked cute, tiny kittens as much as the next person, Jenni reckoned he was right. Plus, she was tickled by the thought of big, strapping Matt holding a tiny, delicate kitten. "I'm sure I will. You should have brought her over."

"I didn't want to impose." He cast a look at her mother.

Mamm shook her head in mock aggravation. "Matt, you know you're practically family. You don't have to ask about bringing over a kitten for Jenni to see. Of course you may."

"I'll bring her next time, then."

"Do you have a name for her yet?" Daed asked.

He blushed. "Not yet."

Mamm chuckled. "Matt, you've got to name her something."

"I will. I . . . I guess I was hoping for a perfect name."

"It's just a cat, Matt," Kevin teased.

"I know." He slumped slightly.

"What about Valentine?" Jenni asked. "Or Heart?"

Matt smiled at her. "Which name do you like best?"

"Valentine."

"Then that's what I'll name her," he said. "My kitten's name is Valentine."

Jenni felt something shift inside her. Maybe it was hope. At last, they'd made a connection. Maybe they did have a future together after all.

Looking impatient, her father crossed his legs. "Was that the big news you had to share?"

"Jah."

"Now that that's taken care of, do you still want to go ice fishing tomorrow with Kevin and me?"

"Of course."

And then they were off and running. Discussing locations and supplies and thermoses. Eventually, her mother brought out snacks, and a full hour passed.

It was all very nice, but Matt hadn't proposed. He hadn't even come close.

Chapter 2

Matt had stayed at the Millers' house as long as he dared. Even though Hank and Beth Miller always acted as if he was part of the family, he definitely wasn't. From the time he'd met Kevin and Jenni on the first day of school, they'd been close friends. That had been more than enough, because their friendship had meant everything to him.

Now, of course, he was courting Jenni. Well, he was *trying* his best to do that. She was so far above him, Matt never knew what to say to her.

How could he tell her that he'd always had a crush on her but never had the nerve to admit it? Or that he'd liked the way she'd helped the younger children in the Amish school but had never mentioned that he noticed. Or that he admired the way she interacted with her parents. She let them shine and respected their words but also made sure to let her opinions be known. She had a gift for making everyone around her feel needed and important.

At least, she'd always made him feel that way.

What did he have to offer Jenni that she couldn't already get from her family? He couldn't think of a single thing. He came from a dysfunctional home, and that was putting it lightly. Not only was his father abusive and his mother needy and distant, but their parents also depended on Matt and his sister, Rachel, to support them. Most women looked for men who could offer them a stable, happy future. He had neither the means nor the experience to give her either.

Jenni could do so much better than him.

If he was being honest, Matt knew he wasn't giving himself enough credit. He was smart, and he was a hard worker. He also thought the world of Jenni. He didn't care that she was quiet or that a lot of their friends overlooked her or thought she wasn't all that pretty. He'd always thought she was.

Honestly, he was kind of glad all the other men in their circle of friends had never thought too much about her. If they had, they'd see what he did—that Jenni was head and shoulders above every other woman in Apple Creek. She was sweet. So sweet. Kind to everyone. Accepting of other people, even when they didn't have much. Like him and his sister.

They'd also see that her brown hair was glossy and smooth. He'd known her so long, he'd seen it down when he'd spent the night at their house. The last time he'd seen it, the ends of her hair had reached her shoulder blades. It was gorgeous. He'd always liked the way she was built, too. She was the feminine version of her brother—which was obvious, given that they were twins—but he loved the fact that she wasn't bone-thin and delicate-looking. He loved the thought of holding her in his arms and not being afraid of hurting her.

Not that he ever would.

Now that they were courting, he knew he should take her walking or on a buggy ride, or do something romantic with her outside their house. Sure, it was January, but they'd experienced some mild days recently. Mild enough to be able to bundle up and go for walks together.

But asking her for a walk in the early evening in the middle of winter seemed rather awful. She'd be shivering by the time they made it to the end of her driveway. In addition, he didn't have a courting buggy, so that was out of the question—unless he wanted to drive Jenni's family's buggy and horse.

Finally, whenever he did come calling, both Kevin and their parents acted as if it would be best to sit together. For the entire time. And when they were all together, Kevin and their parents led most of the conversations. Sometimes Jenni barely got more than a few words in. And usually they weren't actually directed at him.

To make matters worse, none of their conversations were in private.

Matt didn't know a lot about courting, but even he knew that was no way to sweep a woman off her feet. He didn't know how to change things, though. He was so afraid of losing Beth and Hank's respect that he never tried to see Jenni alone.

But it was becoming frustrating.

Now he was walking along with his hands stuffed in his pockets, preparing himself for what he might find at home. He and his older sister, Rachel, had learned that if they wanted anything good to happen, it wasn't going to come from their parents.

When he saw Rachel sitting wrapped in a blanket on the front porch steps, his heart stopped. The temperature was in the thirties, and it was dark. There was only one reason she'd be outside waiting for him. It must have been a really bad night.

"Hey," he said as he strode forward. "Rach, you okay?" He scanned her face. "Are you hurt?"

Her mouth tightened before she shook her head.

He didn't believe her. He sat down by her side. "Sure about that?"

She released a ragged sigh. "Jah. I mean, it's nothing."

Rachel was as good as he was at pretending the things that happened inside their house weren't all that bad. He hated that, and he knew her boyfriend, Caleb, felt the same way. More than once he'd seen Caleb pull Rachel off to the side when they were walking or into the barn just to make sure that the bruises she hid weren't serious.

What was ironic was that once, back when they were all in school and Rachel and Caleb were just fourteen, their teacher had caught him inspecting her. She'd made an example of them, practically giving the class an hour-long lecture about acting modestly. What Ms. Elizabeth had never taken the time to understand was that Caleb was checking Rachel for cuts and bruises, not sneaking kisses.

Hating the direction of his thoughts, he kicked out his legs and faced forward. Even though they'd long stopped pretending that either of them were fine, Matt had decided that dwelling on things they couldn't change wouldn't make anything better.

"I thought you were seeing Caleb tonight."

"I did." Her voice cracked.

Afraid she was more upset than he'd realized, he turned to face her. "What happened?"

She bit her lip.

"Rachel, tell me the truth. Did Caleb hurt you?"

"Of course not."

"Then, what happened?"

Please God, he prayed, *don't let them have broken up.* Caleb was a good man and Rachel adored him. But he'd sometimes gotten the feeling that maybe Caleb's family didn't feel the same way about her. There was also the fact that Caleb wasn't perfect. He was like every other twenty-year-old man. Sometimes he said or did things without thinking.

She chuckled. "Matt, what am I going to do with you? Even though you're two years younger than me, you love to act as my protector."

If he wasn't so worried about what she was holding back from him, he would have made a joke. Instead, he spoke from his heart. "You know I'll protect you any way that I can, Rachel."

All the humor in her eyes faded. "That's what I wanted to talk to you about."

"Just say whatever you need to say. We'll figure out how to deal with it then."

"Caleb proposed to me this evening. He asked me to marry him, and I said yes."

Matt stared at her for a long moment. *That* was what had gotten her so upset and worried?

Leaning close, Rachel nudged him with her shoulder. "Say something. You're making me worried."

At last he was brought out of his trance. He gently pulled her into his arms. "Congratulations. I'm mighty happy for you."

She pulled back so she could see his eyes. "Do you mean it?"

"Of course I do. Rachel, Caleb is a good man. I know he cares about you."

"He loves me. He told me."

He raised an eyebrow. "Are you in love with him?"

"You know I am."

"Then, that's all that matters, jah?"

She nodded. "Jah."

"This is happy news. Why were you afraid to tell me?" Before she could answer, he asked, "Does it have to do with his family?"

"Nee." Looking a little stunned, she added, "Matt, Caleb asked me in their hearth room. There were candles all around and a fire was burning bright. We were alone and he got down on one knee."

"He stepped up, hmm?"

"Stop. It was so romantic." She shivered, no doubt remembering how perfect the moment had been.

"Has he told his family yet?"

"That's what I'm trying to tell you. They were all in the other room, waiting for me to say yes. When Caleb called out to tell them the news, his mother brought out a cake!"

"She made an engagement cake already?" That seemed a bit presumptuous.

But Rachel was all smiles. "She did. And, John, Caleb's daed, said that they'd already spoken to him about remodeling the *dawdi haus*, so it will feel fresh and perfect when we move in. I'm so happy."

"It's everything you've ever wanted. I'm really happy for you."

It wasn't an exaggeration, either. When they were younger, they'd spent many nights talking about how they would one day leave the house where they'd known such unhappiness. Rachel used to say she wanted someone who would treat her better than their father. And now she had found that man.

"Danke. But I don't want you to worry. I told Caleb that we'd need to wait until you were settled and happy, too."

"No, you don't. There's no reason for you to wait."

"There's every reason, and you and I both know it. I'm not going to leave you here."

"I'm a grown man, Rach. I'll be fine."

"You would be, but I'm not going to abandon you. There's no way you'd leave me here."

"You're right. I wouldn't."

"See?"

"You're a woman. You're my sister. I would never leave you here."

"Well, I feel the same way as you do. I'm not going to leave you here to deal with them on your own."

"You know I'm courting Jenni."

"Have you gotten serious?"

He wasn't sure. "Pretty serious. I'm going to propose soon."

Finally, finally his sister's eyes lit up. "You mean it, don't you?"

He nodded. "I know Jenni is the one for me."

"Because you're in love, right?"

"Jah."

She studied his expression. Whether Rachel was completely satisfied with his answer or not, he wasn't sure. But it must have been close enough because she shifted. "It's getting late."

"Do you think they're asleep yet?"

"They should be. It's been dark out for a while. Hey, did you get anything to eat at the Millers'?"

"I had supper with them. What about you? Did you get anything to eat besides cake?"

"Cake would've been good enough, but Caleb saved me a plate. He always makes me eat the minute I get there. I can't wait until Caleb doesn't have to worry about feeding me anymore. I'll be able to cook for him."

"I think he's always going to worry."

"You know what I mean."

He stood up. "Jah. I know what you mean." He reached down for her hand and pulled her up. "Ready? I need to check on the kitten. I left her in our room."

"I checked on her earlier. She was curled up in a ball." Taking a breath, she lifted her chin. "Let's get this over with."

He opened the door and went in first. Good manners usually meant that the woman preceded the man. Here, the opposite was true. The moment he'd gotten bigger than Rachel, he'd begun walking in first.

Bracing himself, he saw the house was dark and silent. "We're good," he whispered.

"Thank God."

Some people might have thought she was merely uttering a phrase. Matt knew different. He knew those words were spoken from Rachel's heart.

Chapter 3

F<small>our</small> days later, Matt came calling again. For once, her family didn't seem more excited about Matt's visit than she was. Kevin had elected to visit some of his work friends and told her to tell Matt that he'd see him another day. While it wasn't unusual for Kevin to visit with friends from work, he didn't do it all the time. Especially not when he knew Matt was coming over. Plus, Matt was bringing over Valentine. Jenni had known Kevin would want to see the kitten—if for no other reason than to tease Matt about his new pet.

So the evening did seem like it was off to a strange start. More than a little strange.

Things got stranger when Mamm told her that she and Daed were going to sit in the living room that evening but Jenni should take Matt into the hearth room on her own.

When Matt arrived, for once Jenni was right at the door to let him in.

And she saw the kitten! "Matt, look at Valentine! She's so sweet."

He'd wrapped the little creature in a towel for the walk.

After placing the towel on the floor, he handed her to Jenni. "She is at that."

She carefully enfolded Valentine in her arms. The little black cat was only about the size of her father's hand. And so light! She was tiny, perfect, and had bright eyes and the softest paws. Jenni loved her already.

"I'm so glad you brought her by."

Matt was smiling at her. "Me too. I like making you happy."

"A baby kitten does make me happy . . . but you do, too, Matt."

Something flickered in his eyes. "I hope so. Do you mind holding her for a little bit longer? I need to take off my coat and boots." He frowned at his feet. "The snow is melting on the floor."

"The floor is fine. Just put the boots in the boot tray like always." Cuddling the tiny cat to her chest, she watched Matt shrug out of his coat. He really had become such a handsome man. His work at the lumberyard had bulked up his muscles, and he had an air about him that was so much more mature than most men his age.

When he turned back to her, she held Valentine a little more closely. "I think I'm going to have a difficult time giving her back."

"I had a feeling you might feel that way." As if he'd suddenly realized they were still standing alone, Matt looked around. "Where is everyone?"

"My parents are in the living room, and Kevin is out tonight."

"Ah. So it's just the two of us."

"Jah. I set up everything in the hearth room." She smiled at him, but the slight tightening of his features told the same story that she was feeling. It felt a little awkward to be alone. How could that be?

"You lead the way, Jenni."

Still holding the kitten, she turned and started walking, but once again it felt odd. "Help yourself to coffee and a snack," she said when they arrived. She'd taken care to put out a thermos of hot decaf coffee, cups, cream, and small sandwiches and cookies.

"It looks wunderbar."

She shrugged. She was a pretty good cook and usually made the treats for Matt's visits while her mother made most of supper.

"Did you make all of this yourself?"

"Jah, Matt. Why?"

"You usually are the one making everything, aren't you?"

She nodded again. Staring at him curiously, she said, "What's going on? I don't think it looks much different from the other times you've visited."

After pouring himself a cup of coffee and a plate of food, he sat down. "I started to realize that I never gave too much thought to all the effort you've made for my visits. I should've thanked you more."

"That wasn't necessary. Besides, it was something I wanted to do."

The kitten was sound asleep. Jenni set her on a chair, and she stayed in a neat little ball. After preparing her own cup, she said, "Now, tell me about life with a kitten."

"It's good. Valentine stays in my room most of the day. I put a litter box in the corner of the room. It seems to be working out."

"I bet Rachel loves her, too."

"I think so." Matt looked away.

He was acting so uncomfortable as Jenni continued to sip her hot drink. She wasn't really sure what else to say.

What did they usually talk about?

Matt cleared his throat, bringing her attention back to him. "Jenni, as you probably guessed, I asked your father if I could speak with you alone tonight. I didn't know we'd spend the whole evening alone, but I'm glad for this moment right now."

It all made sense. She clasped her hands together. "Why?"

He chuckled softly. "For the obvious reason. I'm asking you to marry me, Jenni. Will you?"

This was the question she'd been anticipating and hoping he'd ask for a very long time. She'd always imagined she'd respond with tears of unbridled joy.

But that was the problem. She didn't feel very unbridled.

Because she didn't know Matt all that well.

"Jenni?" He flashed a smile. "This can't be coming as a big surprise. Is it?"

"Nee. I knew you'd likely ask me soon. And you're right. My parents' absence clued me in as well."

"Then why haven't you answered me yet?"

"Because I'm not sure what to say."

"How come?"

Backing away from him, she sat down. "Matt, you know I like you. We've been friends a long time. I also had thought you might propose soon, and I'd planned to tell you yes."

"What's wrong, then?"

"I don't think I'm ready." She shook her head. "Nee. I mean, I don't think either of us is ready to be engaged. Not yet, anyway."

A line formed between his brows. "Why on earth not?"

She'd hurt his feelings. She hated that. But there was something missing between them. Jenni was no expert on love, but she knew enough to expect more from a suitor. "I just don't think we're prepared to be married."

"We're not prepared? Or do you mean me?" He scowled. "Are you waiting for me to be rich and buy a house to give you?"

"Nee! Not at all. You know I don't care about money and houses, Matt."

"Then what is the problem?"

"The problem is that I don't know how you feel about me. Do you love me, Matt?"

He stilled. Seconds passed. "Yes."

"Really?"

"Really." He picked up his coffee cup, almost took a sip, then set it down again. "I love your whole family, Jenni."

There was her answer. He might be saying different words, but she now knew that her fears were justified. He didn't love her the way a man should love his wife.

"Matt, you've been coming over to this house for most of my life. You're Kevin's best friend, and my parents love having you here. But I've never felt courted by you."

"I've been coming over here several times a week for six months. I made it obvious to everyone we know that I'm courting you. What more do you want from me?"

More. She wanted more. "But when you're here, you and I barely say anything to each other."

"That's not true."

"What do you like best about me?" she asked. "What is it about me that makes me different from all the other women you know?"

He opened his mouth, then shut it quickly. Then he frowned. "I didn't come over here to be quizzed, Jenni."

"It's not a quiz. But, Matt, you're asking me to spend the rest of my life with you. Aren't you supposed to know me so well you don't want to be without me?"

He took a bite of his sandwich. Swallowed. "Jenni, really?"

Oh, but he sounded put-upon.

Maybe that was good, because she was feeling a little bit annoyed. As far as she was concerned, he was being purposely obtuse. "Matthew Lapp, I like you. I'm glad we're friends. I even think I want to marry you. But right now, what I want is to get to know you better."

He lowered his voice. "How do you propose we do that?

It's the middle of January, it's freezing cold, and your family likes us all to visit together." He tugged on the collar of his shirt. "Plus, I've never been an especially chatty person."

He made a lot of good points.

Her heart sank . . . until she remembered her journal. It had been so easy to write her feelings down . . . maybe that's what they needed to do.

"Write me a letter," she blurted.

"Huh?"

"I mean, I think we should write each other letters."

His blond eyebrows rose. "And say what?"

Jenni felt a little foolish—especially since she was making this up as she went along—but there was no going back now. "Write whatever you want to write. Tell me things about yourself. I want to know about you, Matt. About your home and Rachel and your parents."

A muscle in his jaw jumped. "I don't want to talk about them."

"I realize that, but I don't know anything about your mamm and daed, Matt."

"You don't need to know them."

"Yet you want them to be my in-laws?" She leaned closer to him. "Matt, please, try to see things from my point of view."

His cheeks flushed. "You're right. I . . . I should've thought about that."

"All I'm asking for is a month."

"It's January fifteenth today." He chuckled. "That will mean we end this on Valentine's Day."

"That's perfect, don't you think? On Valentine's Day, we'll either know that we're in love and should get married. Or that we're better off being just friends."

"All right."

"All right? You'll agree to exchanging notes?" She'd never thought he'd agree so easily.

"Yes. I'll write you a letter this evening."

"I'll write one to you, too."

His expression warmed. For once he was looking at her the way she'd always hoped he would. "I guess I'll start checking the mailbox every day when I get home from work."

"Me too."

Just then, Valentine woke up, looked at them both, and meowed.

"Oh, Matt, she woke up!" Reaching over, Jenni cuddled the kitten and sat her on her lap.

Valentine meowed again.

"Do you think she's hungry?"

"Maybe."

Jenni picked up an empty saucer and poured a little bit of cream in it, then put both the saucer and the kitten on the carpet. After a few tentative sniffs, Valentine began lapping it up.

"Look at her go! She's adorable."

"I think so, too." He reached out and linked his fingers through hers.

"Knock, knock," her mother said. "Have we waited long enough?"

Startled, Jenni pulled back her hand. "For what?"

Mamm turned to Matt. "I thought—"

Jenni felt like screaming. Why did her parents believe they needed to be an active part of this courtship? "Mamm, I'll speak to you about this later."

But her mother continued to frown. "Matt, is everything okay?"

"Mother, stop."

"Shh, Jenni." Keeping his voice low, Matt added, "I know this is uncomfortable, but we might as well get it over with, jah?"

"I don't know about that."

Her mother looked from her to Matt and then back again. "Do you want me to leave again?"

Mamm looked impatient! "Mother—"

Placing a hand on Jenni's shoulder, Matt said, "You don't need to leave, Beth. After discussing our relationship, Jenni suggested we wait a bit until we know each other a little better. I think she's right."

"How much longer?" Daed asked as he entered the room.

"Father, I really would appreciate it if we discussed this another time."

"I would agree—if things were secret. But they are not."

Which, as far as she was concerned, was part of the problem. "Daed, you are embarrassing me."

He threw up his hands. "All I'm saying is that I'm finding this delay a surprise. After all, you've known Matt practically all your life, Jenni." Smiling at Matt, he added, "We all know each other very well."

Out of the corner of her eye, she noticed that Matt was squirming as uncomfortably as she was.

But . . . perhaps he was right. It probably was better just to put everything out in the open.

She turned to face both of her parents. "I know I've known Matt for most of my life. I know he's best friends with my twin brother. I know you and Mamm love him like a son, too. But I want a husband. I want Matt to want to marry me, not just to be a part of this family."

Her father sighed. "Come now."

"She's right," Matt said. "She and I haven't spent that much time alone together. It became very obvious this evening."

Her mother stepped forward. "So, you two are going to do what?"

Jenni couldn't take it anymore. "We were just about to discuss that when you came in." She looked at her parents pointedly and waited.

Beside her, Matt appeared to be hiding a smile. To his credit, he didn't say a word.

Her parents exchanged a look. "I'll just, ah, go back to the kitchen," Mamm said. "Come on, Hank."

When they were out of sight, Matt chuckled. "Your parents look as if they're lost."

"I'm sure they are. They look forward to your visits as much as I do, Matt."

He stared at her intently. "Is that true?"

"Is what true?"

"Do you look forward to my visits?" He leaned forward, his elbows resting on his knees. "Jenni, are you really sure you want me courting you? You're not just biding your time until you can let me down gently?"

Jenni waited a moment to reply. She wanted to respect his question and ponder it carefully. But after closing her eyes and searching her heart, she knew her answer. She wanted Matt in her life, and she wanted her future to be entwined with his.

"I do think we could have a good future together." Hearing how tepid that sounded, she shook her head. "Nee, I want a future with *you*. But I need the chance to know you better before we promise to live together for the rest of our lives."

"Then that's what you will have. We'll spend the next month writing notes." Reaching for her hand, he threaded his fingers through hers again. "We'll have a love letter courtship, Jenni." He smiled suddenly. "I like the sound of that."

"I do, too. I think it sounds perfect."

Chapter 4

Sitting on his bed, Matt stared at the blank sheet of paper. Why had he agreed that writing notes to Jenni was a good idea? He'd never been good with words. Plus, he couldn't remember the last time he'd written a letter to anyone.

It wasn't as if he had scores of relatives or even grandparents to exchange notes with. Or maybe he did and he didn't know it.

His parents, Aaron and Rose, were the black sheep of their families. Years ago, before he'd realized just how dysfunctional their homelife was, Matt had asked his father where his parents were.

Of course, his father had erupted into anger and lit into him something awful. Matt had made sure never to ask about his grandparents again. He later realized that they lived only an hour away but had given up trying to help their son—or Matt and Rachel. That had hurt.

"How's the letter going?" Rachel asked from her bed across the room. Valentine was alternating between cuddling her side and playing with a stuffed mouse on the floor.

"Not good."

"How much have you written?"

"Nothing."

She chuckled. "Matthew. Come on. I know you can write. Ms. Emma said you were 'a mighty gut writer.'"

He grinned at his sister's impression of the formidable Ms. Emma. While most Amish schools had young teachers—they'd had a cantankerous grandmother with a passion for education. All the students in their school had loved her. Ms. Emma had made them think, try harder, and behave. Compliments were given out like precious pieces of candy. The day she'd told him he was a good writer had been the highlight of his fifth-grade year.

Tapping the end of his pen on his knee, he said, "Though I don't want to disagree with Ms. Emma, I'm afraid she'd be ashamed of me tonight. Putting my thoughts to paper for Jenni is tying me up in knots."

She frowned. "Maybe Jenni was right. Maybe you really don't have anything to tell her."

That was a bitter pill to accept, but he was beginning to think the same thing. "Maybe not."

"If that's the case, I think you should consider what Jenni said. Ain't so?"

As much as he wanted to disagree, he nodded. "Maybe. I guess it was never like that with you and Caleb?"

"Come on. You know Caleb. He's a pretty direct fella. From the very first, he made sure I knew that he was serious about me."

Still thinking about their father's anger over his question about grandparents, Matt looked at Rachel. "Have you ever met any of our extended family?"

"What made you think of them?"

"I don't know. I guess I was thinking about how we've never had a reason to write to aunts or uncles or grandparents."

"Well, ah, yes. I did meet a bunch of family once."

"You did?"

She waved the toy mouse at Valentine and grinned when the kitten hopped back on the bed. "You did, too. You were probably only four years old, though."

Indecision warred within him as he debated about whether to ask what had happened. Like everything else about their parents, even the memories brought pain.

But here he was, planning to marry.

Didn't he need to know such things? Yes. Yes, he did. "What happened?"

She sighed. "I was only about seven, of course, so everything is fuzzy, but basically everyone in Mamm's family came over to try to talk some sense into our parents."

"I wonder what they focused on—the fact that Mamm and Daed ignored us or that they did as little as possible to make a living."

"Matt, I think you know as well as I why they came over. They'd seen Mamm's bruises. And your bruises." Her voice cracked. "And my broken arm."

"Obviously the abuse didn't make much of an impression."

"Maybe it did? Mamm's mother offered to take us. No, I mean, she tried to take us. Said we shouldn't have to live here, but that didn't go over well."

"Let me guess, Daed got violent?"

"Like I said, it's fuzzy, but I seem to remember Mamm being the one who got angry that time. She said something that was bad enough to make them all leave."

"And never come back." Matt felt more than a little bit betrayed by the story. He must have been really young because he didn't remember anything about the visit. "Don't you think they should've done something?"

She shrugged. "What could they have done?"

"Oh, I don't know, Rachel. Maybe gotten us out of here?"

"Maybe they should've tried harder to help, but I don't know. I think it was easier for everyone to pretend that we were okay."

"Which means we were left alone here."

"Jah, we were. But we're adults now. We could've gone already. If we had really wanted to."

He sighed. "I hear you."

"Try not to dwell on things you can't change, brother. The past is the past, ain't so? I hate wishing things were different."

"Yeah. I know." Looking down at his blank sheet of paper again, Matt realized what his problem was. "Rachel, I've spent most of my life shielding Kevin and Jenni from what really happens here."

"I know. That's why you like going over to their house."

"Do you do the same thing with Caleb?" He waved a hand in the air. "You know, try to keep all of what goes on here separate?"

"I do the opposite."

"For real?"

"Caleb was inspecting my bruises when I was just eleven or twelve, Matt. Of course he knew how bad things were."

"I've never been ready to share that much."

"Maybe you didn't have to."

When he frowned, she groaned.

"Come on, Matt. You don't really think that Jenni and Kevin have no idea what our lives are like, do you?"

"I . . ."

"I'm sure they've talked about the old clothes or the bruises or the fact that we're always hungry. That's why Caleb started walking with us in the first place, Matt. Both he and his parents hated what was happening here. So he decided to look out for me more." She lowered her voice. "Every night when I go see him, he makes me give him a report."

"A report? That sounds pretty rude, don'tcha think?"

She shook her head. "Every time I share a secret, I feel it can't hurt me anymore. Sharing helps."

"Doesn't he look at you differently because of it?"

"I don't know. All I know is that he always gives me a hug, then gives me something to eat." After a pause, she added, "He used to put ice on my bruises and wash my cuts."

"He patched you up?"

"Jah. Matt, if you've never shared any of our life with Jenni, it's no wonder she feels she doesn't know you."

"There's more to me than what takes place in this house."

"There is. But it is part of you." When it was obvious that he was going to argue with her again, she added, "Matt, do what you want. But I think you might want to consider what kind of husband you intend to be."

"I'm not going to be the kind who hurts Jenni."

"Of course you won't. But if you never share your feelings or your thoughts, she might get upset about that."

"Yeah. I guess that's true."

When Valentine pranced across the room to the side of his bed, Matt bent down and picked her up. He ran his hand along her side and kissed the top of her head when she purred with happiness.

Rachel picked up her book. "I'm going to read for a little bit before I go to sleep. I have to be at the bakery at five tomorrow morning."

He knew she'd barely get through three or four pages before falling asleep. Half the time she fell asleep with her flashlight still on and he'd have to walk over to her bed and turn it off.

"Okay. Night, Rach."

"Night. And, Matt, you don't have to tell Jenni everything all at once. Maybe just a little bit, jah?"

"Jah."

His sister was right. He needed to put an account of his life in this house on paper. If for no other reason than that Jenni would know for certain what kind of man he was.

> *Dear Jenni,*
> *It's late. After we talked, I walked to the phar-*
> *macy and found a letter kit. Did you know they*
> *had those? It's four pieces of paper, two envelopes,*
> *and two stamps. I guess it's for people like me who*
> *don't have anything to write a decent note on.*
> *Honestly, I'm kind of surprised I even had a pen.*
> *Our haus isn't exactly the type of place that has*
> *writing supplies sitting around.*
> *Although I think you know this, my house is*
> *about as different from yours as possible.*

Forcing himself to continue, he started another paragraph.

> *Jenni, the truth is that I haven't wanted to tell*
> *you much about my life. It's not because I don't*
> *trust you. It's that I'm embarrassed.*
> *No, it's also because I don't like to think about*
> *how things are here. If I think about it too much, I*
> *get depressed or, worse, angry. So I try to pretend.*
> *If I talk about my homelife, it feels too real. But*
> *Rachel pointed out that a woman deserves to know*
> *the man she's going to marry. So I'm going to share*
> *some things. I hope I don't scare you away.*
> *So . . . here's one truth. I share a room with my*
> *sister. We have a small house. There are just two*
> *bedrooms, one bathroom, a kitchen, and a living*
> *room of sorts. Rachel and I have always shared a*
> *room. We each have a twin bed, and we've put*
> *them on opposite sides of the room. When we were*
> *younger, we used to pretend there was a curtain be-*

tween our spaces. Maybe it worked, I don't know. We sometimes tell each other if we don't want to talk or need privacy. When that happens, we do our best to pretend the other one isn't nearby.

But even though there have been a lot of days when I wished I didn't share a room with Rachel, she makes life here bearable. We keep our room really clean and have our special belongings hidden underneath the floorboards or in an old coffee can on someone else's land. We learned that anything nice is too much temptation for our parents.

He went on to describe some of his parents' problems.

I hope this letter didn't make you upset. I'm pretty scared of doing something to turn you away, Jenni. When I look at you, I see someone who is shiny and beautiful. Sometimes when you talk, I just stare at you.

Here's another secret. That isn't something new. I've liked you for a long time, Jenni. A lot longer than I reckon you'd even imagine.

Write back soon so I don't feel stupid.

Love,

Matt

He folded the paper into thirds and carefully tucked it into the envelope. Then he sealed it, put a stamp on the outside, and neatly wrote her address. He realized that Jenni probably didn't know his address because he'd never wanted her to know exactly where he lived. Or maybe she did but had never felt comfortable stopping by. Just in case she wanted to write him back, he wrote his address on the top left hand corner.

Yet again he was reminded of just how guarded he'd been

about himself. He'd been so afraid of giving her a reason to reject him that he'd kept far too many secrets. But instead of making him seem more approachable, the opposite had occurred. Jenni didn't know him well at all.

Why had he imagined that would be good enough for a marriage?

Did he even know anything about what constituted a good marriage? Probably not.

Which meant, unfortunately, that he had even further to go than he'd first imagined in this letter-writing courtship.

He hoped he was up to the task.

The next night, he decided to stay home. Jenni wouldn't have gotten his letter yet, and he wanted to give her time to read it and think about his words.

He also wanted to give the Miller family some time to themselves. He'd been over there so often, he'd probably taken advantage of their kindness.

But although he knew he was doing the right thing, as Matt walked into his house after work, he couldn't hold back his feeling of dread. Being home around five o'clock was never a good thing.

"Rachel, did you bring home groceries?" his mother called out.

He walked into the kitchen. "It's me, not Rachel, Mamm."

His mother, always so pale and thin, stared hard at him. "What are you doing here?"

"I live here, last time I checked."

"You are never here, Matt. Especially not for meals."

He realized belatedly that she was at the stove. "What are you making?"

"Nothing much at the moment. Your sister said she'd buy some chicken on her way home."

Noticing the silence, he said, "Where's Daed?"

"He got some work today."

"Ah." That was a surprise. Rarely did his father work much anymore. Several years ago, he'd fallen from a roof and had sustained a lot of injuries to his back. He'd been in so much pain that the doctor had prescribed painkillers. They'd seemed to be the only thing that helped him at all, so the doctor kept refilling the prescription.

And then his father couldn't make it through the day without his pills.

His parents had never been very self-sufficient to start with, but his daed's pill addiction had made everything worse. His mood swings had become violent. In addition, he'd been in too much pain to work, and their mother, used to doing everything that he told her to do, couldn't seem to function without him continuing to do that.

Rachel had started working just to provide food for them. Then he'd started working too.

The only time the four of them looked like a normal Amish family was when they went to church every two weeks. Somehow they got themselves together and their parents were able to pretend to be their old selves. Or they had up until a few months ago.

"Would you like me to go get some chicken?"

"The store is too far. We have to wait for Rachel."

He opened the cupboard doors and found some bread, crackers, and peanut butter. "When was the last time you ate?" he asked.

"Why?"

"Because I'm curious. When did you eat, Mamm?"

"Yesterday."

"Come sit down and at least have some peanut butter and crackers." Taking her arm, he guided her to a chair at the table.

She didn't fight him, but it was obvious that she didn't want to sit. Her mouth pinched. "Matthew, I have to make supper."

"Please, just eat something." Opening the refrigerator, he was glad to see that there was still some milk left in the container he'd bought three days ago. He poured some in a glass and brought it to her. "Here. Drink some milk, too."

She took a tentative sip. "Where do you think Rachel is?"

"She's probably at the store, Mamm. Don't worry."

Mamm sent him a look that spoke volumes. Her eyes were clearer than he'd seen them in weeks. Was it because she was having a good day? Or was it because he'd been so preoccupied with the Millers that he'd hardly paid any attention to his own family?

It was difficult to accept, but he was pretty sure he knew which of the two scenarios was more likely to be true.

He walked to the stove and saw that celery, carrots, some cabbage, and an onion were in the broth. "What are you making?"

"Chicken and dumplings. Hopefully."

"Try to eat another couple of crackers, Mamm. I'll go straighten the living room."

"Why?"

Because it was a mess. Because he should've been doing more to help out before now. "I have time."

The look she sent him practically burned a hole in his skin. She was completely confused by everything he was doing. And who could blame her?

Yes, it had only been natural to find comfort and kindness at the Millers' house. But while he'd been doing that, he'd missed a multitude of opportunities to practice kindness here in his own home.

He needed to make things better and learn how to go forward.

Chapter 5

Jenni's mouth was dry, and she felt kind of sick to her stomach. Looking down at Matt's first letter, she resigned herself to feeling that way. How could she not? She'd been friends with Matt for most of her life. Even when the two of them hadn't been close, he'd been good friends with her brother.

Why had she been so oblivious to his problems? Had she really been that self-centered? She was ashamed of not being more aware of how things really were at the Lapp house.

All the time he'd been coming over, eating every bite of his supper, looking so pleased with her parents' kindness, she'd almost accepted it as his nature.

Now she knew that he'd been eating so much not just because he was hungry for a good meal but because he didn't have any food at home. He drank in her parents' kindness because his own parents weren't kind at all. He enjoyed their warm living room chats because that wasn't the norm in his house. It never had been.

Yes, she could blame some of her insensitivity on the fact that she'd been just a girl during much of that time. Most children didn't think too much about what happened in other people's homes. Not really.

But that didn't excuse her actions during the last five or six years. A better woman would've made note and realized that she should try to help him in some way.

Jenni never had.

Instead, she'd taken his interest for granted. Almost had acted as if his fascination with her family and life was to be expected. She had done so many things she wasn't proud of. It was time to make things right.

But what to do?

Closing her eyes, she prayed for the right words. She wanted to let Matt know she was glad he'd shared so much with her. She also needed to reassure him that there was nothing he could divulge that would change her opinion of him.

Can you help me, God? she prayed silently. *I don't want to make things worse or uncomfortable between Matt and me. I want him to trust me to always love him as he must know You do.*

Opening her eyes, she waited and hoped to suddenly feel a new sense of calm and security. Nothing happened, but perhaps that wasn't a bad thing. It could very well be that the Lord had been with her this whole time. She had, after all, suggested they write love letters to each other.

Even though she wasn't feeling all that confident, she picked up her pen and began her letter. Writing Matt back right away was better than waiting, she decided.

> *Dear Matt,*
> *The last thing you ever need to worry about is feeling stupid around me. You are one of the best people I've ever known.*
> *Matt, I'm going to be honest. Your letter shamed me. It made me realize how much I've*

*taken for granted. Not just here at my house but
also your feelings about my family. I should've
given more thought to why you never talked about
your parents or home at all. I think it shows that I
still have a lot of growing up to do. I will get better,
I promise. I want to one day be the partner and
wife you can count on—not just for the good times
but the bad, too.*

*Since you have shared so much, I feel I should
do the same. I have a secret, too, though it hardly
compares to the things that you've kept to yourself.
My secret is that I still get nervous around you. I
wish I was prettier or had more to give you than
my family. I guess that's the root of it all. When I
look at you, Matt, I know that just about any
woman in Apple Creek would be thrilled to have
your attention. I often fear that one day you'll decide my family is not enough to hold your regard.*

Then what will I do?

*Ugh. I almost crumpled up this note, but I want
to be as honest as I can with you.*

For better or worse, jah?

Love,

Jenni

After reading her note three times, Jenni forced herself to fold it neatly and place it in the envelope. Finally, she addressed the front, placed a stamp on the upper right-hand corner, and walked it out to the mailbox. The weather was bitterly cold. She'd heard the temperature was going to be in the single digits that evening.

Tossing her thick wool shawl on the back of a chair in the living room, she wondered if Matt would be warm enough.

Her mother poked her head out of the kitchen. "Did you finish taking the laundry down from the line in the basement?"

"Nee."

"Jenni, where's your head? There's a load in the washer needin' to go on the line. Plus, you said you'd help me deliver a meal to the widow Martha."

"I'm sorry, Mamm. I'll work on the laundry right now." She hurried down to the basement and got to work.

She had to do something besides worry and fret about Matt.

Chapter 6

Like the lovesick fool that he was, Matt read Jenni's letter, then put it in his pocket and took it with him to work. He really hoped no one would ever discover he'd done that.

Okay, maybe one day he'd tell Jenni—she might feel it was kind of sweet—but no one else.

Honestly, he wasn't surprised that he'd done such a thing. Though Jenni's letter was the first anyone had written him, he was now hooked. He enjoyed writing and receiving letters.

Well, Jenni's.

Being able to read Jenni's words and reread them again made him feel so much closer to her. Plus, the things she'd written were mighty sweet. And meaningful. He'd learned so much in just a one-page note. Never had he imagined that she got nervous around him.

Now his problem was that the note was practically burning a hole in his pocket. All he wanted to do was think about Jenni and how they were becoming closer. Surreptitiously, he pulled it out and reread it.

Boy, he didn't deserve Jenni Miller. She was so kind. And,

yes, so innocent of the many bad things in the world. While her naivete might shame her, he didn't think it was a bad thing at all. Jenni wouldn't understand, but he liked the fact that she was so sheltered. Her belief that most people were innately good and had safe, happy homes soothed him. He liked her optimism.

Now all he had to do was try to figure out how to address the other parts of her letter. Did she really think that she had nothing to offer him but her family?

Had he made her feel that way?

Maybe he had.

As hard as it was to admit it, her statement might have a grain of truth in it. He did admire the Miller family and had spent more than one night when he was little wishing he could trade places with Kevin. It had been hard not to be jealous of his friend, who had his very own room and access to a kitchen that was full of food.

In his weakest moments, Matt knew he'd been jealous of Kevin's entire life.

Had he inadvertently been so enamored of Kevin's family that he'd courted Jenni so he could become a member, too?

He didn't want to think that was the case, but he wasn't completely sure it wasn't.

"Hey, Matt, come help me, will ya?"

"Yeah, sure." Quickly folding his letter back into his pocket, Matt strode over to Abram's side. Abram was in charge of the Troyer Lumber warehouse. The lumberyard had not only a large mill and carpentry area but also an extensive shipping and receiving yard.

Matt had first signed on with Troyer Lumber when he was barely fourteen. Abram had said he'd needed help cleaning and dusting, but Matt had been pretty sure the kind older man had simply wanted to give him a helping hand.

Matt hadn't taken the offer for granted, though. From his

very first day on the job, he had worked hard. He wasn't sure if Abram had been surprised by his enthusiasm or not. But whatever the reason, the man had kept him on and gradually given him more and more responsibility. Now he was Abram's right-hand man—and the one to whom most of the workers went with questions or concerns.

"What can I help ya with?" he asked.

"I want a few minutes of your time, son. That's what I want."

Some of the ease in his body fled. He tried to think of everything that had been on his to-do list. He thought he'd remembered each one. But maybe he'd forgotten something?

"Boy, you always look like I'm on the verge of firing you. I'm not. Just the opposite."

The opposite of firing? He sat down. "What's going on?"

"We've been so busy lately that I haven't asked how Jenni Miller is."

"She's gut."

"Are you still calling on her quite a bit?"

"Jah."

"I could've sworn you were about to propose. Beth and Hank didn't announce it at church, though."

Figuring there was nothing wrong with swallowing his pride and sharing the truth, Matt said, "I did propose, but Jenni asked that we wait a bit."

Abram blinked. "Why would she want that? You two have known each other for years."

"That's true, but she brought up some good points. She felt maybe we needed to know each other even better."

"Hmm. How are ya going to do that?"

Since he trusted Abram, he told him the truth. "We've started to write letters to each other."

"And do what? Pass them to each other when you go calling?"

Matt could appreciate Abram's joke, but now that he was

carrying one of her letters in his pocket, he didn't want to make light of it. "Nee. We've been posting them."

"Really? Buying postage stamps sounds like a waste of good money."

"It's not. It's money well spent." Since Abram still looked skeptical, he added, "I know our letter writing doesn't make much sense, but it's a good thing. Sometimes when I visit Jenni, she and I don't spend a lot of time alone."

"Her parents don't trust you?"

"I think they do. It's more that they act as if I'm a family friend coming over to visit. I am, but . . ."

Abram nodded. "They didn't give you any time to say sweet things to the girl you're courting."

"Jah. That's what I'm trying to say."

"Hard to be romantic if you're surrounded by a girl's parents."

"It is. Don't get me wrong. I like them a lot. And Kevin is my best friend."

"You're laying the foundation for a marriage. That's a two-person thing, no matter how much one's family wants to get involved."

"Yes. That's it exactly."

"How are you going to change things?"

That was a good question. He had no idea if there was a way to tell the Millers that although they'd made him feel like part of the family in a hundred ways, he wanted them to leave him alone when he was calling on Jenni. He was pretty certain there was no good way to do that.

He was even more certain that even if he came up with the most perfect words, they wouldn't take it well at all.

"We're not there yet," he finally replied. "Jenni and I are letter writing, and it's helping."

Abram looked skeptical, but he nodded. "All righty, then. Well, um, if you need another ear, I'm available. Don't be shy."

"I appreciate that."

"Let's talk work, now. How are the delivery schedules looking?"

Relieved to be switching topics, Matt reached for his clipboard and strode to the whiteboard posted on the wall. "Looks like we might need to look at Thursday's deliveries again. It's going to be tight."

"How so?"

"Diamond Manufacturing is two hours away. Since their order is so big, we won't be able to add another delivery on the vehicle."

"We can't reschedule Diamond."

"I agree," he said, pointing to the map on the wall and the other delivery addresses. He and Abram spent the next two hours hiring another driver, coordinating schedules, and calling customers to confirm delivery windows.

It always took longer than expected and always took more finesse than one might expect. When they finally got things locked in place—at least for the night—Matt was pulling on his coat and grabbing his lunch pail. It was time to go home.

Sometimes he took advantage of the ride service Abram offered, but Matt decided to forgo it that evening. The weather was still cold but had warmed up slightly. Plus, he had a lot to think about. Mainly, what he was going to write to Jenni next.

He was determined to get his next letter in the mail the next morning, and it needed to say something important, caring, and meaningful.

He just wasn't sure what that could be.

Chapter 7

Dear Jenni,

I'm starting to think we should've been writing to each other from the very first. I'm learning a lot about you, and I'm glad about that.

I cannot believe you've ever believed for even a minute that you were lacking in some way. You've always been special. I thought so even when we were young and Kevin and I used to catch lizards and put them in your lunch pail. (That was always Kevin's idea, by the way.) Why would you ever think you weren't pretty enough? You are real pretty, Jenni. Believe it, because it's true. I wouldn't lie about that.

Now, on to the next thing you mentioned in your letter. While I realize it's no secret that I'm fond of your family, it doesn't have as much to do with me courting you as you seem to think. I do like your parents, and Kevin is my best friend. And you've been a good friend to me, too. But no mat-

ter what, I would never start formally courting a woman just to be around her parents. I promise, I wouldn't do that. I just wouldn't.

Do you believe me yet?

I've been attempting to court you because I like you, Jenni. And no, that wasn't a mistake of words. I used "attempting" on purpose. I don't feel I've been a very good suitor of late, but I will improve. I want to improve.

However, I have realized that I need to say something to Kevin about getting more time alone with you. I'm going to talk to him soon—so don't you start thinking that you need to do it. And yes, I know it sounds bossy, but I think it's my job. I might have a lot to learn about being a good suitor, but I am a perfectly good man. And this man knows that tough conversations with Kevin about dating his sister should come from me.

Moving on, I have to tell you that I had a doozy of a day today. See, I'm in charge of the warehouse at Troyer Lumber as well as all the deliveries. Sometimes it's not too difficult to make everything work. Today, that wasn't the case. One of our deliveries this week is to a business out of the way, and they bought a lot of stuff, too. I ended up having to call around for a temporary driver who can drive a big truck but also is willing to help move furniture. That ain't all that easy!

Then after I finally hired someone, I had to move everyone else's deliveries around and shuffle workers and items on the truck. And, of course, one of the trucks was going to be too full!

Do you feel tired yet just reading about all the puzzling I had to do?

If so, then you can probably understand why I walked home this evening instead of taking the ride service. It might be snowy and cold, but I needed some time to relax.

No, to be honest, I wanted to think about what to write you. There's a part of me that is very fond of this new letter writing we're doing. I like being able to read your words over and over again. I like being able to put your note in my pocket. It's a fanciful thing, but carrying around your note makes me feel close to you.

And now that I've probably said too much, I'll let you go. I hope you don't mind that this note is mainly about my day at work.

I look forward to our future when we'll be sitting together at supper and we'll be able to share things in person.

I hope and pray that day will really happen.

Love,

Matt

Jenni ran a finger over the last two words. *Love, Matt.* She thought about what he'd written and the things he'd shared and how they made her feel.

Honestly, every word he wrote made her feel closer to him. His letters made her feel as if she were sitting across from Matt. They were that animated and bright. She loved their intimacy.

She also loved that he was being so honest. At least, she hoped he was. She still didn't believe that she was all that pretty, but perhaps it didn't matter whether she believed it or not. What mattered was that Matt liked her the way she was. That was something to celebrate, for sure and for certain.

Skimming over his words again, she frowned. Was it wrong

of her to really like the fact that he had carried her letter while at work? It might be too prideful. No, it *was* prideful.

But she was only human. Surely any woman would enjoy having her suitor do something like that.

"Is that another letter from Matt?"

Her brother's voice was so loud and clear, Jenni jumped. She turned to him. "Kevin, hey."

"Hey, yourself. Are you all right?"

"Jah. I didn't know you were standing at the door. You startled me. Did you need something?"

"Ah, yeah. I wanted to talk to you." He stepped forward, then stopped. "That's okay, right? I mean, you weren't in the middle of something important, were you?"

She was. She'd been reading Matt's letter. And so far, she'd read it only twice. That wasn't nearly enough times to plant it firmly in her heart. But what could she say? It was obvious that Kevin had something on his mind.

"You know you don't need to worry about that. Of course you can come in."

He sat down on the end of her bed. "Jenni, how long do you and Matt think you're going to be writing to each other?"

"I don't know. A while. Why?"

"I don't know." He averted his eyes. "It just seems odd."

"Really? How come?"

"Because don't you two know each other pretty well by now?"

"Not enough to get engaged."

"Come on." His voice turned impatient. "Jenni, you're being ridiculous. You're making Matt jump through a bunch of hoops that aren't necessary. I think you're wasting his time, and he's too nice to tell you."

Stung—and more than a little irritated, Jenni turned to face him. "Let me get this straight, Kevin. You think I'm making Matt work too hard to court me. That I'm wasting his time."

She lowered her voice. "Do you even hear yourself? What's wrong with you?"

Kevin averted his eyes but didn't back down. "I'm only trying to help. Don't make it sound like I'm invading your space or something, Jenni."

She raised her eyebrows. "Or Matt's space, right?"

He waved a hand. "Yeah. Or Matt's, but whatever. All I'm saying is that Matt has a lot going on at his house."

"I know he does." She had a feeling she now knew more about his house than Kevin did.

"Plus, Matt has a demanding job. He comes over here to relax and get a good meal. After he comes over, he walks back home. I don't think he should have to start worrying about writing you letters, too. The man only has so many hours in a day."

"You've certainly given my relationship with Matthew Lapp a lot of thought."

Not catching the warning tone in her voice, he nodded. "I have. That's why I think you should let him off the hook and give him a break. Tell him that you don't want to exchange letters anymore."

"Nee."

He stood up with a scowl. "No? That's it?"

"Jah. Well, pretty much, anyway. Because you are forgetting that Matt's courtship with me is none of your business."

"You might think that, but you're wrong. He's my best friend. Just because you want some extra attention right now doesn't mean that's going to change."

Jenni felt like shaking him. "Kevin, I don't want to be one of the reasons he comes over here. I want to be the main reason he visits. At least sometimes," Jenni added, since she realized she was sounding rather selfish.

"That's unreasonable."

"It's not. Kevin, we're courting."

"Well, he and I are best friends."

"Maybe you should think about putting more effort into your friendship, then. I know you can't go over to his house, but why do his visits have to be the only time you two catch up?"

"I don't see why not. It's always been like this."

"Well, maybe you should shake things up, too."

He stood up. "What? Like write him a letter?"

Oh, but she hated how full of himself he sounded! "Yes. Like that," she retorted. "Or not!"

"I'm not going to write him a letter, Jenni. Don't be foolish."

"Then stay out of my business! If you're missing your time with him, figure it out."

"I just might do that."

"Gut."

"Jenni! Kevin!" Mamm called out. "What in the world are you two arguing about?"

"Nothing," Kevin said.

Nope. No way was she going to let her twin simply sweep everything she'd said under the rug. "It was something," she countered when her mother joined them. "We were arguing about Matt's visits here and his courting me."

Their mother blinked. "What about it?"

Kevin folded his hands. "Jenni wants his visits to be all about her. Not only does that seem selfish, but I told her it's a little late for that. Right?"

Boy, she sure didn't like his tone of voice. Jenni was tempted to ask Kevin if he'd planned to take her along whenever he got up the nerve to finally call on Sally but held her tongue. Barely.

"Hmm. Well, I don't know." Studying Jenni's face, Mamm softened her voice. "I was talking to your father, and I did tell him that I could see why you might want a different type of courtship, daughter."

"You understand how I feel?"

"Of course. Every woman wants to feel special when she's being courted. There's nothing wrong with that."

"But it's Matt. He's been my best friend since we were four or five years old," Kevin pointed out. "Mamm, don't you think that makes everything different?"

"It makes things more complicated, but not really different. Courting is courting."

Jenni raised her chin. Sure, she was acting a bit spoiled and childish, but it couldn't be helped. She and her twin had a long history of bickering with each other. It was a hard habit to break.

Kevin sighed. "Fine. But let's all hope that you don't decide he's not the man for you after all, Jenni."

"Why?"

"Because if Matt really does love you and you decide you don't love him, you're going to break his heart."

"That's not going to happen."

"But it might," he warned. "And if it does, then Matt's heart will be broken and he won't come over here anymore."

Her brother was making up trouble. "Kevin, stop."

"Nee. You need to listen to me. What I'm trying to tell you, sister, is that it's going to crush Matt if he doesn't have these visits to look forward to. He needs us. All of us."

She sighed. "You can't put Matt Lapp's future happiness on my shoulders."

"You're right. I can't. But that's where it sits. I don't think he has much besides our family. I don't want him to be hurt."

Her brother's words rang in her ears as he walked away. She wasn't sure what to do with his comment, beyond hope and pray that he wasn't right.

The last thing on earth she wanted to do was hurt Matt.

That said, she also meant to have a husband who wanted her as much as she wanted him.

"Jenni, dear, you know Kevin didn't mean that the way he said it."

"I know. But I also think he has a point. This courtship has just gotten a little bit more complicated."

Wrapping her arms around Jenni, her mother pulled her into a hug. "Dear, it might seem that way, but it isn't. Love is love, right?"

Comforted by her mother's warm embrace, Jenni shrugged. "I guess. I don't know for sure."

"I do." Mamm lowered her voice. "Kevin is feeling jealous and left out, Jenni. He's worried that you and Matt are going to be so close that there won't be any more room in your lives for him."

"That doesn't make sense, though. He's my twin and Matt is Kevin's best friend. They'll always be close."

"You know that, and I know that. I think Matt even knows that." Pulling back, her mother smiled at her. "One day your brother will realize it, too."

"I hope so."

"He will. I just hope it will be sooner rather than later."

Feeling better, Jenni nodded. "Me too. You're right. I'll try to be more patient."

"Danke, child. Now come help me with dessert for to-night."

"What are you making?"

"Chocolate cake with a cherry sauce and whipped cream."

"That's Matt's favorite."

"Is it? Hmm." Her mother walked down the hall, leaving Jenni to carefully put away Matt's latest note . . . and come to terms with the fact that her mother might be a lot more aware of how Jenni was feeling than she'd thought.

Chapter 8

Matt had come over for supper every Thursday evening for the last three years. It was such a habit, she didn't even think twice about setting an extra place for him at the dinner table. Jenni didn't imagine this week would be any different.

What was different, however, was the change in their relationship. Now that they'd been exchanging notes, she felt closer to him than ever before. Now, whenever she thought about him, her insides felt a little bit fluttery. Her skin felt a little sensitive.

Now, when she imagined being in the same room, she blushed.

After six months of courting, Jenni counted the minutes until he was at her door. She had suddenly become a giddy girl. She might have been embarrassed except for the fact that all these feelings were what she'd been missing. At long last, she was a woman in love.

As she continued to watch the clock, anxiously awaiting his arrival, Jenni felt compelled to give thanks.

"*Danke, Gott*," she whispered. "You've blessed me with

both the opportunity and the time to grow closer to Matt in a way that has been comfortable for us both. I'm so grateful for this gift."

Keeping her eyes closed, she breathed deep. Imagined the Lord hearing every word she said. Being pleased.

"Matt is walking up the driveway, Jenni!" her father called out from down the hall.

Her eyes popped open. "Danke!"

"Would you care to greet him at the door?"

"Jah," she whispered. She did want to do that.

"Stop yelling down the hall, Hank!" Mamm chided.

"Fine." His heavy boots clomped closer on the wood floor. "Jenni, what do you want to do?"

"I'll greet him, Daed. I'll be out in a second."

"Gut."

Hearing his footsteps turn, she hurried to the bathroom and studied her reflection in the dim light. She looked the same but . . . maybe a little bit brighter, too? Remembering Matt's sweet words about how he thought she was pretty, she felt a little flutter inside her tummy. Yes, she knew she shouldn't dwell on such things as her looks, but she couldn't seem to help herself. She longed to be the woman Matt wanted in his life. And though she knew he liked the person she was inside, she hoped he would like the person he saw with his eyes as well.

Hurrying down the hall at last, she passed Kevin.

He was sitting on the couch in the living room with a book in his hands. He wasn't looking at it, though; he was staring directly at her. Almost as if she'd become a person he didn't recognize and was trying to figure out.

She didn't dare meet his gaze. If she did, she'd probably turn beet red. That would be awful! She certainly didn't want Matt to see her "bright" like that!

After her discussion with Kevin and Mamm, her father had also come to speak to her. He'd been the easiest to talk to, mainly because he'd kept their conversation short. "I agree that no man should have to deal with his girl's entire family when he pays a call. We'll take care to stay in the background from now on."

She'd been taken aback by his words. And, perhaps, had felt a little awkward, too. Yes, she'd wanted to feel special and have most of Matt's attention, but she hadn't intended to stop the other three people in her family from talking to him. She knew Matt needed all of them in his life.

"Danke, Daed," she'd finally said. Because, after all, there wasn't a whole lot else she could say.

Now, standing at the door, Jenni realized her palms were damp. She was actually a little bit nervous about being the sole recipient of his attentions with her family observing it all.

That was almost embarrassing. Shouldn't she be pleased that she'd gotten her way at long last?

Then, there was Matt. Looking as he always did in his dark gray pants, work boots, blue shirt, and heavy black coat and gloves. The only thing different was that he was wearing a black knit cap instead of his usual black felt one.

She opened the door and stepped outside to meet him.

"Hi."

"Hiya." His eyes seemed to scan her body, finally resting on her face. He was frowning. "You don't have a cloak on."

"I know."

"It's cold out." He held out his palm, capturing tiny snow-flakes on the dark fleece glove. "Flurries are in the air, Jen."

"I know that, too."

He tilted his head to one side. "If you're such a smart woman, then why did you come out? You'll catch your death."

"I wanted to speak to you in private for a moment."

He stepped closer, pulled off a glove and ran a finger along her cheekbone. "Snowflakes are landing on your skin."

She trembled. "I'm fine."

His green eyes warmed. "All right, then. What did you want to talk about?"

Jenni forced herself to concentrate on something other than how gorgeous his eyes were. She realized that there was a wealth of other options, all very Matt. For instance, even though he'd been out in the weather, heat radiated from him. And he smelled so good, too. "Did you shower before you came over here?"

He stiffened slightly. "Why do you ask?"

What could she say to that? "No reason. I mean, I'm sorry. That was rude. Forget I said anything."

"I don't think that's possible." A half smile hovered at the corners of his lips. It was so obvious that he was trying not to smile. "To answer your question, yes, I did shower recently."

"You had time?"

"I took the time. It gets pretty hot working in the warehouse, even in the winter."

"I guess it does."

"Jenni, why did you ask?"

"No reason." Other than the obvious one, of course. Which was that she'd somehow lost her mind now that she saw him in person. Looking down at her feet, she shifted.

Matt wrapped his bare hand around her chin and lifted it up. Miraculously, his hand was still warm, and the rough texture of his fingers spurred another round of chill bumps.

"Oh, Jenni." When she met his gaze, he added, "You're going to get chilled. What did you want to talk to me about?"

Now she just felt foolish. "Nothing in particular."

"Are you sure about that?"

"Jah." The hand that had just cupped her face traipsed down one of her arms before he linked his fingers through hers.

A shiver raced through her. Even though she had on a wool dress, she could feel his touch through the fabric.

"You're trembling. Are you nervous or just cold?"

She was neither. She was reacting to him in the way that she'd been hoping to for years. But how could she say that? "You're right. We should go inside. My parents are probably wondering why we haven't come in yet."

"Are you sure you're ready to go in?" he pressed. "Are you sure there wasn't something you wanted to say to me in private?"

"There wasn't anything specific. I . . . I just wanted to be with you for a moment. Just the two of us."

His eyes darkened as he swallowed. "It was a gut idea. A very good one. I'm, ah, real glad you came outside to greet me."

She smiled at him. "Me too."

"I'd pull you into my arms and hold you tight if I didn't think your father would give me a talking-to. Let's get you inside before he comes out to investigate."

"I have a feeling that Kevin is the one who would be doing that."

"Kevin? Really?"

"Never mind."

He opened the door and gestured for her to precede him. Jenni walked in front of him and even smiled when her brother sauntered over to shake Matt's hand and claim his attention.

But inside, his words continued to run through her head. *I'd pull you into my arms.*

She wanted that. She wanted to be wrapped up close to Matt. To feel warm and protected and breathe in his scent. But most of all, to feel special. To know that no one else had claimed his attention. To know that no one else had such a special place in his heart.

Twenty minutes later, after she'd helped her mother carry the dishes to the table, poured water in everyone's drinking glasses, and told the men it was time to eat, they at last sat down at the dinner table.

As she took the chair directly across from Matt, their eyes met. He was looking at her intently, and there was a faint smile playing on his lips.

When she closed her eyes for prayer, she felt her cheeks heat. Because she'd just realized that she no longer had to wonder if there was anything special between them.

Matt had just let her know—in front of her family—that she was special to him and that he only had eyes for her.

Chapter 9

Jenni had handed him a letter just as he was telling her good night. It was now safe in his pocket. In spite of the cold, both the note—and the time he'd spent in her company—were keeping him plenty warm.

Things were surely different between them now.

He felt empowered by the words they'd shared. Not just the things she'd written him but also the words that he'd shared with her. Though he'd taken care not to divulge anything too shocking, he had shared a little bit more about his life at home.

A sixth sense—or maybe it was simply common sense—told him that Jenni was going to have to know more about his parents if they were to have a solid foundation for a life together. As much as he and Rachel liked to pretend that they hadn't suffered too badly, Matt reckoned he'd be a fool to imagine he didn't have scars.

Because he did have scars—both on his body and in his soul.

Pushing aside those dark thoughts, he stepped under an Englischer's streetlight and took advantage of walking in its beam for a few feet. The illumination helped clear his head so he could focus on how soft her skin had been when he'd curved his hand around her jaw. How right it had felt to hold her hand for those few moments. The look of happiness that had shone in her eyes when he'd fussed about her getting cold.

She'd been pleased about his concern. She was fine with him being a little overprotective. He'd never thought he would be the type of man to tell his girlfriend or wife to put on a cloak, but it seemed he was.

For a second, he feared his need to care for her was going to one day make him start ordering her around. He would hate to be anything like his father. But he knew their relationship would never be like that. Not only did he not want to boss her around, but also Jenni was not the type of woman to put up with such treatment. Neither was her family, for that matter. Matt knew without a doubt that if her parents or Kevin even suspected Jenni was being mistreated, they'd put a stop to it right then and there. He wouldn't blame them, either.

Returning to more happier thoughts, Matt focused once again on their evening together.

After Beth's delicious supper of lasagna, garlic bread, and salad, he'd helped clear the table and dry dishes with the rest of the family. Then Hank had told them to sit in the hearth room for a spell. Just the two of them.

Jenni had blushed but followed him there. She didn't move an inch when he'd not only taken a seat next to her on the couch but also had situated himself close enough to feel her leg next to his.

Thinking of the many opportunities he'd taken to touch her, even if it was just a brush of his fingers against hers when they passed dishes at the table, Matt chuckled.

"You practically did everything but a backflip to show Jenni how much you're attracted to her, you fool," he mumbled.

He didn't care, though. He never wanted her to have a single doubt about the way he felt about her.

It had been a very good visit.

Except for the way Kevin had acted. He'd almost been sullen during supper. Whenever Matt or Jenni had asked him something, his answer had contained a hint of sarcasm.

Jenni had looked so hurt, Matt had been tempted to call Kevin out but knew it wasn't the right time or place.

He didn't understand Kevin's behavior, either. Though Jenni had written that Kevin was feeling left out, Matt was sure that wasn't the case. Kevin knew he'd liked Jenni for years. He'd also been very receptive to Matt's visits. Why would he now be jealous of something that he'd help put into place?

Coming upon his house, he drew up short when he saw Rachel sitting out front with a quilt wrapped around her. She didn't lift her head when he approached, which made his heart start beating faster.

"Rachel."

She raised her head. "Hey."

Even in the dark, Matt could tell she was very upset. What he didn't know was why. Had their father hurt her? It had been a while since he'd raised a hand to either of them, but that didn't mean it wasn't a possibility. Asking her point-blank if Daed had hurt her was too blunt. She was so used to hiding hurts, it was second nature to lie.

Instead, he asked a different question. "Why are you out here?"

"Do you really need to ask?"

Ouch. Her tone was bitter, and she looked near tears. Maybe she really was hurt. Maybe something even worse had happened. They'd learned a long time ago that just about anything was possible in their home.

Right away his mind went to all sorts of worst-case scenarios, each one uglier than the last—and each putting his nerve endings on edge. He chose his words carefully. "Jah, I need to ask, Rachel. I know it must have been bad." He swallowed.

"All I really care about, though, is if you're okay. Are you okay?"

She waited a moment to answer. As if she needed that brief respite to think about it. "I'm okay."

"Are you sure?" As much as he wanted to rush to her side or march in the front door to get answers, Matt knew neither was a wise choice. Rachel looked as though she was barely hanging on. If he pushed too hard too fast, she'd likely shut down. Going inside would likely tell him next to nothing. It would only make him wish that God would finally help his parents or compel them to get help.

She nodded. "I'm as good as I can be, because tonight was so bad." Meeting his gaze, her expression softened. "Don't worry. I'm not in danger of falling apart. Not really."

Matt sat down next to her at last. "I'm sorry I wasn't here."

"I know you are. I'm kind of glad you weren't, though. There was no reason both of us had to deal with them tonight."

As he put his arm around her shoulders, she leaned in close.

"Daed hit Mamm, and she fell on the ground. When I tried to stop him, he grabbed me."

"Where?"

"Just my arm."

"Are you hurt?"

"Nothing bad. But I'm going to be bruised. Caleb's going to be so upset."

"He's going to be worried about you, sister. That's what he's going to be upset about, right?"

When she nodded but didn't say anything, he turned so she had no choice but to face him.

"You are going to show him your bruises, aren't you?"

"I don't know."

"Rachel, he's going to want to know if you're hurt."

"He will, but it's not going to help anything."

"You can't keep what happens to you a secret. That doesn't help you or Caleb."

"I know. It's just that Caleb keeps threatening to come over and yell at Daed." She sighed. "Or worse, give him a taste of his own medicine."

"You know Caleb wouldn't do that." But Matt wouldn't blame him if he did.

"I'm not so sure that Caleb wouldn't. He doesn't like our life here."

Matt couldn't help himself. He laughed. "That makes three of us then."

"Hey, Matt?"

"Yeah?"

"Sometimes, when I'm feeling really blue, I kind of wish he would," she said in a small voice. "I don't know why we're even still here. We could have moved away years ago."

"We're here because someone needs to care for them, especially Mamm. If we didn't, then no one would."

"I resent it, though." She tilted her chin up to the nighttime sky. "I know that makes me sound like a horrible person."

"No, you sound honest. I think that's a good thing. You know I feel the same way, Rachel."

"Jah."

"So . . . want to tell me why you are sitting outside?"

"After the big blowup, Daed went to their bedroom. Then Mamm got mad at me."

"Let me guess—it's your fault that Daed was upset."

She chuckled, a bitter, dry sound. "Nee, she tried out a new excuse tonight. She said it was your fault."

"Because?"

"Because if you'd been here, everything would have been better, of course."

Her derisive tone told him that she didn't believe their

mother's words one bit. He didn't, either, but he couldn't help but feel a little guilty. "I wish my being here would make everything all better. I wish it was that easy."

"Me too."

With a reluctant sigh, he got to his feet. "It's freezing and spitting snow. I'm going to go on in. Do you want to come?"

"Not yet."

She was huddled under that quilt.

Knowing better than to try to convince her to follow him inside, he carefully took out Jenni's letter and then pulled off his coat. "Here." He wrapped it around her shoulders.

"Danke."

Opening the door, he braced himself. But there was only silence. As much as he yearned to go to his bedroom and read his letter in private, Matt made a short tour of the house. The last thing Rachel needed when she came inside was another disaster.

He did a quick scan of the living room. Beyond a plate on a table and a dish towel, nothing was out of place. He picked up both and carried them to the kitchen . . . and found their mother asleep at the table. She was slumped over and had her arms folded underneath her head. She was very still but breathing. Her dress was stained, and there was a faint mark on her arm.

Matt knew he should feel pity for her, and he supposed he did to some extent. But he also had long ago run out of sympathy or even much compassion where she was concerned. She'd never protected them when they were small and always tried to blame their father's temper and drug problems on them. It was almost a joke between him and Rachel.

For a second, he allowed himself to imagine seeing Jenni like this. Without a doubt, he knew he would have gently woken her up and gotten her something to drink, then made sure she went to her bedroom to sleep. He'd do the same for Rachel.

Even Kevin or Mrs. Miller.

It seemed only where his parents were concerned was he lacking in proper sympathy.

After making sure his father hadn't passed out in the bathroom, he quickly brushed his teeth and washed his face and then headed to his bedroom. Valentine was sitting on his bed. She raised her head when he entered and meowed.

"Hiya, kitty," he said as he sat on his mattress and pulled off his boots. "How are you doing tonight?"

She meowed again as he scooped her up in his arms and nuzzled her neck. Valentine did the same, purring softly.

Matt never thought he'd enjoy having a kitten, but he truly did. He liked having something to cuddle and care for. Plus, her silly antics lifted his spirits. She was good medicine for a troubled soul.

When she grew heavy, he set her back on his quilt so she could sleep in peace. Then, finally, at long last, he lay down on his bed and opened Jenni's letter.

> *Hi Matt,*
> *I know you'll be coming over, but I couldn't help writing to you. For some reason, writing these letters makes me feel closer to you. Selfishly, it also makes me feel better inside, since I tend to keep so much of myself carefully locked up.*
> *Do you know what I mean?*

Her words cut straight to his heart. This was why he knew Jenni was the right woman for him. It wasn't her looks or her smiles or her family. It was because she understood how he felt deep inside. The way no one else seemed to understand him. God had not only found the perfect wife for him, He'd even placed Jenni within walking distance of his house. He was so good.

He blinked back a tear that had formed in his eye and swallowed hard.

"Jah, Jenni," he said at last. "I know exactly what that feels like."

Hearing the front door open and shut, then Rachel's footsteps into the bathroom, he relaxed at last. His sister was inside. Everything was as peaceful as it was ever going to be in this home.

He picked up the letter and started reading again, prepared to savor every word.

Chapter 10

Dear Jenni,

The letter you handed me yesterday was the reason I was able to sleep last night. I'm going to be honest—things were bad at my house when I got home. Rachel was sitting on the front porch wrapped in a quilt. Our father had gotten really mad and lashed out at Mamm. When my sister tried to intervene and protect Mamm, he pulled at Rachel hard. She now has dark bruises on her arm.

I felt so guilty. You see, I used to go to your house to escape mine. I know you know that by now, but maybe what you don't know is that sometimes there's still a part of me that seeks solace when I walk to your front door. Maybe that wouldn't be so bad if I didn't leave my sister here.

Anyway, I ended up going inside, prepared to make things safe for my sister, but of course everything had calmed down. Our father was in his bed-

room, and my mamm was passed out at the kitchen table. Before even taking a shower, I went to my room to read your note.

And now, here I am, anxious to write back even though I saw you just an hour ago.

I'm not a very good brother, am I? I tell myself that all this avoidance is my method of survival, and that Rachel does the same thing. She sees Caleb whenever she can, and the only reason they haven't married yet is because he's trying to save enough money for them to get a good place to stay. They are engaged now, though. They're determined to finally be man and wife, and I don't blame them one bit. As tempting as it is to put off plans for the future, it's not possible. Years ago, Rachel and I promised each other we would move on at the same time.

And now, here I am, burdening you with my dirty secrets. I hope you aren't too shocked.

Honestly, Jenni, the more I write to you, the more I understand why I kept things so superficial. There's no reason for you to want me, is there? You need someone better. Someone who can give you everything you deserve.

If you feel that way now, all you have to do is tell me. Even though I would be upset and disappointed, I will understand. I'll even try my hardest to be happy for you when you find someone else. Although that won't be easy, I'll try. Even though I didn't grow up learning how to be kind and selfless, you are my exception. I want the best for you, and tonight I realize that the best ain't me.

Matt

Jenni was pretty sure that by now she knew each word of his note by heart. It was clear the letter had been painstakingly wrenched from his own heart.

Swiping yet another stray tear from her face, Jenni released a ragged breath. She needed to see Matt soon. That very afternoon. Standing up, she paced in her room. It was unlikely he'd come over that evening. Not after what had happened when he'd left last time.

Or what had happened between them. He'd almost kissed her in the hearth room, and she would've let him. That wasn't shocking, but the time and place certainly had been. Her parents could have walked in and seen them. Or her brother.

No, it was time she took some of her own advice and went to his house. Sure, she was a little afraid about what she'd find there, but she could take it. She wanted Matt to understand that she wasn't the timid, needy girl he seemed to think she was.

Though life at his house sounded really bad, she knew his parents. They went to church on second Sundays. Though neither of them had gone out of their way to talk to her, both always said hello or nodded in her direction from time to time. She'd pay a call and pretend that she was doing nothing more than being a good neighbor. Sure, her act wouldn't fool any of them, but that was okay. What mattered was that she had shown up.

With her visit in mind, she walked to the kitchen and pulled out a mixing bowl. She'd planned to make a loaf of almond pound cake. She could easily double the recipe and take one of them to the Lapp family.

The gesture would serve well enough. If they needed more information, she could say she was making loaves of bread for every family in their church district and that they were the first recipients.

All that mattered was seeing Matt. At the very least, he'd have something to eat.

Pleased with her plan, she pulled out the ingredients and a big mixing bowl and got to work. Each time she measured an ingredient or stirred the batter, she took the time to say a prayer for Matt, Rachel, and their parents. It was going to be the edible equivalent of a prayer shawl, she decided. This gift of food was going to be so full of hope and God's love that the Lapps would feel blessed by Him. Once the pans were filled, she set the timer and then got started on the dishes.

She'd just finished putting away the last of the dishes when Kevin walked in.

She knew he'd been working with their new horse, getting him used to their buggy and grooming him, too. His cheeks were pink from the cold.

"Mmm. It smells so good in here, Jenni. What did you make?"

"Almond pound cake."

He peeked in the oven. "You made a lot of it." He grinned. "I might just take a whole loaf for myself."

"That won't be possible. One of the loaves is for the Lapps."

He frowned. "Are you expecting Matt tonight?"

"Nee. I'm going to go over to his house as soon as the pound cake is cool enough to wrap in paper."

"No, you're not."

Even though she'd known he would have a problem with her plan, she shook her head. "Of course I am."

"Okay, fine. If you are going, then I am, too." He shook a finger at her. "And don't even think about refusing. You need a chaperone."

"Matt lives with his parents, Kevin." And yes, she knew she was being purposely oblivious. "Rachel is there, too."

"I hear ya, but I'm still going, too." Lowering his voice, he added, "Jenni, you know that haus ain't no place for you."

"That's where you're wrong. If Matt is there, then it is most definitely the place for me." That was the truth, too. Even though it felt almost too late, she was determined to make amends. Matt needed to stop hiding his homelife from her. He definitely needed to stop being embarrassed about something he couldn't change.

The timer went off, its shrill *ding* making her jump. Grabbing two pot holders, she pulled out the two bread pans and set them on the counter. In a few moments, she'd remove the cakes from the pans, wrap one of them in parchment paper, and then head to Matt's house.

"You're not going to change your mind, are you?"

"Nope."

"And you know where he lives?"

"I do." She'd always had a pretty good idea. Now she had his address memorized.

"Fine. Give me ten minutes to take a shower, and I'll go with you."

"Are you sure? Matt might be upset if we both just show up."

"I'm positive." When she was about to protest yet again, he added, "Jenni, I'm not going to let you go by yourself. Having a chaperone is the proper way for a woman to call on her boyfriend. You and I both know that."

"We both also know that no one sticks to those rules all the time."

"Perhaps not. But most young women would agree to have a chaperone for their very first visit. You know I'm right." After a pause, he added, "You aren't the only person feeling guilty for never going over to Matt's house, Jenni."

Kevin's eyes were filled with the same regret that she was feeling. It was wrong of her to imagine that she had a stronger connection with Matt than her brother. It was different but just as filled with mistakes.

She nodded. "All right. You can come with me, but don't go tattling to Mamm and Daed."

"You don't think they'll allow this visit?"

She couldn't tell if he was joking or not. Had her parents

been just as unaware of how bad things were at Matt's? Or was
it the opposite? Maybe there was a reason they'd encouraged
Matt to come over so much. Not just because he was their son's
best friend but because they knew he needed a place to feel safe
and secure. "I don't know if they will or they won't. But with
my luck, they'll decide they want to go with us."

Kevin's eyes lit up. "You know what? I can almost see that
happening."

"I can see it, clear as day."

"Danke. When do you want to go?"

"Maybe in thirty minutes?"

"I'll be ready." Walking closer, he rested both of his palms
on the tops of her shoulders. "I always knew you were a good
person, but now I realize that Matt is blessed to have you.
You're going to make him a fine frau one day."

Glad things were better between them, she closed her eyes
when he kissed her brow.

"Let's hope so," she said at last. She might make Matt a good
wife one day . . . if he ever asked her to marry him again.

An hour later, Matt's house was in sight. It might have been
in need of a coat of paint and perhaps a little bit of care with the
front yard, but it didn't look much different from a lot of the
other houses in the area. The paint was white, the door was a
natural wood color, and the front porch had been painted gray
or it had faded over time. She imagined it would be darling with
some bright green boxwoods, garden beds filled with blooming
impatiens, and a fresh coat of white paint.

"Are you ready?"

"Of course." She was armed with a pound cake and a host of
good intentions. Plus, she was eager to see Matt again.

The door opened just as they approached the front porch
steps. Matt's sister, Rachel, stepped out. As always, Jenni was
struck by Rachel's beauty. She had Matt's unusual green eyes

and blond hair. Complementing those features were perfectly bowed lips; a slim, almost delicate build; and a quiet manner that was alluring. She was currently staring at them in confusion.

When a few seconds passed, Jenni cleared her throat. "Hiya, Rachel," she said. "How are you today?"

"I'm all right. Why are you here? Is something wrong?"

Jenni's face heated. Of course Rachel would think that the only reason they would come over was because there was a crisis. "Nee."

"Jenni wanted to pay a call on Matt," Kevin supplied. "Is he around?"

"He is, but now isn't a good time."

"Are you sure? I won't stay long." Jenni held up the pound cake. "I brought your family a cake."

Rachel neither stepped closer nor looked all that pleased by the news. Actually, she looked as if she was about to go back inside and leave them standing on the steps. "That wasn't necessary."

Suddenly the door opened, and their father stepped out. His appearance was so shocking, Jenni couldn't help but stare. Aaron Lapp's clothes hung on his frame, and his skin looked sallow. Jenni tried to recall when she'd seen him last. She couldn't.

Maybe he hadn't gone to church in several months?

"What do you want?" he asked.

Kevin took charge. "Hiya, Aaron," he said. "Jenni's been baking cakes for everyone in our church district. It's your week."

Yes, Kevin had lied, but it was a good lie. At least, she thought so, since Aaron's body relaxed. Motioning to Rachel, he said, "Take it, daughter."

Dutifully, Rachel stepped down to meet them and took the cake out of her hands. "Danke."

When it looked as if they were both going to simply turn around and close the door, Jenni spoke up. "Wait. We also came to see Matt. May we come in?"

Aaron shrugged before walking back inside.

Giving Jenni a look, Kevin stepped forward. "Where's Matt?"

"He's in our room," said Rachel.

"We'll go there, then."

Rachel sighed. "I know you two think Matt's going to be okay with you coming inside, but he isn't."

Jenni reckoned Rachel was right. Matt had taken great care to make sure she never visited his house. She and Kevin had cared about him so much that they'd accepted his wishes without argument.

Now, she didn't think that had been the best thing for any of them. She needed Matt to realize that she was going to love him even if his parents weren't all that lovable. That she would stay by his side even if staying there wasn't always the most comfortable place to be.

"He might not want us here but I'm coming in anyway."

"Why?"

"Because I love him," Jenni said simply. "I love him, and one day I'm going to be his wife. Now, please, let us come inside."

Still holding the cake, Rachel held the door open for them. "Our room is the last one on the right."

"Danke," Kevin said.

After seeing neither Aaron nor Rose Lapp, Jenni followed her brother down the hall. She hoped and prayed she wasn't making a huge mistake.

Chapter 11

Three light raps on the bedroom door were accompanied by two voices that Matt had never wanted to hear in his house.

"It's me, Matt," Jenni said, sounding a little breathless. "Me and Kevin."

He opened his mouth, but no sound came out. It was as if his whole body had frozen while it attempted to process that his best friends in the world had come over.

After another second passed—or maybe a minute?—Kevin spoke. "We talked to Rachel outside. She said to come on in. She told us this was your room."

Matt couldn't believe it. He'd spent the last hour half-heartedly reading a book and watching Valentine bat at a rolled-up sock. He'd also been wondering what to do about Jenni. Over and over again, he'd reviewed all the things he'd said in his letter.

Wished that he hadn't been so honest. He'd probably scared her away. Or, at the very least, he'd likely made her think twice about wanting to spend the rest of her life with him.

Now, here she was. With Kevin.

Had Jenni brought her brother along so she wouldn't have to worry about him getting upset when she broke things off? If that was the case, it crushed him. He would never hurt her. Never.

Did she not know that?

"Matt, come on, buddy. Let us in," Kevin said.

"Please?" Jenni added, further ripping open his heart.

He stood up at last. "It's not locked," he called out.

The doorknob turned, and the door swung open slowly, as though his friends were worried about what they might find inside.

If so, they shouldn't have worried. It was just him, trying to hold himself together.

Jenni stepped in first, looking as tentative as a groundhog on the first day of spring. "Hi," she said.

He surged to his feet. "What are you doing here?"

Obviously stung by his tone, she drew back. "You're mad."

He'd scared her. Never wanting to do that, he gentled his tone. "I'm not mad. I promise. I'm sorry I snapped."

He glanced at Kevin. His friend looked both apologetic about coming over uninvited and wary. Like he was afraid Matt was going to snap at him, too . . . and, maybe, displeased? No doubt Kevin didn't appreciate Matt speaking harshly to his sister. If so, he didn't blame Kevin.

"Hey, I'm, ah, sorry for making you two stand out in the hall. The truth is that you guys took me off guard. I never expected either of you to come over."

"I figured as much," Kevin said. "I told Jenni I didn't think coming here was a good idea, but she insisted."

"I told him that I was coming over to see you and that I didn't need his company."

Jenni's words were so tart, Matt almost smiled. "Let me guess, that's what changed his mind?"

Her eyes brightened. "Maybe."

"I'm glad I came with her," Kevin said. "Jenni was right. We've been good friends for a long time, Matt. I should've come over long before now. I'm sorry I didn't."

Matt knew they could keep apologizing to each other, but there was no reason to go on. All that mattered was that they were there.

"So, this is my room. As you know, I share it with Rachel."

"And now Valentine," Jenni said with a smile. Kneeling down, she wiggled her fingers. "Hello, kitty."

Valentine carefully stepped forward, got almost close enough to brush against Jenni's leg, then darted back to him.

Petting her soft fur, he chuckled. "Valentine's such a tease. Don't worry, she'll come over to see you again in a few minutes. She plays this game with Rachel all the time."

The door opened again as Rachel joined them. "She does enjoy playing hard to get, there's no doubt about that."

Kevin sat down on the floor next to Jenni. "Here, Valentine. Come sit with me."

"She's a kitten, not a trained dog, Kev," Matt said. "Cats don't come when called."

Then, to everyone's surprise, Valentine gracefully stepped toward Kevin and hopped into his arms.

Kevin laughed. "Did anyone just see that?"

"Of course we did," Jenni said. "It's poor manners to point it out, though."

"Is it? Even though it's obvious?"

"Oh, brother," Rachel said. "I can see it's good I came inside to join you, Jenni."

Jenni smiled at his sister. "I'm glad of it."

Relieved that the four of them were doing their best to act as if nothing out of the ordinary was happening, Matt moved to Jenni's other side. "Don't let Valentine's antics get you down, Jen. She knows you have my heart."

Jenni blushed. "Truly?"

Gazing into her eyes, Matt nodded. "Always." And, just like that, the atmosphere in the room changed yet again. The light, irreverent banter had been replaced with a sweet, romantic tension between him and Jenni. Suddenly, all he wanted to do was tell her how much she meant to him. Admit how many nights he'd dreamed of being her husband.

"Don't you two start saying mushy things to each other," Rachel blurted. "There's nowhere else to go besides outside."

"I agree," said Kevin. "Plus, let's all remember that you're talking to my sister."

"Stop complaining, you two. I would never embarrass my almost fiancée that way," he teased.

Jenni giggled. "Almost fiancée?"

"Well, jah. I mean, that's what you are . . . ain't so?"

"I guess so. For now, at least."

His heart just about stopped. "What do you mean by that?"

Kevin and Jenni did that twin thing. A knowing look, accompanied by a smile and nod from her brother, and Jenni seemed to relax.

When she spoke again, splashes of color flushed her cheeks. "Only that I'm an almost fiancée for now."

"Until?"

"Until you are ready for that to change," she replied.

Her hazel eyes were shining. There wasn't a trace of doubt in their depths. But this was too important to him not to be sure.

"Jenni, do you mean it?"

Biting her bottom lip, she nodded. "Jah."

A dozen choices raced through his head as he stared at her. What to do? What to do? Was he actually thinking about proposing marriage to Jenni right there?

"Ask her, silly," Rachel whispered.

"Now?" he whispered back. But, unfortunately, not softly enough.

"Jah," Kevin said. "Haven't you waited long enough?"

The four of them were sitting on the floor of his bedroom. Kevin was holding his cat. Two of them were looking at him, obviously silently prodding him to ask the question.

And Jenni? Well, she was sitting as still as a statue, her hazel eyes staring at him intently.

Yes, it seemed as if there was no time like the present. "Jenni, I promised myself that the next time I proposed, we would be alone, we'd be somewhere romantic and beautiful, and I would kneel at your feet and speak all the pent-up words that have been in my heart." He waved a hand. "I never imagined I'd ask while you were sitting on my floor. It don't seem right."

"I canna think of a better place," she whispered.

"You could kneel, if you wanted to do it right, I suppose," Kevin said.

"Hush, Kevin. You're ruining the moment," Rachel hissed under her breath.

Kevin grinned. "Sorry, guys." Waving a hand, he spurred them on. "Please continue."

Well, Matt supposed there was no time like the present. And now that they'd been sharing their letters, Jenni already knew what was in his heart.

"Jenni Miller, I promise to take care of you, even though I doubt I'll ever do as good a job as you do taking care of me. I promise to guard your heart and keep it safe. I promise to do my very best to make you happy and make sure you never regret agreeing to share your life with me. I love you, Jenni. I love you enough to ask for your hand while you're sitting on the floor of my bedroom. Enough to ask with both your brother and my sister looking on." He took a deep breath, and reached for her hand. "Jenni, will you marry me?"

She smiled. "Yes, Matt. I will."

He could hardly believe it. "You're sure?"

"I'm sure."

"Cover your eyes, Kevin," he said as he turned to Jenni.

"Why?"

Smiling into Jenni's eyes, he replied. "Because I'm about to kiss your sister."

Matt wasn't sure if Kevin covered his eyes or not. He had no idea if Rachel was looking on or had turned away. All Matt cared about was that he was holding Jenni's sweet face between his hands and she was looking at him with so much trust, he felt he must have done something very right in his life to deserve her.

"Kiss me, Matt," she whispered.

He pulled Jenni into his arms and did just that.

It was the best moment of his entire life.

Chapter 12

Valentine's Day

She'd woken up late. Jenni supposed it couldn't be helped, given the fact that she and Matt had celebrated their engagement the night before.

What a party they'd had! Because the party had been planned on the spur of the moment, her parents had invited all of their friends and family to the house and they'd held it in the basement.

Jenni had worried the basement would be too cold and chilly, but Mamm had assured her that the battery-operated candles, portable heater, and the crowd of people would warm the space up in no time. She'd been right.

All told, fifty people had come over in the late afternoon, all bearing gifts and good wishes for her and Matt. To everyone's surprise, even his parents had come for a short time. Rachel had whispered that her and Matt's engagements had been a wake-up call for their parents. They'd finally taken the bishop up on his offer of help. No one but the Lord knew if Aaron and Rose

Lapp would ever completely change, but it was a step in the right direction.

The party had lasted until late in the evening. All of Jenni's parents' friends had brought plates of appetizers and cupcakes. She and her mother had arranged the appetizers on the basement kitchen counters and displayed all the cupcakes on a tiered cupcake holder. It had been so very beautiful.

However, the best part had been at the end of the night when Matt had held her in his arms before leaving with Caleb and Rachel in Caleb's buggy.

In a secluded spot, they'd kissed and whispered and made plans until Kevin had called out for them to stop.

She'd giggled about that all night.

When she walked into the kitchen, she found Kevin and both of her parents sitting around the table holding cups of coffee. Each of them looked as exhausted as she did.

"Gut matin," she said. "Is there any kaffi left?"

"I just made a fresh pot," Mamm answered. "Go help yourself."

After pouring herself a generous cup, she joined them. "I'm sorry I slept so late."

"We just got up, child," Daed murmured. "No worries there."

"I'll go downstairs and start cleaning soon."

Mamm smiled. "I know you will. But first, I think you need to open this." She pointed to a red envelope with her name written on it. "Matthew brought you a valentine this morning."

"Really?"

"He brought you flowers, too," Kevin said. "They're on the counter."

Sure enough, there was a glass milk bottle filled with roses.

"Matt is so wonderful."

Both her mother and father looked as if they were trying hard not to laugh. Jenni didn't care if they were amused by her lovestruck happiness or not. All that mattered was that she'd soon be Matt's wife.

Standing, she picked up her coffee and card. "I think I'm going to go read this in my room."

"That's probably a gut idea, sister," Kevin said. "There's only so much of your romance I can take at a time."

She figured he had a point but couldn't resist ribbing him a bit. "I can't wait until you're the one writing valentines, Kevin."

"You're gonna be waiting awhile!"

Once she was in her room, she sat on the side of her bed and opened the envelope at last.

Inside was a card with bold red hearts and a drawing of a black cat on the front. It was so goofy and sweet and unlike Matt, tears filled her eyes.

But what he wrote would stay in her heart forever.

> *You've made me the happiest man in the world, Jenni.*
> *From now until the end of time, you will always be my valentine.*

She couldn't think of a better way to end their courtship— or begin the next chapter of their life together.

S.W.A.K.

CHARLOTTE HUBBARD

For Neal,
who's written some fine love letters over the years

Chapter 1

"Well, well, little brother. You got two letters today—and the *F* inside the heart where the return address should be means they're from Fannie Lehman, *jah*?" Vera teased. "What's your secret?"

Eddie Brubaker looked up from painting the white latticework beneath the front porch of the house. His older sister's knowing smile made him wish he'd gone out to get the mail before Vera had seen those two pink envelopes. At least she wasn't the type to secretly steam them open before she handed them over.

"I have no idea," he insisted. "I thought moving away from Clearwater would make her lose interest—but who knew she'd be at Danny Yoder's wedding last month? You'd think she would realize I'm not interested when I don't reply to her letters."

"How many have you gotten?" Vera teased, raising an eyebrow.

"Who's *your* letter from?" Eddie countered quickly when he saw her breaking the seal on a plain white envelope.

"Aunt Minerva. Don't change the subject, lover boy."

As Vera perched on the top step to read Minerva's letter, Eddie set aside his paintbrush. They razzed each other a lot, but Vera was considerate enough not to blab to the rest of the family when he confided some of the adventures he'd had on the painting jobs he drove to for a few days at a time. Hopefully she'd keep his problem with Fannie under her *kapp*, as well—although she had to have noticed all the hearts Fannie had drawn along the two letters' seals.

Eddie sighed as he tore open one of the letters.

> *Dear, dear Eddie!!*
> *It's not the same in Clearwater now that you've moved to Bloomingdale. None of the guys around here interest me—they seem so childish that I don't even want to ride home from singings with any of them. What would be the point? When I saw your new wagon, outfitted so you could move from one painting job to the next, it seemed even clearer that you're a man with a purpose. A man with a future!*
> *I really, really wish you'd answer my letters, Eddie. You have no idea how much I miss you— and seeing you at Danny Yoder's wedding has only made me more aware of what a wonderful man you are and how lucky any girl would be to marry you. . . .*

Exhaling hard, Eddie stuffed the letter back into its envelope.

It was worse than he'd imagined. He wished he'd never given Fannie a ride in his specially designed wagon, but she'd worn him down with her wheedling. She was spinning her happily-ever-after around him, and he'd been foolish enough to follow her behind the Yoders' barn and share a few playful kisses at Danny's wedding. Fannie was a cute little blonde, but at seventeen, he was *not* interested in courting her, let alone marrying her.

He glanced at Vera, who was still engrossed in the long letter from their aunt, Minerva Kurtz. Minerva, her husband, Harley, and his family had moved to Promise Lodge in northern Missouri a couple of years ago, and she served as that community's midwife as well as their schoolteacher. Minerva—Dat's sister—always wrote long, newsy letters, so while Vera was engrossed in reading, he opened the second pink envelope from Fannie. He shook his head again at the *S.W.A.K.* she'd written along the back seal, not to mention the string of *X*'s and *O*'s. Didn't she have anything better to do than write to him every day?

> *Dear, sweet Eddie,*
> *I still have such vivid memories of kissing you behind the barn at Danny's wedding. I can't help having hopeful, romantic thoughts about how fine life would be if we were together. Weddings make you think about how wonderful the world is when you fulfill God's intentions for men and women . . . me and you, Eddie . . . in that bunk in the back of your wagon.*
> *When will you be in the neighborhood again? It would be so much fun to ride with you—even be your assistant as you go around to your painting jobs—*

"Eddie, listen to this! Aunt Minerva wants me to come to Promise Lodge!" Vera said excitedly. "She thinks I could be the new teacher there and bring my pottery wheel and—"

"Oh *jah*? What's she say?" he asked hopefully.

As his sister pushed up her glasses and began to read aloud,

Eddie folded Fannie's second letter back into its envelope and slipped both pink missives down the front of his loose shirt. Maybe Vera would forget to quiz him about their content.

"'Because now that I'm in the family way, I would love to have you here as my mother's helper, Vera,'" his sister read in a low, clear voice. "'After losing two previous little souls, I want to do everything possible to birth a healthy, full-term baby this time, so you would also be taking my place as the Promise Lodge schoolteacher when classes resume this fall. Folks here are open to artistic talent expressed in useful ways, so I bet you could make and sell your pottery pieces in our new bulk store.'"

The lilt in Vera's voice was music to Eddie's ears. Vera *loved* dabbling in pottery, so much so that their stepmother, Amanda—who made and sold beautiful sets of hand-thrown dishes—had bought Vera a wheel for her nineteenth birthday. It was no secret, however, that many of their conservative church leaders considered decorative artwork a sinful waste of one's time, so his sister received little local support for her talent.

Eddie smiled when Vera looked at him. "Promise Lodge sounds like a great place—"

"And maybe I would meet a nice guy there," she whispered wistfully. "There's certainly nobody for me here."

"You'll meet somebody, sis. Don't you worry," he murmured, squeezing her ankle gently. "God's got someone wonderful in mind for you. I just know it."

Vera smiled over the top of the letter she was holding. She was a pretty brunette, tall and slender, and her years of experience with their younger siblings—and running the household after their *mamm* had died a few years ago—would make her an ideal wife. She wasn't one to flirt or play up her abilities—

She wouldn't write letters like Fannie's in a million years.

"Maybe that's why girls have always flocked to you, Eddie. You're a *gut* listener and very kindhearted," Vera remarked softly. She smiled as though she'd saved the best part of Aunt Minerva's letter for last. "Listen to this!" she said as she found her place on the page again.

"'And if you'd feel better having Eddie come with you, he could find painting jobs in this area—some of them right here at Promise Lodge. We've had several couples marry recently, and their homes will need to be painted, not to mention the repairs and painting the lodge building requires after a tornado destroyed—'"

Eddie's eyes widened. God and Minerva Kurtz had come to him in his hour of need with the perfect solution to his problem. "Who are we to argue with Aunt Minerva?" he blurted out. "We're going to Promise Lodge, Vera, as soon as you're packed and ready!"

Vera sucked in her breath, staring at him. "Eddie, we haven't even mentioned this to our parents, or—"

"Dat helped buy my new wagon because he wants me out working, making my way in the world, *jah*?" Eddie reminded her happily. "You're nineteen, Vera, ready for a new challenge. And the parents know Minerva and her family will keep an eye on us—her father-in-law's a preacher at Promise Lodge, after all. We're outta here!"

Chapter 2

Two days later, Eddie clucked to his gelding to keep the family's farewells from dragging on into the morning. From the wooden bench of his wagon, he and Vera waved to their parents and their five younger siblings until they reached the paved road. When they both turned to face forward, his heart began to dance.

"Mark this day, Vera!" he crowed, urging Tucker up to street speed. "Friday, June the first—our great escape! Promise Lodge, here we come!"

Vera was toying with one of her *kapp* strings, a sure sign she was nervous. "I—I believe we're doing the right thing," she said softly. "But now that we're on the way to a whole new life—at least for the foreseeable future—I hope we won't regret dashing off without thinking our decision through."

"No sense in overthinking the obvious," Eddie said with a chuckle. "Aunt Minerva needs your help, Promise Lodge will need a new teacher soon—and me, I'm feeling like a free man!"

The morning air cooled his face and smelled of freshly cut grass and the lilacs growing along the fence row. Eddie could feel his sister's gaze as they passed the familiar white farm-houses of their nearest neighbors.

"What are you running from, Eddie?" Vera asked. "What on earth have you told Fannie that makes her think you want to marry her?"

"*Nothing!* She's just got it in her pretty, clueless head that I'm the perfect guy—"

"So why haven't you answered her letters and told her you're not interested?"

Eddie let out an exasperated sigh. "I don't know what to say!"

"Think of something! Don't let Fannie believe you want to be more than a friend!"

"But she's so set on marriage, she won't even hear me if I tell her no."

Vera threw up her hands. "Pay her a visit and state your case, Eddie. If you don't answer her letters, she won't know how you feel. And she won't stop writing to you, or dreaming about a wedding. The higher you let Fannie fly, the farther she'll fall."

Vera was right, but that didn't mean he could follow through with her suggestion.

"How long has this been going on, Eddie? How many letters have you received?"

Eddie stalled, but there was no ignoring his sister's question. "Since the Yoder wedding last month, she's written me six letters. Or maybe eight. I could've lost track."

"Oh, my word," Vera murmured. "You really do need to talk to her. But you might have a point about Fannie spinning pretty pictures in her head if she's doing all that writing and not hearing back from you."

Eddie cleared his throat, trying to think of a solution that didn't involve seeing Fannie in person. She had a way of twist-ing his words around to her own way of thinking, as well as the pluck to grab his hand and lead him down her own suggestive, romantic path.

"Fannie's known you for years, so that's part of it. From what I hear, she's dated a few other guys, but nothing clicked," Vera put in thoughtfully. "Could be, now that you've set yourself up in your own business, she sees you as a man who can take *gut* care of her. Solid husband material, even though you're only seventeen."

"Even though I've never taken her on a date," Eddie pointed out. "And then came Danny's wedding, and who knew she would be there . . . motioning for me to follow her behind the barn?"

"And?" Vera demanded.

Eddie's cheeks tingled with heat. "Okay, so she kissed me a couple of times," he admitted. "It was nice, but I walked away without a second thought. I didn't make any promises. I didn't say I'd take her out or go back to Clearwater to visit her—"

Eddie shook his head, focusing on the road so he wouldn't miss his next turn. "I never figured on Fannie closing in on me with such *expectations*. I'm too young to get married and settle down! And so is she!"

Vera shook her head in disbelief, and maybe a bit of envy. The *clip-clop, clip-clop* of Tucker's hooves on the pavement punctuated their silence until she finally said, "You really do need to figure out a way to wrap this up, Eddie. Escaping to Promise Lodge won't solve your problem. Mamm or Dat will forward her letters to you, most likely—and they'll certainly wonder why you're getting so many of them."

Eddie grimaced. He hadn't thought about the mailbox revealing his secret to his parents, because he—or Vera—usually fetched the daily mail. After several moments of squeezing and releasing his grip on the leather lines, he sighed.

"I . . . I don't want to hurt Fannie's feelings," he admitted softly. "I don't want to disappoint her or make her cry. And I don't want to go away feeling lower than a worm's belly after I let her down. I don't know what to *do*, Vera."

Vera didn't drop her gaze, yet the softening of her expression told Eddie she believed his heartfelt confession.

"Well, no one's ever asked me to marry him, so I'm no expert," she murmured. "But if I were in Fannie's place, I'd want to know sooner rather than later—straight from the horse's mouth—that my dreams of life as Mrs. Edward Brubaker weren't going to come true. That way I could get over my disappointment and find a man who loved me the way I wanted to be loved."

Eddie blinked. His sister's wistful tone spoke volumes about how badly she wanted to become a wife, yet they were both aware of how few eligible young men lived in the church districts near their home in Bloomingdale.

"I can see your point, Vera—and you're usually right about such things," he added with a rueful smile. "But as we make our three-hour drive to Promise, there's nothing I can do about it, *jah*? Shall we change the subject?"

Vera shook her head. Her younger brother was blessed with an effortless appeal: Eddie attracted girls without even trying. Even as a wee boy, he'd had all the older ladies pinching his cheeks and making a fuss over him because he possessed an irresistible combination of modest charm, good looks, and courtesy. She, on the other hand, felt tongue-tied and inept when it came to making conversation with young men. She hadn't had much practice at flirting, and her new glasses did nothing to make her more attractive.

Deep down, it struck Vera as shallow and insincere, the way some girls played up their looks and poured on the charm to make guys notice them. She wasn't interested in relationships that were built upon superficial gestures, false impressions, and pretty promises.

And yet, as she considered the way Fannie Lehman had initiated those behind-the-barn kisses, Vera felt a little envious. Never in a million years could she do such a thing!

But she and Eddie were putting his troublesome relationship behind them for the moment, so Vera considered other topics of conversation.

"Aunt Minerva says things are different now from when we visited them last year," she remarked as they passed a large white barn surrounded by black-and-white Holsteins. "A tornado ripped through Promise Lodge a couple of weeks ago, and they're rebuilding several structures. Two huge trees fell on the back side of the lodge, and that big dairy barn near the entrance was destroyed, along with the little cheese factory and the bakery beside it."

Eddie's eyes widened. "Was anybody hurt?"

Vera shook her head again. "Miraculously, no. The lodge residents were in the basement when the storm passed through."

"Sounds like we'll be arriving in time to help out," he put in with a nod. As he directed Tucker to turn at the next intersection, his expression suggested he was already thinking in a new direction. "As I recall, they have several experienced carpenters there, but another set of hands—younger hands, handling a roller or a paintbrush—will surely be welcome. I'm glad Aunt Minerva suggested I come along with you!"

"Me too," Vera admitted. "Having you around will make it easier for me to meet all those new people—"

"Oh, you'd do fine without me!" he insisted.

"And I really appreciate having you to move all my pottery supplies, so I didn't have to hire a driver," Vera finished. She slung her arm around his broad, muscled shoulders. "You're such a natural at making friends and conversation, Eddie. I wish I wasn't such a mouse. I probably do so well with my pottery because I don't have to *talk* to make the clay behave."

"You'll be a huge hit when folks at Promise Lodge see the cool stuff you make, Vera," Eddie assured her. "And besides, you already know Aunt Minerva's husband, Harley, as well as his *dat*, Preacher Marlin, and Marlin's younger kids, Fannie and Lowell. And Marlin's new wife, Frances, seemed very nice when we met her during our visit last year. You'll fit right in, Vera."

She hoped he was right. The thought of doing something different—helping Aunt Minerva, as well as teaching in the fall—gave her a sense of moving forward in a life that had been feeling stagnant of late.

"Do you suppose you could live in one of those cabins by the lodge, Eddie?" Vera asked. Promise Lodge had once been a church camp, and the large, rustic lodge building with its row of sturdy little cabins had impressed her as wonderful places to stay. "Aunt Minerva's probably figuring I'll be in a guest room at their house, and she'll probably invite you to stay in one, too. But it would be fun to live in one of the lodge apartments—or a cabin—wouldn't it?"

"That's one of the reasons I joined you," Eddie replied with a chuckle. "I've looked inside a couple of those cabins, and they've got everything I'd need to be comfortable—minus the, um, constant watchful eyes of Minerva and Harley. They're nice folks, but I see this as a chance to have a place of my own, without Pete and Lizzie and Dora and Cora—"

"And *Simon!*" Vera chimed in before they both laughed out loud. At seven, their youngest brother was busy and exuberant and quite a handful. "We'll miss them all, but *jah*, having a little place of my own sounds heavenly. A chance to hear myself *think*, and to figure out what I want to do with my life . . . in case I don't find anyone to marry."

Eddie hugged her quickly, grinning. "We'll soon find out, Vera. This is just the beginning of our adventure!"

Chapter 3

Fannie Kurtz glanced through Minerva's kitchen window for the dozenth time, eager for the first glimpse of Eddie Brubaker's wagon—but mostly wanting to see Eddie himself. When her sister-in-law Minerva had announced that Vera Brubaker was coming, and that her younger brother was joining her, Fannie's heart had sprung cartwheels.

Ever since she could remember, she'd had a huge crush on the eldest Brubaker boy, who was a year or so older than she. And now Eddie was coming to live at Promise Lodge!

"How many marshmallows do you think we *need* in that fruit salad, Fannie?" Minerva asked with a chuckle.

Fannie gasped when she glanced at the big bowl of fresh fruits and canned pineapple chunks on the table in front of her. Lost in her daydreams, she'd poured almost an entire bag of miniature marshmallows over the fruit salad she was making for the evening's picnic supper. "Oh my, I didn't intend to—I don't suppose we can pick out all the extras now that they've touched the fruit."

Her sister-in-law laughed knowingly. "Eddie impresses me

as a guy who will eat whatever we put in front of him—and with all the folks from Coldstream helping us today, we have a lot of extra mouths to feed," Minerva added kindly. "Let's add another can of pineapple chunks and cut up this other quart of peaches, shall we?"

Nodding gratefully, Fannie pulled back the tab on the can of pineapple. "I've always liked Eddie," she admitted softly.

"And with *gut* reason," Minerva put in as she opened the jar of peaches. Her face glowed as she spooned the golden-yellow slices into the salad bowl. "When Vera called to say both of them were coming, it struck me as a sign that Eddie's looking to expand his horizons while he's in *rumspringa*—and maybe you'll be part of his new vision, now that you're both a year older."

With a shy shrug, Fannie drained off the pineapple juice before pouring the yellow chunks over the marshmallows. "And maybe I won't," she murmured. "Now that Vera's told us about Eddie's special wagon with the bunk in it—so he can stay at his painting jobs until they're completed—who knows how much time he'll spend around here?"

Before Minerva could respond, the rapid pounding of feet in the mudroom and a familiar laugh announced the arrival of Lavern Peterscheim, best friend of Fannie's younger brother, Lowell.

"Aha! These cookies are for me, *jah*?" he called out as he snatched a brownie from a cookie container farther down the table.

"One's enough, young man!" Minerva warned, pointing her big serving spoon. "Take one for Lowell, and then I don't want to see you boys until we've gone to the lodge to eat, hear me?"

Unfazed, Lavern stuffed the brownie into his mouth. Most of his shirttail was hanging out beneath his suspenders, and he probably hadn't combed his sun-streaked sandy hair all day. He smelled like the horses he and Lowell had been working with, and when he flashed Fannie a grin, wet chunks of brownie were clinging to his teeth.

"Where'd ya get that flashy pink dress, Fannie?" he teased. "You didn't have to get all spiffed up for *me*, ya know!"

"Not to worry," Fannie muttered, focusing on her fruit salad. If she answered Lavern's question, it would only give him ammunition for baiting her later.

"I'm outta here," he announced after a few moments of being ignored. "I'll just grab another brownie for Lowell, and if he's lucky he'll actually get to eat it!"

When he shot off in the direction of the pasture where he and Fannie's brother helped with Bishop Monroe's Clydesdales, Fannie let out a disgusted sigh. "I wish Lavern would pester somebody else," she muttered. "He and Lily might be twins, but they're from different planets. And when Lavern and Lowell are together, they act so *dorky*."

"That comes with being fifteen and male," Minerva remarked as she stirred the big bowl of fruit. When she gazed at Fannie, her expression softened. "I hope you don't mind that I asked Vera to come help me, and to take over as the teacher this fall, sweetie. You're totally capable of handling both jobs, but I could foresee some problems if you had to deal with Lavern and your brother during their final year of classes."

"You have no idea how happy I am not to be their teacher!" Fannie said without missing a beat. "I don't envy Vera for a second."

"*Gut.* I thought you might see it that way."

"And I'd feel odd teaching Lily, too, because she's my best friend," Fannie said softly.

"It would send your friendship in a different direction, that's for sure." Minerva assessed the amount of salad in the bowl. "You've become such a proficient painter, Fannie—and you have so much fun with your friends when you all work together—that I suspected you'd be happier continuing with that. And now that we're rebuilding the lodge and so many of our other structures, the men doing the carpentry work are happy to let you girls continue your painting."

"Considering their progress on the barn and the back wall of the lodge, we'll probably have another painting frolic soon." As Fannie envisioned her friends Lily Peterscheim, and recently-married sisters Laura Helmuth and Phoebe Troyer in their paint-splotched dresses and kerchiefs, she couldn't help smiling. "Of course, now that Laura and Phoebe are married, it probably won't be long before they're in the family way—like you—so they won't be climbing ladders or rolling paint anymore."

"When you consider how many weddings we've had these past months, Promise Lodge might see any number of wee ones appearing," Minerva said with a pleased smile. Her expression softened as she glanced down at her midsection, which hadn't yet begun to expand beneath her blue cape dress. "God's given me another chance at motherhood, Fannie—just when I'd assumed Harley and I weren't meant to be parents. I feel overjoyed and hopeful, yet nervous and scared. Deep down, I'm preparing myself for another disappointment if my body doesn't cooperate any better than it did the previous two times I was carrying."

Fannie wrapped her arms around Minerva's slender body, sending up a prayer for this very special woman. It seemed only right that a midwife and a schoolteacher, already devoted to children, should have babies of her own. "Vera will be such a *gut* helper for you—and I'll be here any time you need me, Minerva," she insisted. "Especially after school starts, when Vera will be busy with the scholars all day."

"It'll all work out according to God's *gut* plan, sweetie."

Minerva returned Fannie's hug and then pointed out the window. The Kurtz home sat on the highest point in Promise Lodge, so they had an unobstructed view of the arched metal sign at the community's entryway. A large green wagon was turning off the county blacktop onto the private road that meandered between the dairy barn and the lodge and past most residents' homes.

"Wow," Fannie murmured, gazing intently at the vehicle and the young man and woman on its driver's seat. "Now *that's* a fine wagon! Look at that big yellow lettering on the side. 'Brubaker Painting and Staining.'"

"I told Vera they should drive right on up to the house," Minerva said as she reached for the plastic wrap. "Let's put this fruit salad in the fridge and walk out to meet them, shall we?"

Chapter 4

A few hours later, Eddie found himself at a picnic. Despite the recent tornado that had tossed two huge trees into the back of the lodge, leveled the barn, and destroyed two smaller buildings, the mood was amazingly upbeat.

"Folks, before we give thanks for this fine food," Bishop Monroe Burkholder called out over the crowd, "we also want to express our appreciation to the work crew from Coldstream—"

Loud applause filled the air as the residents nodded gratefully.

"And we want to welcome Eddie and Vera Brubaker, who've just arrived from Bloomingdale," the burly bishop continued as he came over beside them. "Vera will be assisting Minerva Kurtz, and Eddie operates a painting and staining business. The talents they'll share with us are surely gifts from God, for which we're also thankful. Let's bow in prayer."

As Bishop Monroe gave thanks for the food that filled three entire serving tables, Eddie thrummed with a sense of purpose and unexpected excitement. The folks were eager to meet him and Vera—and the heartfelt way many of them were thanking the workmen from Coldstream, who were headed home for a few days, warmed his heart. Rather than dwelling on the devastation of their property, these folks were focused forward. Despite the stress some of the residents had to be feeling after the loss of their apartments and businesses, their smiles impressed Eddie immensely as he and Vera took their places in the serving line.

"You've arrived just in time, young man," Preacher Amos Troyer remarked as he stepped behind Eddie and picked up a clean plate. "We've been replacing the hardwood floors of the lodge apartments that were destroyed, and they'll soon be ready to stain. Since that's your business, we certainly wouldn't expect you to work for nothing—"

"Oh, but I'd be pleased to finish your floors," Eddie put in immediately. He spooned potato salad and some baked beans onto his plate, hoping to make the right first impression because Amos was the lead carpenter in this community. "I'll eventually look for paying jobs around the area, *jah*, but for now, I want to help you folks any way I can."

As Amos held Eddie's gaze, approval glimmered in his coffee-colored eyes. He was a compact man with some silver in his dark beard and hair. The lines around his eyes and mouth deepened when he smiled. "I know Harley and Minerva have offered you a guest room," he said in a low voice, "but I'm betting a fellow your age might enjoy staying someplace that's not right under his kinfolks' noses, *jah*?"

Eddie laughed out loud. The preacher's insights were keen after many years of leading congregations here and in Coldstream. "I'd hoped to bunk in one of the cabins," he admitted as he took a fresh dinner roll. "But I guess the storm took them out?"

"Most of them required extensive repairs, so Rosetta Wickey—the gal who owns the lodge property and those ten cabins—had them razed," Preacher Amos replied. "Dale Kraybill, who owns the bulk store, has spoken for part of that land, and we'll be starting his new house after the lodge is put back together—as well as building a few new cabins. For now, I was thinking about that tiny home on the shore of Rainbow Lake."

Amos turned, nodding in that direction. "My son, Allen, builds tiny homes as his business, and this one's sitting empty right now. It was the first one he designed—his model home, which he shows to potential customers."

Eddie followed Preacher Amos's gaze. When he and Vera had driven in, they'd assumed the small blue structure must be a fancy storage shed. It was about the size of a railroad car, with a boxlike section on top, set back from the road behind the newly rebuilt dairy barn. It was far too small for an Amish family, but it seemed perfect for a single person.

"I could stay *there*?" he asked excitedly.

"Rent-free, in exchange for your staining and painting. If that suits you."

The preacher chuckled as he heaped potato salad on his plate. "The place has quite a history as a bachelor pad. Lester Lehman lived there most recently, but he's married now and lives in a new house. After supper he'll show you where everything is and how it works."

Lester Lehman's last name reminded Eddie of the young woman he was trying to forget—but not for long. His imagination was already off to the races as he envisioned the possibilities of living in the miniature blue home.

When someone grasped the other side of his plate, Eddie refocused. Fannie Kurtz was spooning up a hefty serving of colorful fruit salad loaded with marshmallows.

"Here you go, Eddie," she murmured. "Enjoy your supper."

Fannie's cheeks had turned nearly the same shade of pink as her dress. Shyly, she lowered her long lashes and looked down at the salad.

"I'm sure I will, Fannie. Everything about Promise Lodge is

better than I'd anticipated." When he and Vera had arrived at the Kurtz house that afternoon, Fannie had hung back—as she'd always done when his family and hers had been together at weddings and funerals over the years. "*Denki* for your help. It's *gut* to see you again."

She gazed at him briefly, her brown eyes sparkling. Then she greeted Preacher Amos and his wife, Mattie, spooning up more fruit salad as though her life depended upon it.

After they'd filled their plates, Vera went to sit with Aunt Minerva and Frances Kurtz, who was Preacher Marlin's wife and Fannie's stepmother. Eddie headed for an empty chair near some of the men he'd seen working on the back wall of the lodge. When he met Lester Lehman, they talked about the experience of living in a very small space. After supper, the two of them strolled across the private road and past some mailboxes to look at the little blue home.

"This place teaches you to be tidy, because you have no room for clutter or extra stuff," Lester said with a chuckle. "Allen installed several ingenious space-saving features—not to mention a microwave and other conveniences his English customers expect. It's the perfect place for a young fellow on *rum-springa!*"

"It's electrified? And Bishop Monroe and the preachers allowed you to live there?" Eddie asked. The expanse of grass they were crossing was freshly mowed, and as they approached Rainbow Lake, a large trout surged up out of the water and splashed down.

"*Jah*, but it's powered by a solar panel on the roof—and the church leaders knew I wouldn't have a TV or a computer in there," Lester replied. "And that trout we just saw? Plenty more where that one came from, as the lake is restocked each season. You'll find fishing poles in that red shed farther back, and you can use the rowboat tied at the dock, too."

"This is amazing," Eddie murmured, admiring his new surroundings. "Way better than one of the cabins would've been."

As they stepped onto the home's small front deck, Lester gestured for Eddie to precede him inside. "It's an adjustment for us folks who're used to a full-sized house," he admitted. "For instance, your bed is that narrow bunk up the ladder, in the loft that sits above the rest of the place. And the table folds out from the wall, with space for one or maybe two people. In a pinch, you—or a friend—could sleep on this wee little couch, but I don't recommend it."

Eddie was nodding as he eagerly took in the details Lester pointed out. The kitchen had the tiniest sink he'd ever seen, and beside it, the microwave sat on top of a small refrigerator. The bathroom's shower, toilet, and sink were arranged so compactly that he barely had room to close the pocket door when he stepped inside.

"One of the advantages to living here is that—after the lodge is rebuilt—you can walk over there for your meals." Lester pointed to the timbered building that was visible through the small kitchen window. "Ruby and Beulah Kuhn have apartments upstairs, and they're fabulous cooks! They'll try to keep tabs on your private life, but that's a common hobby for gals their age."

Eddie shrugged. "I won't have much for them to keep track of. Sounds as if I'll be busy staining floors and doing whatever the carpenters ask of me."

And wasn't it liberating to say that? And to know that he'd escaped Fannie Lehman by coming to this wonderful community?

Chapter 5

Sunday morning, after Fannie Kurtz settled into her lawn chair in Bishop Monroe's side yard, she peered between the older women in front of her. This was the second time they'd held church outdoors after the tornado had demolished the back of the lodge building, and the uneven rows of chairs made her search more difficult. But there, behind the older men and the fellows who'd recently gotten married, she spotted Eddie. Like all the men, he was dressed in his black vest and pants with a fresh white shirt, and he was chatting with her younger brother, Lowell, as though they'd been best buddies for years.

Fannie sighed, envious. Both her brother and Eddie Brubaker could talk to anyone they met, effortlessly. Why hadn't she been blessed with a more outgoing personality? Fannie savored a few moments of watching Eddie's animated facial expressions, until the bishop stood up to begin the service.

"As we behold the wonder of this early-June morning, we're mindful of God's glory and presence," Bishop Monroe said as he looked out over the crowd.

Two of Harley's sheep bleated loudly in the pasture to their left, which caused folks to chuckle and turn their heads. Outdoor worship afforded many distractions, so the bishop waited patiently as he, too, glanced toward the pasture—a setting that always reminded Fannie of the twenty-third psalm.

"We're also thankful that—according to Preacher Amos and our other carpenters—we'll probably hold our next church service two weeks from now in the lodge, Lord willing," he announced.

Members of the congregation nodded eagerly at his good news.

"That said," Bishop Monroe continued in his resonant voice, "if anyone prefers to return to more traditional worship held in our members' homes, this is the perfect time to consider that option. Most of us recall that we've held our services in the lodge's meeting room because two years ago, when the three Bender sisters and Preacher Amos acquired the abandoned church camp to start a new community, they had no homes to worship in. We've come a long way, friends."

Fannie nodded, loosely following the bishop's upbeat remarks—but her attention was on Eddie. His sandy-brown hair was cut shorter—and less boxy—than most Amish guys wore theirs. The way it framed his handsome face suggested that he paid more attention to his appearance, too.

How was he adjusting to the tiny home? She'd peeked inside after Allen had completed it, and she had to wonder if Eddie opened the bathroom door when he stepped out of the shower, so he had enough room to—

"This morning's words of wisdom come to us from the New Testament book of Matthew, the seventh chapter, verses seven and eight," her father said in a voice that carried over the crowd. "Hear the word of the Lord!"

Fannie snapped to attention so thoughts of Eddie in the shower wouldn't distract her further. Dat often quizzed her and Lowell on Sunday afternoons, asking about the day's Scripture lesson and what they'd learned from the sermon. In their previous church district, Dat had been a preacher—which meant he would always serve in that capacity for which God had chosen him—but Promise Lodge already had two preachers by the time the Kurtz family had arrived, so Dat served as the district's deacon. He oversaw the congregation's money, read the Scripture from the Deutsch Bible at church, and sometimes took a turn at preaching a sermon.

"'Ask, and it shall be given you,'" her father read confidently. "'Seek, and ye shall find; knock, and it shall be opened unto you: For everyone that asketh receiveth; and he that seeketh findeth; and to him that knocketh it shall be opened.'"

Around her, the women were nodding at the familiar words as Dat closed the huge Bible with a *whump*. As Preacher Amos rose to deliver the first sermon, the folks on the lawn settled into their chairs to listen.

"Ask and you shall receive. Knock, and the door will be opened," Amos began, confidently rephrasing the verses as he looked around the crowd. "We know these words like the backs of our hands, yet maybe it's time to reexamine them. Does this passage really promise that every time we ask for something, we'll get it?"

Preacher Amos paused, allowing folks to ponder his question. "And what about those times we *don't* ask for something—like that tornado, for instance—but it hits us anyway? All right now, fess up—which one of you prayed for that devastating storm?" he teased.

Fannie chuckled along with the women around her. Amos Troyer had a gift for homespun humor and down-to-earth wisdom that resonated deeply with the people of Promise Lodge. It was also a blessing that he didn't speak on and on, rambling down rabbit trails that didn't seem to lead anywhere.

"And let's not forget the flip side of the coin," Amos continued earnestly. "Sometimes we beg and plead for what we want so badly, and we don't receive it. And then, years down the road, we look back and realize that God, in His infinite wisdom, has given us what we truly need rather than what we'd probably be sorry about in the long run."

Fannie blinked. The preacher's words made her ponder her life, now that she was sixteen and had joined the church. What did she want more than anything else in the world?

I want Eddie to love me as much as I love him.

Her breath caught in her throat. Would God consider that a worthwhile request? Was Eddie Brubaker the man He'd intended for her to marry? After all, they hadn't even gone out on a date or spent any time alone together.

Fannie sighed as she thought about her blushing, tongue-tied reactions every time Eddie came near her. He was friendly enough—but he was nice to *everyone*. He apparently had no idea about her feelings for him; he could look right at her, and she felt as though she blended in with the scenery. She sensed that she could keep on praying about Eddie, as she'd done for the past several years, and get nowhere . . . unless she found a way to make him notice her.

For several minutes Fannie let the timbre of the preacher's voice lull her into her own imaginary world, where she and Eddie were talking freely and laughing together. In her fantasies, she always found the right words and Eddie's replies were positive and uncomplicated, as though they already shared an effortless, fulfilling form of love she'd witnessed between many of the married couples living around her.

"In closing, I'd like to leave you with this thought," Preacher Amos said, turning toward the men and then the women. "When Jesus preached that we should ask and seek and knock, He was telling us to *believe*—to have faith that God would hear our prayers and respond with His best answers."

Fannie's eyes widened. Had Preacher Amos tapped into her thoughts and told her to *believe* she could win Eddie's affection? All her life she'd known that God heard her prayers, but would He listen more closely if she took some sort of positive action? What could she do? Was it true that God helped those who helped themselves?

Her pulse kicked into a higher gear. When Eddie finished staining and painting the various rebuilt structures at Promise Lodge, he'd probably hit the road in his wagon and take other jobs—because he had a business to run, after all. And if Bishop Monroe was correct, work on the lodge would be completed in the next two weeks.

I've got to get my act together! If I snooze, I'll lose him to some other girl.

"Ask the Lord for what you deeply desire, my friends," Amos encouraged with outstretched hands. "But be careful what you ask for. *Be careful what you ask for.*"

Fannie sucked in her breath. As Preacher Amos sat down, it once again seemed he'd been preaching directly to her. How did he know what was on her mind and in her heart?

Be careful what you ask for.

His final words rang with a challenge. And a warning.

The rest of the service was a blur. Fannie went through the motions of kneeling for the prayers and singing the hymns while remaining mentally disconnected from the age-old order of their worship. Try as she might, she couldn't come up with an effective way to get Eddie's attention without the risk of tripping over her tongue or trembling like a scared rabbit.

Fannie considered baking him some brownies, but what if he didn't like them—or wouldn't even accept them? Lots of girls had probably baked goodies for him, so that gesture might not set her apart.

She and her good friends had painted several new homes over the past several months, so she could offer to help Eddie with his staining and painting—but that seemed like an even bigger risk. What if he didn't like the way she worked? And while they were painting in the same room, what if Eddie felt she was ridiculously immature, unable to hold even the simplest conversation with him?

When Bishop Monroe sat down after preaching the morning's second, main sermon, Fannie realized she hadn't heard a word he'd said. Folks around her began shifting in their lawn chairs, anticipating the end of the service. After nearly two and a half hours, everyone was ready for the final prayer, the benediction, and the closing hymn—and, of course, the common meal.

I've got to figure out my plan—and fast! Once Eddie's on the road in his wagon, he might meet any number of girls who could steal my one chance for happiness.

Chapter 6

Eddie whistled a cheerful tune on Tuesday morning as he crossed the lawn from the tiny home, carrying a big bag of clean rags. After discussing his work with Preacher Amos and the other carpenters the day before, he'd gone into Forest Grove to pick up several gallons of stain. In the morning, he'd meticulously removed the dust from the sanded floors and woodwork of the four upstairs lodge apartments, and he'd taped along the walls above the baseboard, so he was ready to apply the stain. He was making good progress, and Bishop Monroe, Lester, and the other workmen had been quick to compliment him.

Coming to Promise, Missouri with Vera was the best thing he'd done since he'd opened his painting business. He'd begun a whole new chapter of his life, and he'd never felt happier. He felt he had a *purpose* at Promise Lodge.

As an older-model car rumbled under the arched metal sign at the entry to the community, Eddie saw a magnetic sign that read "US MAIL—RURAL DELIVERY" on its side.

"*Gut* morning!" he called out.

The bushy-haired driver stopped the car before he reached the post that held the mailboxes for the tiny home and the lodge. "Say there, you folks must have a new resident," he said as he leaned out the window. "This manila envelope is addressed to an Eddie Brubaker at Promise Lodge, but there's no box number. Know where I might find him?"

Eddie dropped his bag of rags and hurried toward the car. "That's me! I'm staying in the tiny house for a while—"

"Then you should tell folks to mark your mail as box number two. Your place comes right after the Peterscheims' home, and they're number one—and box number three is for all the ladies who rent apartments at the lodge."

Nodding, Eddie accepted the six-by-nine-inch manila envelope. He recognized his *dat's* handwriting and the return address immediately. "*Denki*, sir. I appreciate it!"

"Quite all right, son. I'll make a note of you in my directory. Have yourself a good day."

After the postman dropped a couple of envelopes and some ad flyers into the lodge's mailbox, he drove slowly up the private road. Eddie tore open the clasped, taped envelope. What sort of news did his father have? Eddie had called his parents on Friday evening to tell them of his and Vera's safe arrival, and Dat hadn't mentioned any mail of importance then.

At the sight of three pink envelopes with hearts and *S.W.A.K.* written along their seals in red ink, Eddie groaned. As he removed them from the manila envelope, a loose piece of paper came out with them.

> *Better tell your girlfriend you've relocated!*
> *Hope things are going well for you and your sister.*
> *We miss you—Dat*

Fannie Lehman's feelings for him were no longer a secret. And his parents were probably speculating about why she'd written to him *so* many times during the previous week.

Eddie could already guess what these letters said. He wanted to get the wood in the four apartments stained before the end of the day, so he stuffed the pink envelopes into a back pocket of the splotched English-style jeans he wore to apply stain. Why ruin a perfectly wonderful day by reading about how excited and determined Fannie was to latch on to him? Truth be told, each insistent letter he read made him less inclined to pursue a permanent relationship with her.

As he entered the lodge, he paused in the lobby to take in its rustic splendor. To his right sat a massive stone fireplace, alongside the arched entryway to a dining room that could easily accommodate a hundred people—and the long wooden tables that had been pushed toward the front windows probably dated back to when Promise Lodge had been a church camp. Beyond the dining room, he heard men's voices in the kitchen, where all the cabinets and walls were being rebuilt. Off to his left he saw a large meeting room, also under partial reconstruction. A huge chandelier of antlers hung from the ceiling two stories above him, and a curved double stairway led up to the mezzanine-style hallway of the second floor.

Eddie sighed with appreciation. It was a blessing that the glossy wooden stairways and railings had survived the tornado; the two uprooted maple trees behind the building had devastated the apartments on the back side as well as the kitchen, but the front half of the building had remained intact. The lodge reminded him of a similar structure he'd seen in a state park when his family had gone to Colorado for a reunion, and it was nothing short of *glorious*. He felt honored that the residents wanted him to help restore it.

Laughter rang out above him as Phoebe Troyer, Laura Helmuth, Lily Peterscheim, and Fannie Kurtz leaned over the upstairs railing to wave at him—three blondes and one brunette wearing kerchiefs and big smiles.

"Hey there, Eddie!" Lily called out.

Laura raised her roller in salute. "*Jah*, we're having a painting frolic—"

"But we're working in the hallway so you can get the apartment floors stained," Phoebe finished. "Preacher Amos said the stain needs to dry for a few days before we walk around in those rooms with our ladders."

"But don't worry," Laura put in cheerfully. "We'll cover them with our drop cloths and work *very* carefully when we paint the apartments. We pride ourselves on only putting the paint where it's supposed to go!"

Eddie grinned at them. Rosetta Wickey had told him these girls had painted inside most of the homes at Promise Lodge, so he was pleased to share the work with them. It was a fine thing when young women could laugh and have fun while they went up and down ladders spreading fresh paint.

"That'll be fine. But once I finish each apartment and close the doors, don't peek inside," he said. "We don't want any dust—or your footprints—drying on the fresh surface. Please and *denki*," he added so he wouldn't sound so bossy.

"Anything for you, Eddie!" Lily teased as they turned and went back to work. At fifteen, she was the youngest—and most playful—of the group, whereas Phoebe and Laura had gotten married within the past year.

With a chuckle, he ascended the stairs and entered the apartment at the back corner to his right. He'd met the tenant, Irene Wickey—who was Rosetta's mother-in-law—at the picnic Friday evening, and she'd already thanked him for helping to restore her home. The wide windows afforded Irene quite a nice view, so Eddie could understand why she'd chosen that apartment.

After he strapped on his knee pads, he started in the bedroom at the back, working on a small section of the baseboard at a time. He quickly found his rhythm, brushing on the rich maple stain and then wiping it off with a clean rag. As he worked, he couldn't imagine the heartache Irene and the other renters had endured when the tornado had ripped the back walls from their homes and gutted them. When he'd completed the baseboard, Eddie rolled the stain onto sections of the floor, going with the grain and wiping it before any drips could mar the beautiful variations of color in the natural wood.

It was painstaking work, with a lot of up and down as he stood to apply color with a long-handled roller and then crouched to wipe it off. As Eddie began in the back corner of Irene's big sitting room, working his way toward the apartment's front door, he felt a deep sense of satisfaction.

When his work was going this smoothly, he could forget about everything else—including Fannie Lehman. It felt exactly right to be doing work God had given him the skills to accomplish.

"Time for a break," Phoebe declared. Fannie agreed: they had completed two of the tall hallway walls, applying new paint the color of pale sunshine.

"*Jah*, let's go out on the porch for some fresh air and lemonade," Laura suggested. "It's stuffy up here. I suppose Eddie's got the windows closed to keep any dust from coming in."

After the four of them had covered their paint trays and rollers with foil, they started toward the stairway—but, of course, they had to peek in at Eddie as they passed Irene's apartment.

"Bye, Eddie!" Laura called out.

"Break time for us," Phoebe chimed in.

"Can we bring you back some lemonade and cookies?" Lily offered as the three of them crowded around the doorway.

"*Denki*, but I'll get something when I come to a stopping point," he replied.

Hanging back as her friends started down the stairs, Fannie took her turn at peering into the apartment. When she saw that Eddie was applying stain only a few yards away from the door, with his back to her, she kept quiet. She told herself she didn't want to startle him, yet deep down she didn't want him to catch her lingering, watching his agile movements as he set aside his long-handled roller to kneel with a rag.

Eddie's muscular shoulders strained against his stain-splotched shirt as he wiped the wet floor with firm strokes, huffing with the effort. His backside filled out his faded English jeans so nicely—

And then Fannie spotted the pink envelopes sticking out of his back pocket—*three* of them. All along the seals, red hearts and *S.W.A.K.* announced that the letters were from a girl. She couldn't see a name or an address, but she didn't have to.

Anyone who'd send Eddie *that* many letters had to have serious feelings for him.

Backing away from the door, Fannie swallowed a sigh. She sagged like a balloon with a slow leak, blinking back tears.

Of *course* Eddie would have a girlfriend. He was attractive, he ran a successful business, and when he traveled to his painting jobs, he had lots of opportunities to meet girls.

It had been part of her naive fantasy to believe that she could become the love of Eddie's life, just as he'd been the young man she'd adored for years. But another girl had beat her to him. It took a few moments of deep breathing at the top of the stairs to compose her feelings and her facial expression before she joined her friends outside.

The shade from the enormous trumpet vines at each end of the front porch felt heavenly. As Fannie stepped toward the pitcher of lemonade on the table near the swing, Laura and Phoebe were choosing cookies from a plate and chatting—but Lily, Fannie's best friend since she'd moved to Promise Lodge, had been waiting for her.

"Eyeballing Eddie, were you?" Lily teased softly. As she poured a glass of the cold lemonade and handed it to Fannie, she watched for a reaction.

Fannie knew better than to deny what she'd been doing, because Lily would only tease her more. She shrugged, hoping to hide her deep disappointment that Eddie was in love with someone else. "For a minute, maybe. Sure is hot upstairs."

Not wanting to say anything else in her dangerously tremulous voice, Fannie closed her eyes. She held the cold glass of lemonade against her forehead and cheeks.

Lily cleared her throat ceremoniously. "I suppose you saw that wad of letters in his back pocket," she murmured.

Fannie sighed, sipping her cold drink. If she said anything, she'd only get more upset—and if she started crying, Phoebe and Laura would join the pity party.

The *last* thing she wanted was for her friends to hint to Eddie that she was sweet on him. If his girlfriend was writing him so many letters, he wouldn't be the least bit interested in a mousy girl who found spreading paint much easier than speaking coherently to him.

I'll keep my chin up this afternoon and lick my wounds this evening, behind my closed bedroom door. No sense in making a bigger fool of myself.

"Just a guess, but whoever wrote them likes Eddie a whole lot more than he likes her," Lily remarked with a short laugh. "He hasn't even opened them."

Fannie gazed at her best friend. A bright light pulsed inside her, as though Lily had thrown open the barn door and a shaft of sunshine had pierced her gloom. "I—I suppose you could see it that way," she murmured.

"And why would Eddie want the mailman—and everyone else—to see those silly hearts? And *S.W.A.K.* written all over the place?" Lily mused aloud. "That seems so childish, like something you'd do for Valentine's Day when you're twelve."

Fannie's pulse pounded more hopefully.

Maybe I shouldn't give up. Maybe Lily's right about the reason Eddie hasn't read those letters—

And maybe I should fight fire with fire instead of limping away, assuming I'm a loser.

Fannie's eyes widened. Where had such a challenging thought come from?

Ask and you shall receive. Knock, and the door will be opened.

Preacher Amos's words came back to her in a rush. He'd said that Jesus wanted His followers to *believe*—and that incredible things happened to folks who sought the power of God's love when they prayed for what they wanted most.

Fannie's thoughts took off like runaway horses. Suddenly an improbable romance didn't seem impossible anymore.

I want Eddie to love me as much as I love him. But how can he do that if he doesn't know how I feel? I'll have to stick my neck out—take some risks. Nothing ventured, nothing gained.

"Fannie, are you okay?" Lily stepped closer to study her face. "Maybe you'd better drink another glass of lemonade— get rehydrated—before we go back upstairs."

Fannie smiled as a simple plan formed in her mind. Lily didn't know it, but she'd provided the perfect insight—and now Fannie knew how she would indeed fight fire with fire.

After all, Eddie had come to Promise Lodge instead of going wherever that other girl lived, hadn't he? Couldn't she use that to her advantage?

Chapter 7

That evening, after supper with Vera, Aunt Minerva, and Uncle Harley, Eddie returned to the tiny home. He'd stained the floors in three of the four rebuilt lodge apartments, and every muscle in his body ached. He'd showered quickly before going up the hill to eat, but a longer hot shower would help prepare his tired body for staining the fourth apartment's floor in the morning. He would spend the rest of Wednesday applying the sealant to the other three apartments.

As he eased onto the chaise lounge on the dock, enjoying the twilight breeze off Rainbow Lake, Eddie sighed. He'd brought Fannie's letters outside with him, but he already knew what they said, didn't he?

He tore open the first one—the earliest, according to the postmarks.

> *Eddie, Eddie, Eddie!!*
> *Why are you being so mean to me? Why don't you respond to my letters when you surely must realize that I love you and that we were meant to*

be together? I can't believe you've been busy every
single minute since we were at Danny's wedding, so—

Irritated, Eddie stuffed the letter back into its envelope. Was there any point in opening the remaining two, which had both been mailed to Bloomingdale last Thursday? He wondered about Fannie Lehman's mental state. There'd been a time when he might've dated her, but she'd blown all possibility of that with her demanding letters and those silly red hearts on the envelopes.

"Might as well get this over with," he muttered as he opened a second letter. The evening was tranquil and soothing, with the gentle lapping of the lake against the shoreline. The long shadows of houses and trees stretched over the grass across the road as the sun sank in the sky, but the sunset's beauty was lost on him.

> *Dearest Eddie,*
> *Can you forgive me for writing such an impa-*
> *tient letter yesterday? Can you understand that I*
> *long to see your face and hold your hands because*
> *I'm so lonely without you? I think about you riding*
> *around in your wagon, going to your jobs, and I*
> *know my life would be complete if I could be your*
> *wife—*

Why did Fannie think he wanted to marry her? What girl in her right mind would believe a few stolen kisses behind the barn could be the basis for a satisfying, forever relationship? Eddie shook his head as he tore open the third letter.

> *Dear Eddie,*
> *My parents are getting worried, because I'm los-*
> *ing weight and losing interest in normal activities—*

because I can't think of anything except you.
You're the light of my life, Eddie, so please, please
call me or write to let me know you still care—

Annoyed—and concerned about where Fannie's intensifying feelings would lead if he *did* respond to her letters—Eddie rose from the chaise lounge. The sound of birds nesting for the night, along with the chirping of crickets, would ordinarily have soothed his soul after a tiring day, but Fannie's letters had made him too anxious to appreciate the peaceful evening. Before he headed into the tiny house, Eddie paused to inhale the cool night air. He looked up into the sky.

The pale crescent moon resembled a smile. And it seemed to be mocking him.

Eddie exhaled hard, trying to rid himself of his negative mindset as he stepped inside. At least Fannie Lehman had no idea where he lived.

As he settled into the narrow bunk in the loft, Eddie prayed for God to show him a quick, sensible solution—a way to douse the flames of Fannie's one-way romance before they both got burned. And he thanked God for leading him to Promise Lodge and giving him meaningful work among folks who appreciated his skills.

After breakfast at Aunt Minerva's with Vera and Uncle Harley on Wednesday morning, Eddie was eager to get to work. As he reached the front porch of the lodge, he gazed at the fragile bands of pink and peach that glowed on the eastern horizon, glad to be getting an early start. The temperature upstairs would rise quickly as the day's heat set in.

He peeked into the three apartments he'd stained the day before. The deep luster of the maple color, which matched the double staircase in the lobby, made him smile. By the time he was finished, the woodwork in the apartments would be restored to its original beauty and he was pleased to be part of that process.

When he reached the fourth apartment, Eddie paused at the door. A folded piece of paper had been taped to the top of his stain bucket. When he opened the note, the bottom dropped out of his stomach.

> *Eddie, I just want you to know how happy I am to be here with you. I hope we can spend lots of time together and become much closer friends.*
> *Truly yours,*
> *Fannie*

Eddie's head swiveled as he searched the hallway for signs that someone else was upstairs with him. How on earth had Fannie Lehman taped this note to his stain bucket—unless she'd come to Promise Lodge? How had she found out where he was? How could she have arrived without anyone knowing it? The penmanship left no doubt that she had written the note, so—

Is she hiding in one of the apartments? Or in a closet? She could be holed up in any number of places here, because all the residents have been gone since the tornado hit.

Eddie stood still, not breathing—listening for a floorboard shifting with someone's weight. As hard as his pulse was pounding, he might not hear her—

She could be in the basement—or anywhere on the Promise Lodge property, lurking where she can watch every move I make. And she knew exactly where to put her note so I'd find it before I started work this morning.

Exhaling harshly, Eddie suddenly wished he'd called Fannie a long time ago to set her straight. Vera had been right about that. There was no telling how many more letters had arrived at the house in Bloomingdale; his parents had to be wondering what was going on between him and Fannie.

Or maybe she stopped writing letters when she came to Promise Lodge. No need to write when she can walk right up to me and demand attention in front of everybody—

There could be no more maybes or second-guessing. Eddie was spooked—this situation with Fannie was spiraling wildly out of control. He crammed the note into the back pocket of his jeans and jogged down the hallway. Taking the stairs two at a time—with his thoughts racing even faster than his feet—he burst out of the lodge. He sprinted across the lawn and past the neat rows of vegetables Preacher Amos's wife, Mattie, was growing to sell at her roadside stand. At the tiny home, he grabbed the stack of pink envelopes he'd received.

If Fannie Lehman was indeed watching him, she must be having quite a laugh. He probably resembled a frantic rabbit.

But Eddie didn't care. By the time he'd jogged up the private road to the little shed where Uncle Harley had cleared a space for Vera's potting wheel and kiln, he was completely winded and totally *ferhoodled* about the note he'd just found.

His sister looked up from the bowl she was forming on her wheel, so startled that she jerked. "Eddie! What's the matter? You look like you've seen a ghost."

"Oh, it's worse than that," he said, gasping for breath. "Fannie Lehman's here at Promise Lodge! Wipe your hands—you gotta read this."

Frowning, Vera reached for her towel. "But that makes no sense," she said as she removed the wet clay from her fingers. "You haven't told her we were moving—have you? And you received those letters from her before we left home—"

"I got three more yesterday, in an envelope from Dat," Eddie admitted with a miserable sigh. "And just now, when I went upstairs to work at the lodge, I found this on my stain bucket. It was right beside the door where I'd be working—which means she *knows* which apartments I finished yesterday and—"

"Whoa," Vera murmured, holding up her hand. "*Breathe*, Eddie. I've never seen you this riled up."

"I've never had a reason to be."

As he handed her the folded note, he tried to make sense of the conclusions he'd jumped to over the past several minutes. None of his assumptions added up, yet he couldn't think of any other way for Fannie Lehman to have put the note on his bucket.

Vera pushed up her glasses and read the brief message. "How do you know this is from Fannie Lehman? I can't imagine she'd hire a driver to come all this way—"

"Compare the handwriting," Eddie replied as he thrust the stack of pink envelopes at her. "Can't be from anyone else."

He sighed as his sister opened a letter, held it beside this morning's note, and then began to read it. He'd hoped to keep Fannie's romantic rantings a secret, but at this point he was desperate for Vera's help. He certainly couldn't get Aunt Minerva or Uncle Harley—or Preacher Amos—involved in this situation.

After she'd read a few lines, Vera refolded the letter. Her brow puckered in thought. "Has Fannie always been so—so *aggressive*? None of the Amish girls I know would *dream* of writing a guy such insistent letters. It's the young man who's supposed to take the lead—and you haven't even asked her for a date, have you?"

"Absolutely not. Nor have I suggested it," Eddie replied. "Her latest letter said she was losing weight and losing interest in everything except for me—and that her parents are getting worried about her. How can I respond to *that*?"

Vera's eyebrows rose. "I have no idea," she murmured. "Maybe you should call Dat. If he sent you three letters from

Fannie—with those hearts and *S.W.A.K.* written all over the en-velopes—he knows something's going on, *jah*?"

Eddie rubbed his forehead. He had a humdinger of a headache. "Dat included a note that said I should tell my girl-friend I'd moved," he said glumly. "I was hoping Fannie would lose interest—or at least take a hint—after I didn't answer her letters."

"I doubt that's going to happen. Call Dat, Eddie," she added, gently grasping his arm. "He's *gut* at dealing with sticky situations—but you'll need to do whatever he suggests. You can't just keep avoiding Fannie and hope she'll go away."

"See there! You think she's at Promise Lodge, too!"

"That's not what I meant!" Vera retorted. "Call him now. He's probably at the grain elevator office, and he'll pick up the phone."

Eddie could picture his father, Wyman Brubaker, in the no-frills office of the large grain elevator he and his partner oper-ated just outside of Bloomingdale. Although Eddie didn't want to interrupt whatever business his *dat* might be conducting, he stood a better chance of keeping his dilemma man-to-man than if he called the phone at home in the barn, where a younger brother or sister might answer it. And he certainly didn't want to leave a detailed message on the answering machine.

With a sigh, he collected his letters. "You're probably right, Vera. Just like when we were driving up to Promise Lodge and you warned me to make a clean break with Fannie. I'm sorry I made you ruin the bowl you were working on."

Vera shrugged. The limp, lopsided bowl she'd been forming had fallen in on itself, with a gash where her thumb had slipped into it. "I'll just start over. Clay is very forgiving."

"Let's hope Fannie is, when I inform her I'm not going to marry her."

Vera flashed him an encouraging smile. "Tell Dat I said hello."

The phone in the Kurtz barrel factory, where Preacher Marlin manufactured rain barrels and other such containers, was the closest, but the machinery was noisy—and Eddie didn't want Harley or Marlin to walk in on his conversation. He strode down the private road to Bishop Monroe's phone shanty.

Eddie spotted the bishop out in his large pasture, working with a team of the huge Clydesdales he trained, so the coast was clear. Eddie slipped into the small white building, sat on the old wooden chair, and punched in the number for the grain elevator. As the line rang, he tried to think of ways to phrase his questions—

"*Jah*, it's a beautiful day and you've reached Wyman Brubaker at the grain elevator. How can I help you?"

The sound of his father's voice soothed Eddie, as it had since he'd been a boy. But he wasn't a five-year-old curled up in his *dat's* lap anymore. "Dat, it's me—Eddie, that is—"

"Well, now my day's even *more* beautiful! *Gut* to hear from you, son!"

His father sounded so genuinely happy that Eddie hated to spoil the conversation by talking about his problem with Fannie. Beating around the bush would only waste time while their work awaited them, however.

"It's *gut* to talk to you, too, Dat," he began.

"Hmmm. Do I hear a *but* coming?" his father asked gently. "Are things not going the way you'd hoped at Promise Lodge?"

"Oh, it's not that! So far, I've stained the floors of three apartments, and folks here are grateful for my help renovating the lodge," Eddie said in a rush. "It's about those three letters you sent me."

"Ah. From a certain Fannie Lehman, I believe."

He suddenly wished he *were* five again, sitting on his father's knee. From that vantage point, the world had seemed like a safe, uncomplicated place where he'd been surrounded with love and support, and nothing bad could ever befall him.

"*Jah*, her. Um, if you've gotten any more letters, do you recall when the latest one was postmarked?" Eddie asked hesitantly.

Dat cleared his throat as though to disguise a chuckle. "Matter of fact, I've sent you a couple more—but meanwhile, Fannie called us Monday and left a message."

Eddie groaned.

"She was wired pretty tight, wanting to speak with you, son," his father continued in a low voice. "So I called her back and gave her your new address, as well as the Kurtzes' telephone number. I figured you two should leave the rest of us out of your romantic entanglements—"

"I'm not romantically entangled!" Eddie protested. "Fannie's imagination is in overdrive—and the note I got this morning, taped to my stain bucket, tells me she's come *here*, to Promise Lodge! But I haven't seen hide nor hair of her."

After a pause, during which Eddie could almost hear the wheels turning in Dat's head, his father said, "Maybe you'd better start at the beginning. I've got time."

Ruefully, Eddie recounted his fateful afternoon at Danny Yoder's wedding. He also mentioned the stack of letters he'd received before he and Vera had left home, and the way their content was growing more intense.

As always, his *dat* listened without interrupting. Then he paused to mull over what Eddie had told him.

"And you've done nothing to indicate any interest in her?" Dat asked.

"That's right. I've known Fannie for a long time—since back when we lived in the Clearwater district," Eddie reminded him. "But it was those kisses behind the barn that got her going. How can I call a halt to this nonsense? We're too young to get married—even if I liked her that much. And the more I read, the more I'm coming to believe that Fannie's going off the deep end."

"You need to either call her or drive to her house and tell her that in person, son. Soon."

Eddie grasped the receiver, leaning his head on his hand. "But then she'll cry and get all upset because I've spoiled her plans—"

"You can't keep a young woman on the hook without reeling in the consequences," Dat put in firmly. "If you don't state your case, Eddie, someone's *really* going to get hurt. Ignoring this one-sided relationship won't make it go away."

Eddie sighed. After a few more minutes of Dat's gently encouraging him to man up—maybe with Fannie's parents present, so they knew the real story—they ended the call.

He sat for a few moments to consider his father's advice. Then he stepped out of the phone shanty to find Vera waiting for him in the shade nearby.

"Did it help, talking to Dat?" she asked.

Eddie shrugged glumly. "He gave me some things to think about. Come to find out, Fannie called home on Monday, and her message sounded urgent enough that Dat called her back with my new address and the Kurtz family's phone number—which they answer in the barrel factory. Which means she's had time to hire a driver and get up here."

His sister came to stand in front of him, gently holding his gaze. "If Fannie Lehman *had* come to Promise Lodge, she'd be talking your leg off by now, Eddie. The girl who wrote those letters isn't the type to hide herself away. Just my opinion, though."

Eddie blinked. He hadn't considered that angle. "You're probably right. But if she's not here, how did her note come to be taped to my bucket?"

"I never said I had all the answers," Vera remarked with a chuckle. "For now, it's a mystery. Something to ask Fannie herself, perhaps—if you call her, you could at least find out whether she's still at home in Clearwater, *jah*?"

With a sigh, Eddie turned to walk down the road. The sun was high in the sky now, and he had a day's work to do, but he couldn't dispel the feeling that Fannie was lurking behind a tree or watching him from the lodge. He could've sworn he saw a face in the center window upstairs—in the second apartment he'd worked in yesterday—but then it was gone.

Had it been a figment of his imagination? Were the out-of-control, crazy emotions in Fannie's letters rubbing off on him?

He hoped the coming hours of repetitive motion, rolling on stain and wiping it off, would clarify his jumbled thoughts and settle his nerves.

Chapter 8

Fannie Kurtz stepped away from the apartment window before her three painting partners caught her and accused her of mooning over Eddie—even though she *was*. Knowing that Eddie liked to start work early, she'd eaten breakfast and left the house in record time that morning, hoping to catch a few moments alone with him. Ever since she'd slipped into the lodge late the previous evening to put the note on his bucket, she'd had so many butterflies in her stomach that she'd hardly slept.

Writing that note and leaving it for Eddie were the two boldest things she'd ever done. She wanted to be his friend—and gradually become much more than a friend. Yet the idea of talking to him about it scared her as nothing else ever had. But she'd made the first move!

Eddie had found her note. Had he gone rushing up the hill toward Harley and Minerva's house because she'd upset him—because it was supposed to be the boy who took the lead? Or was he agitated about something else?

He'll be here in a matter of moments. Should I let him know I'm here, waiting for him? What if he says that he loves that other girl? What if—

The sound of her friends' cheerful laughter drifted up the open stairwell from the lobby.

"Hey there, Eddie! *Gut* morning!" Lily called out.

Fannie sighed. If only she had half of her best friend's gift of gab.

"I bet your floors look really pretty," Phoebe put in. "I can't wait to see them now that they're dry."

Fannie ducked out of the center apartment and quietly shut the door. She prayed that the stained floors *were* totally dry and that, in her eagerness to watch for Eddie, she hadn't left any telltale footprints. Her heart was pounding as she tiptoed over to where they'd been painting the day before, keeping close to the wall so her friends wouldn't spot her in the open hallway.

She wasn't used to sneaking around, and it was nerve-racking.

Putting on her best smile, Fannie turned toward the railing as her friends reached the top of the stairs. "There you are! I thought you'd already be here, so—so I was checking the walls we covered yesterday. For thin spots, you know."

"Find any?" Lily asked. "Rosetta suggested two coats, so that's what we did."

"In the morning light, the hallway looks fresh and clean again," Phoebe remarked as she gazed at their work from the top of the stairs. "You'd never know a tornado blew through here."

Fannie nodded, trying not to study Eddie's expression too closely as he topped the stairs. Was she seeing things, or did he seem preoccupied? Had her note caught him off guard?

She was wearing her least-splotched painting dress and a fresh navy-blue bandanna around her hair, wishing she looked prettier on what might be the first day of the rest of her life with Eddie, but it couldn't be helped. They both had work to do, and he would understand that. It was an important trait they had in common.

"Um, *gut* morning, Eddie," she murmured, wishing her voice sounded mature instead of like a little schoolgirl's.

He blinked, glancing at her. "Hey there, Fannie. How are you?"

And that was it.

He could've been talking to anyone. And he didn't even await her reply before he opened the door to the corner apartment, the first floor he'd stained the previous day.

Fannie let out the breath she'd been holding. Nothing had changed. She was still invisible to Eddie, even though he'd surely read her note—

But what if someone else spotted it on the bucket before Eddie did? It would be just like that pesky Lavern to snatch it, if he'd been nosing around up here. If he's got my note, I'll never hear the end of it.

The rattle of two aluminum ladders unfolding across the open hallway brought Fannie out of her woolgathering. It was time to get to work, before her friends accused her of lollygagging.

Fannie swallowed the lump that was forming in her throat. She'd put all her feelings on the line—had lost sleep after daring to write that note. And it had apparently come to nothing.

I've knocked, Lord, but the door hasn't opened even a crack, she thought as she poured paint into her tray.

When she'd climbed the ladder to begin at the top corner of the wall she and Lily were working on, the return of routine settled her thoughts. With her trim pad, she deftly applied butter-yellow paint along the line where the ceiling met the wall, and then along the edge of the wall where they'd stopped the day before. She coated a large area with her roller, as far as she could reach in either direction, before climbing down to shift the ladder so Lily could paint the lower section of the wall to the floor.

"Cat got your tongue today?" her friend asked. "You're mighty quiet."

"Compared to you, I'm always quiet," Fannie pointed out, hoping she sounded upbeat. She didn't want Lily prying into her private thoughts in the open hallway where their voices carried, because Eddie might overhear them.

Am I going to remain quiet, like a scared little mouse? Or will I try again? Knock a little louder this time on that door to Eddie's heart?

A wonderful man like Eddie deserved a second attempt, didn't he? After all, if Lavern *had* snatched that note from the bucket lid, Eddie had no idea she'd written to him.

And if that's the case, Lavern's going to get what's coming to him.

By midmorning, the work crew from Coldstream had returned, and Fannie heard many different male voices drifting upstairs from the kitchen. Before her family had moved to Promise Lodge, three then-unmarried sisters—Mattie Troyer, Christine Burkholder, and Rosetta Wickey—had sold their farms in Coldstream, pooled their money, and, along with Preacher Amos, had bought the abandoned Promise Lodge church camp. They'd grown tired of the Coldstream bishop's attitude—which was the same reason Lily's family had moved to Promise Lodge shortly after that, along with other folks. This meant that the workmen from Coldstream were longtime friends, and they were happy to help with rebuilding after the tornado.

Lunch was a big picnic out on the lodge lawn, for which all the local ladies had made casseroles, salads, and desserts that covered three long tables. Laughter rang out as folks gathered to visit and enjoy their midday meal together. After Bishop

Monroe had blessed the food, the workmen started through the line to fill their plates and sit at the dining room tables that had been set outside in the shade.

"Wow, I'm hungry!" Lily exclaimed as she waited with Fannie on the lodge's front porch. "We've already covered a lot of wall space today."

"We have," Laura agreed as she came up behind them. "I was tickled when Rosetta asked us this morning if we could put several coats of floor paint on the new back stairway that leads upstairs from the kitchen, as well as on the old stairs leading down to the basement."

"I won't be a bit surprised if she asks us to paint the dining room, the lobby, and the other downstairs rooms," Phoebe remarked from beside her sister. "That way, the whole building will look fresh and clean."

From the vantage point of the porch, Fannie was listening to her friends as she scanned the crowd to find Lavern Peterscheim. She intended to quiz him about her note before he used it to embarrass her and Eddie in public. "How much of that work do you suppose Rosetta will want Eddie to do?" she asked as she kept looking for Lily's blond twin brother. "He'll soon be finished with the apartment floors."

"Oh, I'm thinking Eddie should paint the ceilings!" Laura piped up with a laugh. "I can't imagine how we girls could reach the lobby ceiling where the antler chandelier hangs. It's two stories above the floor!"

"You won't catch *me* up that high!" Lily blurted out. "Even if we had a ladder that tall—"

"Which we don't," Phoebe interrupted emphatically.

"Not to worry, girls. We've got it covered," Eddie said as he came out the screen door behind them. He, too, began looking out over the crowd, as though hoping to spot someone.

"You've got scaffolding in your paint wagon, right?" Lily asked brightly.

Eddie smiled at her briefly before turning to gaze in the opposite direction. "I do, but Rosetta says her husband, Truman, will rent a portable power lift with a cherry picker cage on it. It'll take me as high as I need to be, so I can reach the base of that chandelier with my roller."

"Wow, does *that* sound cool!" Lily said with a wide-eyed giggle. "I don't suppose you'd take us girls up for rides—"

"I don't suppose he will," Fannie put in, elbowing her friend. The idea sounded like a lot of fun, however—especially if she could ride with Eddie alone.

For the briefest moment, Eddie smiled at Fannie in agreement—but then he waved at someone in the crowd.

"Excuse me," he murmured as he started down the porch steps. "There's Truman now."

And just like that, Eddie went to be with someone else. It made perfect sense for him to join Rosetta's husband in the serving line, of course, because they had business to discuss.

Even so, Fannie sighed to herself. Eddie had worked inside the apartments all morning, and while he'd been standing on the porch just then, he'd still seemed a million miles away, as though her note had meant nothing to him.

Fannie set aside her disappointment, however, when she spotted her brother, Lowell, coming down the hill toward the lodge alongside Lavern. "Go ahead and fill your plates, girls," she said as she started down the steps. "I'll catch up to you in a bit."

As she strode across the lawn, behind the tables where the men were starting to eat, Fannie thought about how to quiz Lavern without blaming him outright for filching her note—just in case he hadn't. He and her brother were best buddies, so she couldn't ask Lowell to leave without raising the boys' suspicions.

When Lavern spotted her, he started right in. "Well, well, if it isn't Fannie Banannie!" he called out. "Let me guess! You knew how hungry we'd be from working with the bishop's horses all morning, and you've already loaded a couple of plates for us!"

"With another plateful of desserts!" Lowell chimed in.

"And you're gonna sit with *me*," Lavern continued, "so I can gaze at your pretty face with all those paint splotches on it."

Fannie's hands flew to her cheeks to feel for paint. She'd worked so carefully, trying to stay clean—

The boys' hoots of laughter exposed Lavern's joke.

Irritated that he'd caught her off guard, Fannie blurted out, "So where were *you* last night, Mr. Peterscheim?"

Lavern's blue eyes widened. "Who wants to know?" he shot back, pleased with himself for dodging her question.

Fannie scowled at his smart-aleck tone. She'd gotten off on the wrong foot with her questioning—until her brother unwittingly came to her rescue.

"Don't you remember, Fannie?" Lowell asked as the three of them continued down the hill toward the picnic. "After we finished mucking out the bishop's barns yesterday, Lavern's *dat* took the both of us into Forest Grove to fetch some welding supplies for the big job he's gonna start next week. And we got our supper in town—"

"And we went for ice cream after that," Lavern added with a nod. "So whatever you were going to blame me for, I didn't do it. This time."

The boys howled with laughter, as only best friends could when they were razzing an older sister. With a shake of her head, Fannie walked away before Lavern took a notion to delve deeper into her query.

As she made her way back to her three girlfriends, her thoughts ricocheted like a rubber ball thrown against a closet wall. Her brother hadn't returned home until after nine the previous night—which was right after she'd taped the note to Eddie's bucket and hurried home herself. Lavern's *dat*, Preacher

Eli, would've had his son unloading the supplies they'd bought and tending the horses before they headed into the house for the night.

Fannie sighed glumly. It was unlikely that Lavern knew anything about the note she'd put on Eddie's stain bucket. So why was Eddie acting as though he'd never read it? Why did he seem so distracted?

Or is he looking around for someone else so he can avoid looking at me?

It was a question she didn't dare ask him face-to-face. What if he said *yes*?

She had to try again, however. Somehow, she had to make her second note so compelling that Eddie would at least talk to her—even if she tripped over her tongue and turned ten shades of red when she continued their conversation.

Her dreams depended upon it.

Chapter 9

By Friday morning when he stepped out of the shower, Eddie had finally convinced himself that Vera was right: if Fannie Lehman had come to Promise Lodge to tape that note to his stain bucket, she couldn't have remained hidden. She would've been pestering him about getting married. He'd received the additional letters Dat had forwarded, not surprised that their messages still sounded urgent and repetitive.

But he'd gotten no letters from Fannie directly, using his Promise Lodge address. He didn't know how to interpret the break in Miss Lehman's letter writing, but he was relieved. And because she hadn't turned up at Promise Lodge, he hadn't had to deal with her drama in person, which was an even greater relief.

But who had written the note on his stain bucket?

It was a sure bet Fannie Kurtz hadn't put it there. She was such a quiet little mouse that she'd barely made eye contact with him during their families' occasional visits over the years. These days she was always with Phoebe, Laura, and Lily while they painted, as though she had no interest in spending time with guys. Nope, Fannie Kurtz was too shy by half to slip him a note about becoming closer friends.

Eddie dried quickly and slung his wet towel over the narrow shower door. He'd noticed that Lily's twin brother, Lavern, had a knack for teasing Fannie to the point that she stalked away looking flustered and irritated with his childish pranks. Could *Lavern* have written that note so Eddie would think Fannie was interested in him? And so Fannie would get even more flustered if Eddie mentioned the note to her?

He pulled on clean painting clothes, wondering if he should call Lavern out. The Peterscheim kid had one more year of school, and he was probably bored enough to liven up his life by teasing Fannie—maybe because he had a crush on her. The more Eddie thought about it, the more sense that idea made.

He laughed out loud. He'd ferret out the author of that note sooner or later but this morning he had bigger fish to fry: Truman Wickey had rented the portable lift with the cherry picker, and it was parked in the lobby of the lodge, waiting for him.

As Eddie microwaved some of the French toast casserole Aunt Minerva had sent home with him, he thrummed with the anticipation of riding all the way to the lobby's high ceiling to paint it. Rosetta had given him a feather duster, too, so he could remove several cobwebs while he was up there. He'd never used a portable lift, and the day's job would give him some good experience at maneuvering the basket—because someday he might be offered a commercial painting job involving heights. A lift was much more economical—and safer and more fun—to rent than scaffolding.

He stepped out the door of the tiny house with visions of riding high in the cherry picker, until a fluttering piece of paper caught his eye. Someone had apparently stuck it in his door—

And once again, Fannie Lehman's pink paper and precise penmanship made the bottom drop out of Eddie's stomach.

Dear Eddie,

*I have to say this straight out: you have no idea
how much I love you—how I've always adored
you, but I couldn't find a way to tell you in person.
My heart and my future are in your hands, Eddie,
and I dream of being your wife someday. Please,
may we talk about this soon? I'll be waiting.*
    Yours,
    Fannie
    S.W.A.K.

Panic shot through him, and he stared across the lawn in all directions, trying to catch a telltale motion—any sign of Fannie Lehman, who had indeed come to Promise Lodge and turned his worst nightmares into reality. No matter how adept Lavern Peterscheim was at pranking, he would *not* have used pink paper exactly like Fannie's—and his handwriting probably wasn't the best, either.

Crumpling the note in his fist, Eddie strode toward the private road, all exhilaration about riding on the platform forgotten. All the way up the hill, past Allen Troyer's place and Preacher Amos's house and Preacher Marlin's home, he swore he felt someone watching him from behind a tree or a phone shack. More than once he turned around in the road to meet Miss Lehman's gaze and confront her.

But she eluded him.

Or else she's not here at all, and my imagination is racing in high gear now.

Luckily, Vera was settling into the seat of her pottery wheel when Eddie reached the little shed behind Aunt Minerva's house.

"I thought you'd be riding the cherry picker by now, Eddie, but you seem to have another bee in your bonnet," she said, her forehead furrowing in concern.

"Another note from Fannie Lehman," he rasped as he tried to catch his breath. "Just when I'd convinced myself that you were right—that Fannie couldn't possibly be at Promise Lodge—*this* fluttered out of my door."

Vera skimmed the note quickly and handed it back to him. "Just a left-field suggestion, but what if Fannie Kurtz is—"

"No way!" Eddie blurted out. "Even if she worked up the nerve to send me a note, she couldn't *possibly* have handwriting and paper exactly like Fannie Lehman's. And she's not the type to bare her soul—or to sneak around putting notes where I'll find them, either! I—I just don't know how to handle this, Vera!"

His sister gazed at him over the top of her glasses before pushing them up her nose. "Has Miss Lehman sent you any more letters, now that she knows your new address?"

"Nope. Which might mean she's not home to write them because she's *here*—don't you see?"

Shaking her head, Vera pumped the pedal on her wheel to start it spinning. As she carefully inserted her thumbs into the center of the clay ball on the wheel's surface, her fingers curved around the outside to form a bowl. She hadn't dismissed him; she was focused on her work to let her mind puzzle out the second riddle he'd brought her this week.

Eddie watched the spinning ball of clay, amazed at the way his sister produced a smooth, round bowl with her skilled fingers and the speed of her wheel. When Vera was satisfied with the piece's base, she moved her hands slightly to form an irregular rim that took on a life of its own. As the wheel slowed to a stop, the bowl resembled a woman's floppy-brimmed summer hat turned upside-down—and it had a sense of artistic whimsy that Eddie recognized as Vera's signature style.

"That is so cool, the way you do that," he murmured in awe.

She smiled. "We all have our talents, *jah*? I have a knack for making pottery that our bishop back home considers too artsy to be acceptable. I believe your talents, Eddie, include spreading paint and stain with incredible accuracy, as well as attracting girls as effortlessly as those coneflowers attract bees."

Eddie followed her gaze to the large clump of purple coneflowers outside the shed door, which buzzed with honeybees. He chuckled ruefully. "I suspect I'm about to get stung, too. The more letters and notes I get from Fannie, the more of a nasty, dramatic spectacle it's going to be when I reject her. Her letters are sounding downright *desperate* these days."

Using a large spatula, Vera carefully lifted the completed bowl from her wheel. When she'd transferred it to a shelf where several other recent pieces were drying, she looked at him again. "I wish I could be more help. Maybe after you ride that lift basket up to the ceiling and begin to work, the increase in altitude will give you some new ideas about how to handle this situation."

Eddie shrugged, unconvinced. "Maybe when Fannie shows herself, I can use the lift to get away from her," he joked. "Even if that trick won't work in the long run."

"For what it's worth, I'd give my five best bowls to ride up on that lift with you, little brother," Vera admitted softly. "But I'd be scared out of my mind before we were ten feet off the floor."

"I could take you up for short trips until you get accustomed to the rise, and then we could go a little higher," he suggested. "After you rode with me several times, it wouldn't feel so terrifying, *jah*?"

Vera's eyebrows rose as she reached for another chunk of clay. "Did you hear what you just said?" she challenged. "Maybe if you practice writing—or saying—what Fannie needs to hear from you, *you* won't be so terrified to face her. You've got to tell her soon, Eddie. You can do this."

Chapter 10

As Fannie watched the lift's metal basket rise, she couldn't take her eyes off its handsome occupant. Eddie stood at the controls, appearing so cool and confident as he steered; she had the sudden urge to vault over the railing to join him when the cage reached the level of the second-story hallway.

She'd never do that, of course. But in her mind, she was every bit as agile and outgoing as Eddie, and when the two of them were alone, high in the ceiling's canopy, they'd be able to talk about all the things that mattered most—the message she'd left him early that morning, for instance.

For a brief and glorious moment, Eddie focused on her from just a few feet away. Time stood still as his hazel eyes glimmered richly, as though to peer all the way into her soul.

Has he read my note? Does he think I'm too aggressive, admitting I love him before we've even gone out on a date?

As he gazed at her, Fannie held her breath and her hands fluttered to her heart. Her cheeks blazed like the burners on the newfangled gas stove that had arrived for the lodge kitchen. Somehow, despite her shyness, Fannie maintained eye contact.

It took all her courage, but she didn't look away until Eddie began to scan the crowd that had gathered to watch him. It wasn't every day that somebody went up in a cherry picker to paint an old ceiling where a huge, rustic chandelier of antlers hung suspended.

When he'd risen high enough to study the ceiling's surface, he tested it with his long-handled broom. "A bunch of grit and grime's going to fall on you folks while I do my cleaning," he called down to the folks in the lobby. "It's a *gut* time to re-member the old joke about looking up with your mouth open when a flock of geese flies over."

Laughter filled the open area as Eddie put on a shop mask and goggles. The workmen who'd come out of the kitchen, as well as other curious residents, stepped back to the edges of the lobby and the nearby meeting room.

As he started sweeping the ceiling's textured surface, Fannie thought she'd never seen anyone work with such effortless poise at such a height. The metal basket's railing went up about as high as his waist, but if he made a careless move—or reached too far with his broom—he could fall to the floor more than two stories below him.

Fannie didn't allow herself to think about that. As particles of plaster and dust fell past the upstairs hallway, she stepped back so the loose debris didn't land on her.

"Who knows how long it's been since that ceiling was cleaned and painted?" Laura wondered aloud.

"Eddie'll have to shower a lot of grime out of his hair," Lily remarked. From her place alongside Fannie, she was watching every move he made. "Maybe one of us should've offered him a kerchief—or a *kapp*!"

Chuckles erupted around her, but Fannie was too absorbed in following Eddie's broom to pay much attention. Over the next half hour, he slowly rotated his basket's position, and when he'd cleaned one full quadrant of the ceiling, Truman cautiously steered the base of the lift along the floor to the next corner of the lodge. After Eddie had knocked off all the ceiling's loose grime, he screwed a feather duster onto the end of the long handle and carefully caressed the cobwebs from the chandelier's antlers.

"*Gut* job, Eddie!" Rosetta called up from the lobby. "I'm glad it's you up there and not me!"

By the time Eddie lowered the cherry picker to exchange his cleaning equipment for his bucket of paint and rollers, some of his audience had returned to their own work. Fannie's three painting partners were headed toward the ladders and paint trays awaiting them in the far corner apartments at the front of the lodge. These rooms had never been occupied, except by wedding guests staying a night or two, but Rosetta had asked the girls to freshen them up. Fannie lingered near the railing, hoping for a few more moments of eye contact with Eddie when he ascended to begin his painting.

But he started on the opposite end of the lobby. Fannie's latest heartfelt note had apparently failed to capture his attention. Or else, in the brief gaze they'd shared earlier, Eddie had seen nothing in her eyes that compelled him to seek her out.

With a sigh, she returned to her work. What else could she do, aside from calling out to him, proclaiming her love aloud? Such a bold move felt far too risky, considering the way he'd all but ignored her two notes—and the fact that so many other people would hear her.

Third time's a charm. When Eddie and Vera come to the house for dinner with Harley and Minerva on this visiting Sunday, I'll have one more chance to plead my case—

If I'm not too scared to initiate the conversation while Eddie's there all day.

On Sunday morning, as Eddie held the door for Aunt Minerva and Uncle Harley, he noted what a fine house Preacher

Marlin had moved to when he'd married Frances Lehman—
which had happened since his family's last visit. Frances's two
daughters, Mary Kate and Gloria, had gone into new homes
nearby when they'd married, which had made plenty of room
in Frances's home for Marlin and his two younger kids. Harley
and Minerva had remained in the house beside the barrel factory, and everyone seemed happy with the new living arrangements.

"*Denki*, dear," Aunt Minerva murmured as she entered the
house with her big bowl of slaw.

"*Jah*, you're a peach, Eddie," Uncle Harley teased as he carried a lidded pan of cake with a bowl of applesauce on top of it.

Eddie nodded his acknowledgment before smiling at Vera,
who'd brought along a box of the colorful bowls and pots she'd
recently glazed and fired.

"Pay attention today," his sister murmured. "You might
find out that *our* Fannie put those notes where she knew you'd
find them."

Eddie shook his head, entering the house behind Vera.
"Nah, she looked like a scared rabbit ready to bolt on Friday,
after I found that paper stuck in my door. Could be the Peterscheim kid is a good enough copycat to prank her—or it's
something else we haven't figured out yet. And besides, if Fannie is Harley's sister, that makes her my *aunt*—"

"Only by marriage, because Minerva is *dat's* sister," Vera
pointed out quickly. "Just keep your eyes and ears open, okay?"

Eddie forced down a sigh. He was tired of puzzling out this
business about the notes. It was time to change his mindset—
his preoccupation with a young woman who perplexed and irritated him—and focus on the day's visit with the Kurtz family.
As he approached the kitchen behind Vera, greetings for Minerva and Harley rang out. He inhaled the aromas of freshly
perked coffee and cinnamon before he spied the large pan of
frosted rolls that spiraled around a filling of nuts, butter, and

raisins—a midmorning snack to tide everyone over until the noon meal was served.

"Vera! And Eddie," Preacher Marlin said as he smiled at them. "As I recall, you kids haven't been to Promise Lodge since I remarried, so I'd like to welcome you to my new home and introduce my wife, Frances."

"Frances and I chatted after church last Sunday," Vera put in quickly. "And she asked to see some of the pottery I've been making—"

"Oh, look at these bright, shiny colors!" Marlin's wife said as she gestured for Vera to set her box on the counter.

Eddie chuckled, knowing that Frances, Minerva, Vera—and even Fannie, who'd been arranging brownies on a platter—would be engrossed in pottery conversation for several minutes. He smiled, pleased that his sister was enjoying some attention for her work—until Fannie set her goodies on the table right next to him.

"I—I hope you like frosted brownies with sprinkles, Eddie," she stammered as her cheeks turned pink. "It's a special day."

He blinked. How should he interpret her remark?

As Fannie turned to join the women's conversation, Eddie picked up a brownie and took a big bite. Harley had beelined toward the cinnamon rolls, asking Lowell about how his work with Bishop Monroe's Clydesdales was going.

Preacher Marlin stepped up to take a brownie, holding Eddie's gaze. "This might be a *gut* time to walk up to the barrel factory," he murmured. "*Someone* left you a message on the phone."

Eddie nearly choked on his mouthful of brownie. Something about Marlin's confidential tone suggested that the preacher had drawn some interesting conclusions about Fannie Lehman—because who else would be leaving a message for him? As they passed through the front room, Eddie's temples began to pound. His mouth went so dry that he didn't want any more of his brownie.

"We're, um, not talking about Dat or Mamm, are we?" he ventured, careful not to let the screen door bang behind them.

"Identified herself as Fannie. No last name. Ring any bells?"

"Oh, *jah*," he replied with a shake of his head. As they fell into step and headed up the hill, Eddie wished yet again that before he'd left Clearwater, he'd found a way to convince Miss Lehman to leave him alone.

"Thought we should listen to it first thing and erase it before Lowell or anyone else checks the messages." The preacher cleared his throat, as though wondering how to finish his story. "I saw the light blinking last night after I finished the horse chores, while Harley was out with his sheep, so I'm pretty sure he hasn't heard it, either."

Eddie squeezed his eyes shut, sensing that Marlin had a very compelling reason for keeping Fannie's message private. They walked in silence, which became more nerve-racking with each step they took; Eddie didn't want to say too much until he'd heard the message. As they entered the small door to the Kurtz Barrel Factory's office, he wondered if Fannie had said something incriminating enough to require a confession to Preacher Marlin.

Marlin pushed the Replay Message button and took a step back.

"This call is for Eddie Brubaker." After a pause—was that a muffled sob?—the message continued. "Eddie, it's me—Fannie—and well, haven't you gotten *any* of my letters? And—and if you have, you surely know how much I love—Well, I really need to say that in person, don't I? So *please* call me back or come see me or—I can't go on without you, Eddie. We have to talk soon! I—"

The message ended abruptly, as though Fannie had seen

someone coming to the phone shanty and slammed the receiver down. Eddie closed his eyes, wishing the floor would swallow him. What must the man standing beside him think?

"Do you need to hear that again, Eddie?"

He shook his head, wondering how to explain his predicament.

Preacher Marlin pressed the Delete button. "I suppose it's none of my business, but I sense this Fannie is—"

"She wants me to marry her," Eddie said wearily. "And I've never had any such intentions, or led her to believe—"

"Have you given this young lady a *reason* to get married?" Marlin interrupted in a low voice. "Does she sound so desperate because you've . . . left her in the lurch?"

Eddie's eyes flew open. "What do you mean, have I—"

"Is she carrying your baby?"

His breath escaped him in a rush. "Absolutely not! I've kissed her a couple of times, but that's—a *baby*?"

The idea had never occurred to him because he'd given Fannie no reason to worry about being in the family way. But what if some other guy had?

Preacher Marlin crossed his arms, holding Eddie's gaze with unwavering brown eyes. He wasn't a large man, but he had a powerful presence about him. "So you've not had relations with her? Tell me the truth, because I'll know if you're not."

Eddie swallowed hard, knowing better than to dodge the question because he was too nervous to think straight. "I have not jumped the gun," he insisted hoarsely. "I have never, um, *known* Fannie Lehman in the biblical sense. But for the past couple of months, she's been hounding me about—"

His own words brought a sickening realization to light. He'd known Fannie for years, but she hadn't begun pursuing him so aggressively until they'd both attended Danny Yoder's wedding. Maybe she'd suspected her condition then and had motioned him behind the barn for those kisses, thinking to entice him into marriage before anyone was the wiser about the baby.

The preacher relaxed, gently grasping Eddie's shoulder. "I don't *know* she's carrying, understand. That might be a long shot. But I experienced something similar when I was a little older than you, and a gal tried to sweet-talk me into getting hitched. The situation spiraled downhill as the next few months went by."

Still reeling from the possibility that Fannie Lehman was following the same pattern Preacher Marlin had described, Eddie took a deep breath to fortify himself. "What'd you do?"

Marlin shrugged. "I could've handled it better. But I'm older now, and I realize that girls caught in that predicament don't have many options," he replied softly. "If the man responsible won't marry this Fannie—and if you won't, either—she'll most likely leave town for several months to stay with a relative, have the baby, and give it up for adoption. If she's lucky, nobody in her hometown will be the wiser when she returns, and she'll have a chance for another man to court and marry her."

Eddie thought hard about what the preacher was saying. "So if I'd fallen for Fannie's sweet talk, I could've been raising another man's baby? And she wouldn't have told me?"

"That's been known to happen, Eddie." Marlin smiled gently. "You have options, and it's best to be aware of them. You can take the higher road and marry her despite what you know, which would give Fannie's child a home and a *dat*."

Eddie was about to protest, until the preacher leveled another probing, brown-eyed gaze at him. "But if you're not to blame for another man's—and Fannie's—premarital behavior, you can go your own way in *gut* conscience, and this young lady will need to find another solution. God knows that we're all actively involved in making our own messes, after all."

Eddie shook his head, still reeling from the possibility Preacher Marlin had proposed. "I'm only seventeen. Too young to support a wife," he said softly. "And even if I were older and more able, I would *not* choose to marry Fannie Lehman! I—you've given me a lot to think about, Marlin, and I appreciate it."

"Here again, we might be interpreting this all wrong," Marlin admitted as he gestured toward the door. "You need to contact her right away and figure out what she's up to. Most girls wouldn't leave a message like that where other folks might hear it. But then, most girls wouldn't need to."

Is Fannie in trouble? Or is she convinced I'm as crazy about her as she is about me, even though I haven't responded? Either way, it's time to straighten this out.

Chapter 11

Peering out from behind the front room's blue curtain panel, Fannie immediately noticed Eddie's pale face and distracted expression—not to mention the way her *dat* was keeping his thoughts to himself. It wasn't like her father to be so somber, so unsmiling, on a visiting Sunday when he had no responsibilities for reading Scripture or preaching a sermon.

What on earth had been so important—and apparently so serious—that her father had whisked Eddie away the moment he'd arrived? Did Dat know something about the very private notes she'd left Eddie this week? Rather than speaking with *her* about them, had he been steering Eddie away from her before a relationship could develop between them?

Too late! I'm already head over heels, even if Eddie still seems clueless about my feelings for him.

Fannie quickly backed away from the window, slipping into the kitchen again. Luckily, Harley and Lowell were at the table, talking about an upcoming sheep auction while her step*mamm* and Minerva were still admiring the colorful details of Vera's pottery. Drawn by the deep greens and yellows of a ceramic parrot on the counter, Fannie joined the women.

"Vera, when you asked for a place to set up your wheel and kiln, I had no idea you were such an accomplished potter!" Minerva said as she examined a large striped platter shaped like a fish. "Look at these colors! Think of how this piece would brighten my kitchen if I hung it on the wall—and I could use it as a cookie tray, so it wouldn't be just for decoration!"

"Usefulness is the key if we don't want the preachers telling Vera she can't make her pottery," Frances agreed as she gazed at the pieces on the counter. "It's never been an issue for us women to enjoy fancy china cups or other serving pieces, after all. *My* favorite is this pretty blue-and-green cookie jar."

"Consider them my gifts to you both," Vera said eagerly. "I can't thank you enough for inviting Eddie and me to Promise Lodge and taking us under your wings. And, Fannie, if you like that parrot vase, it's yours. That's the first one I've done, and the way you're smiling at it tells me I should make more of them."

Taken by surprise, Fannie looked up. "Oh, don't feel you have to give it to me, Vera. I'd be happy to pay you for it."

"*Jah*, we didn't intend to cut into your profits," Frances put in. "You could probably sell your pieces at Dale Kraybill's bulk store and do well at it. Especially if you took orders."

"They're gifts. I insist," Vera said, smiling at each of them. "I'm delighted to make pieces for my family—because where would we be without our kinfolk?"

Fannie couldn't help smiling as she turned the bright green and yellow parrot in her hands to study its details. Its whimsical feathers and facial features had been loosely sketched in black ink. The hole behind its head would hold a large handful of flowers.

"I'm going to put this on the corner of my dresser," she

murmured. "It's exciting to have something new for my room, Vera. *Denki* so much!"

Vera straightened her glasses, holding Fannie's gaze. "Shall we go pick a nice bouquet for your vase after dinner? I've been so busy since I arrived, I haven't caught up with what you're doing these days."

Was it her imagination, or did she hear an unspoken motive behind Vera's suggestion?

"And speaking of dinner," her step*mamm* put in, "how about if you arrange some of Minerva's cake and our cookies on the fish platter, Fannie, and we'll start setting out the food? Lowell and Harley have polished off several of those cinnamon rolls— but that won't stop them from eating a full meal! Eddie and Marlin seem to be waiting for the main event."

As Fannie removed several squares of Minerva's lemon cake from the pan and placed them on the bright striped platter, she glanced over at Eddie. Although he and Dat were rehashing the excitement of painting the lodge ceiling with the cherry picker, Eddie didn't seem fully engaged in the conversation—as though he was still flummoxed about whatever the two of them had discussed when they'd left the house.

She added some of her brownies and Frances's peanut butter cookies to the tray, wondering how she could find time alone with Eddie sometime during today's visit.

Or is this a bad time? Maybe he won't care about my hopes and dreams when he's worried about something else—especially if he and Dat were discussing the notes I've sent him.

When Fannie carried the platter to the counter behind Dat's place at the table, however, Eddie looked over at her. She smiled, holding his gaze for as long as she dared. He nodded before refocusing on what Dat was saying.

At least he doesn't seem inclined to avoid me. But I don't see any new spark in his eye, either.

Fannie busied herself with setting out the cold sliced ham, potato salad, slaw, and applesauce. Although her step*mamm* usually sat at Dat's left, it was no surprise that Lowell and the men took chairs at her father's end of the table so they could hold their own conversation. Frances happily seated herself beside Minerva and asked how she was feeling these days.

The Sunday meal progressed at its usual leisurely pace because it seemed they all talked as much as they ate. Eddie sat on the same side of the table as Fannie, next to Dat, so she had no chance to make eye contact with him.

She watched his sturdy hands, however, intrigued by the way he held his fork in his left hand even though he maneuvered his rollers and staining pads with his right. She'd stolen enough glances at him while he worked that she'd become very aware of the effortless way he moved when he was focused on painting and staining. He was a study in efficiency—just one more reason Fannie admired him.

At long last everyone had eaten dessert. Fannie and Vera scraped and stacked the plates at the table while Minerva ran hot, soapy dishwater and began washing. Frances removed the clean dishes from the rinse water while Fannie and Vera dried and put them away—work that was considered as necessary on the Sabbath as tending the livestock, which the men would do later in the day. When the kitchen was cleaned up, Minerva and Frances went out to the front porch to enjoy some lemonade with the men while they relaxed.

"Where will we find some nice flowers for your vase, Fannie?" Vera picked up the parrot vase, and Fannie found some scissors before the two of them went out through the mudroom. "This will be a *gut* chance for me to look around at places I've not seen yet. Minerva and I have been setting up the nursery, and she's giving me some pointers about taking over as the teacher when school starts."

"And you've been making a lot of pottery," Fannie added. "I suspect Frances got it right when she said your colorful pieces would sell well at Dale's bulk store. You could stay very busy even if you weren't going to be our new teacher."

Fannie gestured to their right, toward the new fences containing Christine Burkholder's dairy herd. Bishop Monroe's wife had been one of the founding sisters of Promise Lodge, and the old barn on her property—destroyed by the tornado—had recently been rebuilt. "Let's check along the fencerows and in the pasture where the Holsteins are," she suggested. "I've seen black-eyed Susans and tiger lilies growing there, along with Queen Anne's lace and bee balm."

Vera nodded and kept pace with her, looking around as they passed Preacher Amos and Mattie's house, walking toward the entrance to Promise Lodge. She inhaled deeply and then spoke in a low voice.

"Fannie, I'm going to ask you about something, and if I'm way off base, just tell me, all right?"

Little red flags shot up in the back of Fannie's mind, but she nodded. She couldn't imagine kind, quiet Vera Brubaker saying anything that might upset her.

"Eddie has been in quite a stew over some letters he's received in the mail, and over two notes he found this week. Did *you* write the two notes and put them where he'd find them?"

Fannie's cheeks burned. She swallowed hard before she was able to answer. "*J-jah*, I did. Did he show them to you?"

Vera slung her arm gently around Fannie's shoulders. "Bless your heart, you surely must wonder what's going on—and why Eddie hasn't responded to you, ain't so?" she replied. "Strange as this may sound, he's been receiving letters from a different Fannie—"

Fannie pressed her lips together, trying not to cry. She clearly recalled those envelopes stuffed in Eddie's back pocket.

"And your pink stationery and handwriting are exactly like

hers," Vera continued in a rush. "When he found your notes, Eddie believed the other Fannie had come to Promise Lodge to get his attention, even though your notes are *nothing* like what she wrote in her letters—"

Fannie quickly swiped at her tears. "*Jah*, I saw those pink envelopes with all the hearts and *S.W.A.K.* written on them," she whispered miserably, "so I knew Eddie already had a girl-friend. But I had to take a chance, Vera. I wrote those notes be-cause I'm too shy to tell him in person—"

"Please don't give up on him!" Vera stepped in front of her, placing her hands on Fannie's trembling shoulders. "That other girl is too pushy by half, insisting that she and Eddie should get married by the end of the summer, but he's afraid to set her straight. He dislikes confrontation—doesn't want to hurt her feelings or cause a big scene—so he hasn't called or written back to her."

Fannie blinked. "*Eddie* is afraid to speak up? I—I had no idea he'd be shy about talking to anyone."

Vera smiled, shaking her head. "And Eddie thinks *you're* too shy to leave those notes for him. He and I have agreed that if Fannie Lehman had come to Promise Lodge to write those notes, she wouldn't still be hiding. But he can't get past your matching paper and penmanship."

Fannie considered what she'd just learned about Miss Lehman—and about Eddie. The situation would be almost funny if she hadn't put her heart and soul on the line and told Eddie she loved him. But apparently that other girl loved him, too.

"You know, Vera, that pink paper and the matching en-velopes are for sale in a lot of Plain stores," she said with a shrug. "And as for the handwriting, I learned it from copying those cursive alphabet charts above the blackboard—"

"Which are in every Amish schoolhouse in the country," Vera put in. "You and Fannie Lehman have mastered your penmanship much better than most folks—including Eddie and me."

Eddie's sister paused, gazing ahead at the pasture dotted by black-and-white Holsteins. "Look at those pretty daylilies and black-eyed Susans by the fence," she said. "What if we let our minds work on a solution to this situation with Eddie while we pick your flowers, Fannie? Maybe if we're quiet for a little while, God will whisper something in our ears."

"*Gut* idea," she murmured as they started across the grass. "I don't have the faintest clue what to do next. Any idea God comes up with will surely be better than mine."

On the way to Christine's new white barn, which was shining brightly in the afternoon sun, Fannie gazed over toward Rainbow Lake and the blue tiny home where Eddie lived. The water shimmered with a million little sun diamonds. A pleasant breeze stirred her *kapp* strings as she kept pace with Vera's longer stride, angling across the grassy lot bordering the lake to fill the vase with water. It was easy to understand why Eddie had jumped at the chance to stay in the tiny home, where he could sit out on the dock or go fishing any time he wanted.

After Vera dipped the parrot vase into the lake, they walked to the pasture fence. Fannie cut a handful of deep yellow black-eyed Susans as well as three large tiger lilies. A sprig of Queen Anne's lace rounded out the bouquet, and looking at it helped Fannie settle her agitated soul.

"I do hope you'll keep trying to win Eddie's attention," Vera said softly. "You and Eddie are well suited—"

"But we're too young to get married," Fannie put in firmly. "Eddie and I need to spend more time together to determine if we could be happy with each other. So far, this is all *my* dream. Maybe . . . maybe he won't be interested."

It was a painful thought, but Fannie resigned herself to it. Perhaps God was telling her to be a more realistic young woman instead of nurturing childlike fantasies.

"Maybe he won't, but you're giving him a chance to find out. The other Fannie has always been a flirt, and lately she's been pushing the marriage issue. I doubt Eddie would be happy stepping to her tune for the rest of his life."

By the time the two of them were within sight of the house, Fannie felt calmer. She had no guarantees that Eddie would come to love her, but at least she knew why he'd been so preoccupied lately—and so confused about the letters and notes he'd been receiving.

"*Denki* for telling me about the other Fannie, Vera."

Her companion nodded. "Shall I tell Eddie we had this talk or keep it between us?"

Fannie smiled as she looked at her beautiful bouquet and vase. "He'd probably rather believe he figured this out on his own—so from here on out, I won't leave him any room for doubt about who's slipping him notes on pink paper."

Chapter 12

Around two o'clock, when Frances suggested they all play Yahtzee, Eddie saw the chance to excuse himself. "I usually give the parents a call about this time on Sunday afternoons," he explained as he rose from his chair on the porch.

"Give them our best," Preacher Marlin said. "Feel free to use the barrel factory phone, and we'll see you later for a little supper, if you're so inclined."

"Invite them up for a visit," Minerva put in eagerly. "It's been a month of Sundays since I've seen that busy brother of mine and the rest of your family."

Nodding, Eddie held Marlin's gaze for a moment. He hadn't fibbed, exactly, because he did phone home on Sunday afternoons, but the preacher's slight nod encouraged Eddie to proceed with the other call he needed to make. He'd felt twitchy all during the noon meal, wondering if Fannie Lehman was deceiving him about her motives for marriage.

Another man's baby was a compelling reason to leave this one-sided relationship. Even if Fannie wasn't in the family way, it was past time to state his case.

As Eddie walked toward the private road, he tried to compose his thoughts. The call he was about to make might be one of the most important in his life—although he was hoping Fannie wouldn't hear the phone ringing in her family's shack out by the road. He would leave her a message promising her a letter, and then he'd write it so he could mail it first thing in the morning. After that, he could breathe a little easier.

The sight of his sister walking alongside Fannie Kurtz, who carried a bright-colored vase full of wildflowers, made him smile. Vera was head and shoulders taller than her companion, and the afternoon sun glinted off her glasses when she turned her head. Fannie appeared calm and relaxed, talking easily with his sister. Her dark eyebrows rose in her slender face and her laughter drifted on the breeze as the girls shared something funny.

Fannie's done some filling out since the last time our family came here. Why haven't I noticed that until now?

Eddie slowed down to better appreciate the way her lavender cape dress swayed with her walk—and then he hurried up the hill. Could it *possibly* be true that Fannie Kurtz had written those notes on his bucket and on his door?

Better call the Lehman place before I get sidetracked or lose my nerve.

When he entered the cavernous barrel factory, Eddie savored the stillness. With the windows closed, the stuffy little office wasn't a place he wanted to linger for long, so he picked up the receiver and tapped in the Lehmans' number. With each ring he felt relieved that he wouldn't have to *talk* to Fannie, because his news was exactly what she didn't want to hear. After the recorded greeting, he kept his message brief.

"Fannie, this is Eddie, returning your call. I'm mailing you a letter first thing tomorrow, so please don't leave me any more messages on Preacher Marlin's business phone, all right? Bye."

When he replaced the receiver, he took a deep breath. He'd

sounded terser than he'd intended. And he hadn't revealed his feelings or the contents of his letter, because who knew which member of the Lehman family might check the messages? At least he'd honored Fannie's privacy—unlike the way she'd given Preacher Marlin plenty to speculate about in *her* recording.

Driven by his mission, Eddie headed back to the tiny home to write his letter. Again, he wanted to keep it brief: every detail he gave her would turn into ammunition when she spoke with him again. There was no point in beating around the bush, either.

> *Dear Fannie,*
>
> *I'm sorry I haven't responded sooner, but please understand: I'm not marrying anyone any time soon. And I've never knowingly indicated that I was interested in a relationship with you. It was sheer coincidence that we were both at Danny's wedding, and those kisses behind the barn were your idea, not mine.*
>
> *This sounds harsh, I know. But please don't call me or write me any more letters.*
>
> *Thanks.*
>
> *Eddie*

He sealed the letter in an envelope, addressed it, and added a stamp, then took it out to the mailbox. Fannie would be upset, but he'd written the plain truth. He hadn't given her the least little reason to think he would change his mind, either.

Eddie spent the rest of the evening sitting on the dock, where the gentle lapping of the lake's waves soothed his soul. It was such a relief that he could face a new week with a clear conscience, knowing he'd spared himself a painful future with the wrong wife. He would be eternally grateful to Preacher Marlin, too, for offering the insight that Fannie might be carrying a baby.

He'd done Fannie Lehman a big favor, too, even if she wouldn't see it that way. He could only hope she would set her sights on some other guy so he and Fannie could both move on. Because he truly wanted things to work out for Fannie, he said a little prayer about the baby's father stepping up and taking responsibility—if indeed, there was a baby. He also asked God for guidance about confirming her pregnancy . . . a ticklish subject for a girl caught in the lurch.

Fannie had always been high-strung and had a flare for dramatizing details, however. She might be writing him such urgent letters because she saw marriage as a ticket out of the Lehman home, where—if rumor had it right—Fannie's parents squabbled constantly.

As the evening's shadows lengthened, Eddie's thoughts wandered to Fannie Kurtz. When he went inside to get ready for bed, he reread the two brief notes.

Vera was right: these messages were written in a totally different tone from the mailed letters. But Preacher Marlin's modest daughter would never declare her love and adoration for him so boldly! And what were the odds that any two girls with the same first name also used the same paper and had penmanship that matched so perfectly? Maybe these notes *were* from Fannie Lehman as she changed her strategy, hoping to catch him off guard—even if he couldn't figure out how she'd managed to deliver them.

It was a mystery. And he hoped to solve it soon.

Very early on Monday morning, Eddie saw Fannie Kurtz closing his mailbox before starting up the road. Had she taken his important letter to Fannie Lehman? Or had she slipped him a note, not planning to get caught at it?

Only partially dressed, he shot out his front door. "Fannie! Fannie, wait—we need to talk!"

She froze, her face flushing pinker than the bands of sunrise on the horizon. She reminded him of a frightened deer, too dazed to dash off to safety yet too frightened to face him. By the time Eddie reached the mailbox, Fannie was gasping for breath. When he removed the envelope on top—a pink one with *S.W.A.K.* written along the seal—he thought she might pass out from sheer terror.

Why is she afraid of me?

Or is she embarrassed because I'm not wearing a shirt?

He ripped open the envelope but didn't read beyond *Dear Eddie.* "These notes have come from *you?*" he blurted out. "How can your handwriting—and your paper—be identical to Fannie Lehman's?"

Fannie swallowed so hard her throat clicked. "I—I don't know this other Fannie, but she probably learned cursive handwriting from the charts at school," she murmured in a nervous rush. "And—and she apparently buys her stationary from a Plain store. Just like me. That might sound improbable to you, Eddie, but it's the truth."

Eddie blinked. He'd never considered those possibilities.

Fannie stood taller, clasping her hands so they wouldn't shake so badly. "You probably have a dozen girls interested in you, but I—I wanted you to know how much I've always loved and admired you," she continued miserably. "I'm obviously invisible to you, however, and your heart belongs to someone else."

Before Eddie could formulate his thoughts to reply, Fannie's velvety brown eyes widened, glistening with tears.

"Maybe my *S.W.A.K.* should stand for 'sealed without any kisses,' because I'm never going to get any of those from you," she continued dejectedly. "I can see that now. And—and I'm sorry I've been such a bother."

As Fannie hurried up the road, her sobs drifted back to him.

Eddie deflated like a balloon. He'd known and liked Fannie Kurtz most of his life—and he'd just treated her very badly. Only an insensitive fool would compare this bashful young woman to Fannie Lehman. Since he'd arrived at Promise Lodge, she'd proven—quietly, without any fanfare—that she was a competent, meticulous painter. A hard worker. A young woman of faith whose actions spoke louder than her tremulous words.

Yet despite her shyness, Fannie had found the courage to bare her soul to him, without demanding anything in return. She'd stated her case—and her love—without wheedling or going overboard with drama.

And he had to admire the direct answers she'd given him under pressure.

When he read the morning's note, he felt lower than a worm.

> *Dear Eddie,*
> *I saw those letters in your back pocket last week, so I know your heart and soul are probably invested in someone else. But I want you to know I've always thought you were the most hardworking, solid, dependable fellow I've ever met, and I have these dreams about being your wife someday, when we're old enough. If that other girl ever disappoints you, I hope you'll give me a chance to prove that we could find the love of a lifetime— even if I'm so shy; I can't string two sentences together when I'm alone with you.*
> *I'm going to seal this note with a kiss for luck, and I won't write you any more of them. If you don't respond this time, I'll accept the fact that you're not interested in me.*
> *I love you, Eddie.*
> *Fannie Kurtz*

Eddie hung his head. This time, Fannie had fully identified herself so he couldn't possibly think she was someone else—not that any fool with eyes could mistake her simple declarations for the demanding, manipulative way Fannie Lehman worded *her* letters. She'd stated her love and admiration for him, and he'd rudely ignored her feelings by challenging her penmanship and paper, of all things.

It occurred to him that his *dat's* warning had come true: someone had indeed gotten hurt because he hadn't stood up to Fannie Lehman. He'd never intended for it to be shy, gentle Fannie Kurtz.

He had some major apologizing to do.

Chapter 13

Wearing a clean shirt and pants, Eddie approached the Kurtz home, knowing he deserved whatever angry words Fannie might hurl at him—if she would even listen to his apology. When he knocked on the front door, however, it was Preacher Marlin who stepped out onto the porch.

"You've broken my daughter's heart," he stated sternly. "From what I could piece together while she was crying, the Fannie who left you that urgent phone message is part of the problem."

"*Jah*, and I've come to apologize and ask your Fannie's forgiveness," Eddie murmured. The brim of his straw hat might as well have been a washcloth, the way he was wringing it, and his voice sounded strangely thin. "For what it's worth, I left the other Fannie a message yesterday asking her not to call me again. And my *gut*-bye letter goes out in this morning's mail."

The preacher's dark eyebrow rose. "You've washed your hands of her?"

"I'm trying, but it may take more than one attempt to convince her," Eddie replied ruefully. "I should've contacted her earlier, before she got it in her head that I intended to marry her. Now I'm paying for my 'too little too late' behavior."

Marlin gestured toward the porch swing, so Eddie sat down. Fannie's *dat* eased onto its opposite end, his expression somber as the chains creaked beneath their weight.

"You're young, and you're entitled to a few mistakes," Preacher Marlin said in a low voice. "But you must decide what—and who—really matters to you, Eddie. God comes first, of course. But then you must find a way to fill His world with peace and to keep Jesus's other commandment, that we love our neighbors as ourselves."

Eddie nodded, grateful that the preacher hadn't lectured him more harshly.

"Fannie's a gentle soul, inexperienced when it comes to young men—and, at sixteen, she's too young to be seriously involved with one," Marlin added in a purposeful tone. "She hasn't admitted it straight out, but I suspect she's always been sweet on you, Eddie. I don't expect you to go along with her hopes and dreams if you don't believe she's the young woman God intends for you to love, but I'd like your word that you'll be more respectful of her feelings in the future."

"That's what I came to tell her. If she'll even talk to me." Eddie shook his head forlornly. "I had no idea that your daughter was hanging her future happiness on me—"

"She's the quiet type," the preacher admitted.

"And I mistook her notes, thinking Fannie Lehman had written them," he finished in a rush. "It was a stupid mistake on my part, Preacher Marlin. If you can convince her to come out and listen to my apology, I'd really appreciate it."

Fannie's *dat* held Eddie's gaze, assessing his sincerity. His rugged face, accented by a dark beard and expressive brows much like Fannie's, eased into a smile. "I'll see what I can do."

When the screen door closed behind the preacher, Eddie gazed out over the Kurtzes' neatly mowed front yard, where roses bloomed in the flower bed. He almost went out and plucked one of the deep pink flowers for Fannie, but it seemed last-minute—and crass—to give her a bloom from her family's rosebush. He should've picked her a nice bouquet of wildflowers at the lake as his peace offering.

I've got to think ahead! I'm already off to a shaky start.

As the minutes dragged by, Eddie wondered if Fannie refused to come out. It occurred to him that he'd never had to anticipate girls' reactions or plan gifts for them—or wait for them to show up—because they'd usually pursued him. No one had forced his hand or gotten serious until Fannie Lehman wrote that she intended to marry him, without giving him any say about it.

But Fannie Kurtz is playing for keeps, too. She's spelled it out, and I need to decide whether I'll follow her plan or let her down. It's all or nothing and—

The screen door creaked.

Fannie's red-rimmed eyes and blotchy cheeks told Eddie just how much he'd upset her. She clutched a handkerchief as though her life depended upon it.

But she'd come out to see him. Her brief backward glance suggested that her *dat* was in the front room, not far from the open window, so Eddie had only one chance to make amends.

Fannie paused in the doorway. She could retreat into the safety of the house, or she could face whatever Eddie had to say. If he was asking for her forgiveness, as Dat had suggested, she was supposed to hear him out. Even if he loved Fannie Lehman.

She'd run away from him before he'd had a chance to explain, after all.

But I brought this on myself, didn't I? Eddie was involved with another girl, and I told him flat-out that I loved him. How was he supposed to handle that when he barely knew I existed?

Eddie rose from the swing almost shyly. "W-would you like to sit down with me, Fannie?" he asked, gesturing toward the padded seat. "*Denki* for coming out to talk to me, considering all the idiotic, thoughtless—"

He drove his fingers nervously through his thick brown hair. "I've gotten myself into a pickle with that other Fannie, because she's convinced herself that I'm going to marry her," he continued in a rush. "I haven't encouraged her, honest! I've called and written to her, insisting I'm not interested, but—well, when I saw your identical handwriting and stationery, I jumped to the wrong conclusion!"

Eddie swallowed hard, entreating her with his hazel eyes. "I got spooked, thinking that the other Fannie was here, to confront me in person. If—if I'd paid attention to what you wrote rather than how you wrote it, I'd have known right off that your sweeter, gentler notes couldn't have come from that other girl.

"I am so sorry, Fannie," he added breathlessly. "Can we clear the air? Can you forgive me for being so clueless and stupid?"

Fannie's hand fluttered to her throat. Never had she imagined that the stalwart, confident Eddie Brubaker of her dreams could act so vulnerable in real life. But then, she'd never envisioned him getting caught in a dilemma involving two girls named Fannie, either.

Cautiously, she perched on the edge of the swing. A thousand reassuring words whirled in her mind but before she could work up the nerve to say them, Eddie pivoted, facing away from her.

"Sheesh, I've really stepped in it now," he said, exhaling in disgust. "Why would you want to listen while I blather on about that other girl, when it's *your* feelings I've trampled on?"

There was nothing funny about Eddie's confession because he was so obviously upset—and sincere—yet Fannie had to clear her throat to keep from chuckling.

"Eddie, I'm not being fair to you," she admitted. "Yesterday your sister told me who those other letters were from—and why you thought my notes were hers, too—so I've had some time to think about your situation. Fannie's a very common name, after all. And why *wouldn't* you get confused if two of us, with identical schoolhouse handwriting, wanted to be your wife?"

Fannie inhaled to sustain herself. She'd just spoken in long, mostly coherent sentences to the young man who meant *everything* to her. She'd exposed her heart and soul yet again—face-to-face this time. And she'd survived it.

When Eddie turned to gaze at her, the wonderment on his handsome face made up for all the times he'd made her feel invisible.

"That's a very kind thing to say, Fannie," he murmured. "You don't have to apologize—"

"Oh, but I do," she insisted, hoping to explain without tripping over her tongue. "It also wasn't fair of me to write you those notes about how I've always dreamed we could—could be together, assuming you would go along with it. I've been writing a romantic play in my imagination for years, expecting you to already know the lines I want you to speak. How silly and unrealistic is *that*?"

Eddie sat down beside her, taking her hand. "I could never call you *silly*, Fannie," he insisted softly. "Believe me, plenty of girls have a script in their heads and expect the guy to follow it—but you've just nailed it. And again, you don't owe me any apologies. But—but I'll accept yours if you'll accept mine."

A rush of sheer love made Fannie feel as though she'd floated off the swing. Eddie's hand was large and strong and calloused yet utterly tender as he enfolded her fingers in his. Her pulse was thrumming with the thrill of sitting so close to him after all the years they'd merely nodded at each other and exchanged short, polite conversation. His tawny, soulful eyes reminded her of a hunting dog's while he gazed at her as though he was seeing her for the first time.

She wanted this moment to last forever.

"Your, um, *dat* has told me you're too young to marry anyone yet, and I agree—because I am, too," Eddie added quickly. "But that still leaves us open to being closer friends—if you're willing—"

"Oh, I'd like that more than anything!" Fannie blurted. "And my note-writing days are over. If we're to grow truly close, we need to talk things out, Eddie—just like we're doing now."

His smile made her glow all over.

"You've got that right. If I'd done more talking to—and less avoiding—the other Fannie, I wouldn't be getting such troublesome letters from her," Eddie mused aloud. "*Denki* for your patience and your wisdom, Fannie. You're way ahead of most girls our age."

Fannie's cheeks sizzled, probably as pink as the rims of her eyes. Yet her shyness was no longer such a stumbling block, was it? If Eddie was complimenting her despite her red nose, still holding her hand and wanting to spend time with her, wasn't she on her way to a fresh start with the young man she loved?

Chapter 14

Tuesday morning, Eddie was lost in a euphoric blur. He was eating a glorious pancake and sausage breakfast in Aunt Minerva's kitchen, inwardly rehashing his amazing conversation with Fannie Kurtz, when Uncle Harley interrupted his pleasant thoughts.

"What would you say to sprucing up the interior of the barrel factory with a fresh coat of paint, Eddie? Dat's been grousing about how dreary it seems in there because we didn't spend much time fixing it up after we built it."

Eddie blinked. In his mind's eye, he'd been watching a mental movie of Fannie in the pretty purple dress she'd worn the day before while he'd held her hand. "Um—what'd you have in mind?" he asked, hoping he hadn't missed the main gist of his uncle's idea.

Uncle Harley's laughter rumbled in his broad chest, as though he'd sensed Eddie was a million miles away. "This would be a paying proposition," he said. "Doesn't have to be anything fancy, understand. Just another coat or two of off-white paint would work wonders, I think."

Vera, seated beside Eddie, elbowed him playfully. "And to *really* spruce things up, I could bring in my paints and freehand a few murals on those fresh walls, *jah*?" she teased. "I'm sure your *dat* would like *that*, Harley!"

As they all chuckled at his sister's suggestion, Eddie wondered if Preacher Marlin had devised this painting project so he'd be working in a separate place from Fannie—but he knew better than to ask.

"I could start as soon as Rosetta no longer needs me to paint or stain anything else at the lodge—"

"We've got you covered," Uncle Harley put in smoothly. "Now that the ceiling and hardwood floors are done, Rosetta's fine with the four girls finishing up at the lodge. Dat chatted with her last night, so you're *gut* to go."

Eddie let his fork rest on his plate, considering his response carefully. As an independent businessman, he usually lined up his own jobs—although Marlin and his son had assumed, correctly, that he didn't have any of those yet. Still, it rankled him that the Kurtzes had planned this project without consulting him.

But it's not worth making objections. If Preacher Marlin wants me to paint the barrel factory, maybe he's got other reasons besides keeping me away from his daughter. After all, he probably listened to our conversation yesterday, and he surely must be pleased with the way it turned out.

"I guess it's settled, then," Eddie murmured. "I'll get some measurements inside your factory this morning and drive into Forest Grove for the paint. Depending on how much scraping and prep work I need to do, I'm guessing it'll take me the rest of this week to complete the job."

"That'll be fine," Harley said with a nod. "Meanwhile, Dat and I will start moving everything away from the walls to clear a path for your ladders."

* * *

That evening, Fannie sighed contentedly as she wiggled her bare toes in Rainbow Lake. Sitting on the dock with Eddie at sunset was a dream come true—and the fish they'd been catching were a nice bonus.

"I can see why you enjoy living here, Eddie," she said softly. When her bobber wiggled in the middle of the lake, she tugged on her rod, but nothing was on the hook. "It's so peaceful by the lake, and the cool breeze makes me want to stay longer than I probably should."

Eddie smiled, reeling in his line so he could recast it. "Stay for as long as you want, Fannie. As warm as it was in the barrel factory this afternoon, sitting here with you has been the nicest part of my day."

His sentiment made her feel giddy all over—and it gave her the opening she'd hoped for. "I was disappointed to hear you wouldn't be painting at the lodge with us girls anymore—"

"Do you know why your *dat* and your brother decided I should paint their factory instead?" he interrupted softly. "I wasn't told a thing about it until Harley informed me that's where I'd be working for a while."

"Ah." Fannie could tell by his tone of voice that he was as puzzled as she was. "When Dat and I talked after you left our porch last night, he seemed satisfied that you and I had mended our fences. But I suspected—he gets a look in his eye and a set to his jaw—that he might be cooking up something he wasn't telling me about."

"I suppose we'll eventually find—oh! You've got one, Fannie!"

With a gasp, she yanked hard on her rod to set the hook. She liked the way Eddie helped her to her feet and let her reel the fish in herself, rather than grabbing her rod away and assuming she couldn't handle it. Instead, he positioned the net at the end of the dock, as excited as she was about her catch.

"What a beauty!" he crowed as he dipped the net underneath

the flopping fish. "I bet this trout weighs seven or eight pounds—more than anything I've caught since I've come here, Fannie! You win the prize!"

Fannie's heart was thumping so fast she could barely breathe, but her joy had more to do with the young man beside her than the trout she'd hooked. She was grinning and laughing and hopping from one foot to the other—so happy that when Eddie hugged her shoulders, she thought she'd pass out.

His kiss caught her totally off guard.

Eddie's warm lips met hers for a few glorious moments before he stepped away, as wide-eyed with surprise as she was.

"Fannie, I—I wasn't planning on—"

"Planning is highly overrated, *jah*?" she whispered. It was a wonder she still had a grip on her rod and that Eddie hadn't dumped her fish from the net.

His soft laughter sounded shaky yet exhilarated. "Um, let me put this fish on the stringer. Don't go away."

Why would she leave when her life had just changed in ways she hadn't anticipated? For years she'd dreamed of the moment she and Eddie would share their first kiss. As Fannie watched him secure her trout on the stringer and drop it back into the water, keeping it alive until they left the lake, she prayed she wouldn't do anything silly like moving her mouth the wrong way or poking her nose into the wrong place or—

After he'd wiped his hands on his pants, Eddie came to stand in front of her. His hazel eyes were like saucers, and his breathing sounded as shallow and rapid as her own. Despite the other girls he'd surely kissed before, he appeared as anxious as she felt about whatever came next.

Fannie stood still, waiting. Not daring to breathe.

"Can we try that again?" he whispered.

She closed her eyes, instinctively leaning toward him. Ever so softly and gently, Eddie pressed his lips to hers. His arms encircled her as her hands found the soft hair falling over his collar. The kiss was longer and sweeter this time, far better than anything she'd ever imagined.

As they stood together for several moments, his warm breath teased her neck and sent goose bumps along her spine. "That was amazing," he whispered.

Fannie sucked in her breath, overjoyed that his assessment matched hers.

"I don't want to walk you home yet, but I probably should," Eddie said with a sigh. "I don't want your *dat* coming to fetch you, thinking I've kept you out too long."

"*Jah*, probably best if we show off our fish and then clean them on the back porch," Fannie agreed. How was it already dark enough that fireflies were twinkling above the grassy lot between the lake and the road?

"Shall we do something together tomorrow night?" he asked as he pulled their stringer of fish from the lake. "It'll give me something to look forward to while I'm painting the barrel factory."

"I can't wait, Eddie," Fannie whispered. "Tomorrow will be the best day ever!"

Chapter 15

By lunchtime on Wednesday, Eddie had painted most of one long wall in the barrel factory. As he worked in an easy rhythm, he still wondered why Preacher Marlin and Harley had been so insistent that he apply two coats to surfaces that appeared perfectly clean and intact. As the three of them ate their noon meal with Vera and Aunt Minerva, he sensed a thrum of tension between father and son—but it wasn't his business to ask about it. Every family had situations they didn't discuss with newcomers, after all.

Eddie was back on the ladder by one o'clock. The heat near the high ceiling slowed him down. The steady whir of Marlin's sander and the rumble of the big solar-powered exhaust fans made him sleepy.

I'll work for an hour and then step outside for some—

Whack! The walk-in door by the office opened so fast it hit the wall.

"Eddie Brubaker, why are you up on that ladder? I left you a message Monday night saying I'd be here this afternoon, and you apparently don't care a *fig* about it!"

The ringing female voice was very familiar, except it sounded shriller and more strident than he'd ever heard it. As his pulse shot into overdrive, Eddie clutched his ladder to keep from falling off it.

What on earth is Fannie Lehman doing here, after I told her not to—

"How was *I* supposed to know you wouldn't be at the lodge building?" Fannie continued angrily. "That's where my driver dropped me off, so I've had to hike all the way up the hill after some girls told me where to find you. And *this* is the greeting I get?"

Somehow Eddie laid his roller at the edge of the paint tray without dropping it. As he turned slowly to look at his unexpected guest, Preacher Marlin and Harley stepped away from their machines to see what the ruckus was about.

Fannie Lehman stood near the ladder with her fists on her hips, glaring up at Eddie as she caught her breath. Her *kapp* sat askew on her blond hair. She looked as thin and bedraggled as an underfed feral cat.

Eddie's throat felt like sandpaper. "Fannie, I had no idea you'd—you'd left another message. Especially after I told you *not* to—"

"The phone's in my office, so Eddie hasn't listened to any messages lately," Marlin put in calmly. "I'm Preacher Marlin Kurtz, by the way."

Fannie glanced at Marlin and Harley, who also stood next to him. She was too irritated to offer them her name, but when she looked at Eddie again, some of her bravado seemed to be slipping.

"After all my letters, Eddie, you surely realize that—I've come all this way to—isn't there somewhere private we can go?" she pleaded in a lower voice. "We *really* need to talk."

Eddie gestured toward the door. "We can step outside, Fannie. Give me a minute to wipe my hands."

As she strode back the way she'd come in, past the duffel she'd dropped by the door, he eased down the ladder on shaky legs—even though he had no reason to feel guilty. Truth be told, he'd suspected Fannie might pull such a stunt—and the two men's expressions told him they must've listened to her Monday night message and anticipated her arrival—as well as her mindset.

"Say what needs to be said, son. We'll stand by you," Marlin murmured.

Swallowing hard, Eddie nodded. As he stepped through the small door, he saw that Minerva and Vera were hoeing the big garden to his left. From beneath her floppy-brimmed sun hat, his aunt's steady gaze told him that she, too, had been warned about what might happen today.

Why didn't anyone tell me what was going on? How could Vera not clue me in about—

When Fannie grabbed his hand and led him toward the big maple tree, however, Eddie didn't have time to fret about being left out of the loop. Her grip was insistent, yet she, too, was trembling. By the time they reached the shade, her face was pale and her blue eyes shimmered with unshed tears.

"Eddie, I couldn't believe the way you talked to me—your *tone*—when you left that phone message," Fannie said with a whimper. "And when I got your letter, I knew something must be *terribly* wrong because you *know* how much I love you, so I, um, borrowed most of Mamm's egg money to pay a driver because I had to hear you say in person that it was all a mistake, what you wrote in that letter, and now that we're together—"

He wanted to slap her to bring her out of her escalating hysterics, but instead he grasped her hands. Up close, Eddie could see how thin and drawn her face was, as though she'd missed a lot of sleep or had suffered an extended flu bug.

"Fannie, listen to me," he said firmly, keeping his voice low.

"I don't intend to marry you because—because I don't love you. You've got these romantic notions in your head—"

When her face crumpled and she began to sob, Eddie felt helpless—until he realized that Preacher Marlin, Uncle Harley, and Aunt Minerva had done him an enormous favor. They'd asked him to paint the barrel factory so they could be with him when Fannie Lehman arrived at Promise Lodge—which told him that Fannie's Monday night message had alerted them to her mental and emotional state.

And hadn't Marlin tipped him off earlier about a possible change in Fannie's physical state, as well?

Say what needs to be said, son, and we'll stand by you.

It was a tricky situation because he hadn't caused that possible change in Fannie. But he had every right to know the truth, didn't he? Fannie was adept at adding drama to her desperation, hoping he'd be too sympathetic—or too clueless—to ask her such a personal question. If she could convince him to marry her, she'd be saving herself a boatload of embarrassment when the baby came. And folks would just assume that Eddie had jumped the gun, wouldn't they?

Thankfully, Preacher Marlin had shared his own experience so Eddie was prepared. Eddie owed him for yet another enormous favor.

He took a deep breath, holding Fannie at arm's length when she wanted to move in for an embrace. Her ashen face was drenched with tears as she continued to cry like a child who'd lost her way.

And maybe she had.

Eddie sighed, praying for the right words. "Fannie, look at me."

Sniffling loudly, she wiped her face on her sleeve and focused on him.

"Fannie, are you going to have a baby?"

The drop of her jaw—the sudden flash of terror in her

eyes—were all the confirmation he needed. "How'd you know?" she blurted. "I haven't told a soul—not even Mamm—"

"But we both know your baby isn't mine, don't we?" Eddie asked in the gentlest voice he could muster. "Why do you think I'd want to raise another man's child, Fannie? If you love me so much, why did you try to deceive me? Why aren't you talking to the baby's father instead of to me?"

"Because he's already *married*!" she shrieked.

Fannie pivoted, folding in on herself as she wailed so loudly that most of the folks at Promise Lodge probably heard her— or so it seemed to Eddie. When Aunt Minerva came around the corner of the house, shucking her gardening gloves and floppy hat, he'd never been so happy to see anyone in his life.

"Fannie, you've every right to be upset, sweetheart," Minerva murmured, slipping her arm around the girl's shuddering shoulders. "I'm Eddie's aunt, Minerva Kurtz. I'm a midwife, and I can help you get through this."

"But I can't tell anybody—and if Eddie won't—I've got nowhere to go and—"

"I've got some options for you, dear," Aunt Minerva murmured. "Have you seen a doctor or a midwife?"

Fannie shook her head miserably.

"Then our first step is to go inside and be sure you're carrying a child. After a quick, painless exam, we can talk, all right?" Eddie's aunt asked in a soothing voice. "You don't have to go through this frightening time alone anymore. Shall we have a glass of cold lemonade and a cookie first? I bet you're thirsty after your trip this morning."

Eddie let out the breath he'd been holding, vastly relieved that his compassionate family had come to his assistance when he'd needed them most. As Minerva coaxed Fannie to sit on the porch and settle herself, Vera came up beside him. Her eyes were wide behind her glasses.

"Did you have any idea Fannie was in the family way?"

"Not until Marlin brought it up as a possibility," he replied hoarsely.

"So now we know why she was so desperate to get hitched," Vera remarked, shaking her head. "She's between a rock and a hard place. And I'm *really* relieved she didn't sweet-talk you into marrying her, little brother."

"That makes two of us."

When Marlin and Harley came outside, he realized that they'd heard everything through the open office window. "Excuse me, sis. I have some man-to-man gratitude to express."

As he started toward the two men, a flutter of gray caught his eye at the corner of the house. Fannie Kurtz, in an old paint-splotched dress and blue kerchief, gazed at him with enormous brown eyes. She'd been at the lodge when Fannie Lehman had arrived, so she'd gotten a taste of the other girl's demeanor—and her flummoxed expression told him she'd also heard an earful a few moments ago.

When Aunt Minerva stood up and opened the door, encouraging her shaken guest to step inside, Fannie Kurtz gave Eddie a little wave.

"We'll talk later," she mouthed before disappearing around the corner of the house.

Eddie nodded, relieved. Then he joined the two men who'd rescued him.

Chapter 16

As Fannie Kurtz returned to the lodge to help her three friends paint, her thoughts were whirling wildly. After she'd heard the other Fannie's outburst—not to mention the tone of voice she'd used with Eddie—she felt like a teakettle that would explode if she couldn't release her pent-up steam.

The loud, rapid *clomp-clomp-clomp* of her feet on the wooden porch stairs made her stop to settle herself. If she was so riled up about Eddie's uninvited guest, she might have an accident on the ladder or cause one of her friends to fall. She had to get control of her emotions before she went inside.

Inhaling deeply, she focused on the orange trumpet vine flowers, and beyond that she saw Truman Wickey driving a large, rumbling machine that would dig the hole for the foundation of Dale Kraybill's new house. Through the screen door, she heard familiar laughter: Rosetta, Christine, and Mattie were helping Irene Wickey move back into her corner apartment, which Fannie and her friends had finished painting earlier that day.

Life is getting back to normal at Promise Lodge.

Fannie felt her sense of perspective returning.

The people of Promise Lodge are moving beyond the tornado's devastation—and Lord, I have to trust that You'll guide that other Fannie beyond her predicament toward a brighter future, as well. And please guide her away from Eddie, while You're at it.

Fannie chided herself for telling God what He should do—it was something Dat often warned folks about in his sermons. But because she'd said a little prayer, she was breathing easier, feeling calmer.

I still don't like what I heard, but I understand now why Eddie said the other Fannie had put him in a pickle.

After one more deep breath, she went inside and up the stairs to Beulah Kuhn's corner apartment, where her partners were spreading paint the color of a pale summer sky. Their chatter stopped when she paused in the doorway.

"What'd you find out?" Phoebe asked.

"*Jah*, why on God's green earth was that girl so rude to us?" Laura shook her head as she shifted her ladder to the next section of a wall.

"And why was she in such a tizz to see Eddie?" Lily demanded with a raised eyebrow. "Is she the one who wrote him those letters with the hearts all over the envelopes?"

How much should she reveal? After a moment Fannie decided basic honesty was best.

"*Jah*, she wrote those letters. She's been trying to convince Eddie to marry her—"

"Puh!" Lily blurted. "Someone should tell her she'll catch more flies with honey than with vinegar."

Fannie smiled at her best friend's observation. "Truth be told, she—she might be in the family way, but Eddie politely called her on it. He asked her why she thought he'd want to raise another man's child and why—if she supposedly loved him—she'd tried to deceive him about her condition."

Her friends gaped. All painting came to a halt.

"What'd she say to *that*?" Lily whispered.

Fannie wondered if she'd already revealed more than she should've—but she wasn't spreading gossip. She'd heard every word Eddie and Fannie had exchanged. And it was too late to stop answering her well-meaning friends' questions.

"The baby's father—if there *is* a baby—is married," Fannie murmured. "When I left, Minerva was just taking Fannie inside for an exam."

"How could she play such a nasty trick on Eddie?" Lily blurted out. "That's the biggest lie I've ever heard!"

Phoebe let out a long sigh. "Maybe it was the married guy who played the trick," she murmured. "In that situation, it's the girl who gets caught."

The room got so quiet Fannie could practically hear the wheels spinning in her friends' heads.

"Wait! That girl's name is Fannie, too?" Laura asked with a raised eyebrow.

"Now *there's* an unfortunate coincidence," Lily remarked. "Thankfully, she's nothing like you, Fannie."

Fannie sighed as she retrieved the roller and paint tray she'd abandoned earlier. "The whole situation is unfortunate," she said softly. "I got so mad I almost slapped her for the way she was treating Eddie, but—but I sure wouldn't want to trade places with her."

Phoebe nodded as she went back to painting. "*Jah*, there's no *gut* direction for this story to go. It's a reminder that we lead blessed lives, girls, and we should be grateful."

Fannie began rolling paint on the lower part of the wall Laura had started earlier. As the four of them worked, the rhythmic swish of their rollers was as soothing as the silence that had settled over the apartment's main room. Physical labor shared with friends was a balm to the soul, and it helped Fannie get past the foul mood she'd been in when she'd left Harvey and Minerva's house.

She turned her thoughts to Eddie, hoping he still wanted to see her later that evening—and hoping Minerva could give Fannie Lehman the help she needed if she was indeed carrying a baby. As Fannie was finishing the bottom half of the wall, voices drifted in through the open window.

"*Please* go home with me, Eddie! *Please* don't make me live without you, now that—"

"We've discussed this, Fannie, and my answer is still *no*," he interrupted. "Now that you know you're not having a baby, you can go to singings again—date other guys—"

"But I want *you*!" she cried out. "Now that there's no baby, there's no deception, *jah*? We can wipe the slate clean and start fresh!"

Fannie Kurtz's eyes widened. She set her roller on her paint tray and covered it. "Sorry I can't be more help today, girls," she said. "Sounds like Eddie's still in a pickle and Fannie's trying to close the jar on him. She hasn't heard a word he's said to her."

She hurried down the stairway and out onto the porch just as Dick Mercer's familiar white van was passing under the Promise Lodge entry sign. Dick was a nice fellow who did a lot of driving for the Amish of this area, and Fannie was glad he'd been available on short notice to take Miss Lehman home.

Eddie, meanwhile, was carrying Fannie's duffel, trying to peel her hands off his arm as she continued to plead with him.

"I'm not changing my mind, Fannie," he insisted. "I'm going to pay your driver, and you're going home. I'm relieved that you won't be having a baby, and that Minerva's given you some information and remedies to help you stop worrying and start feeling better again. That's *gut* news we can all be grateful for, *jah*?"

Was it any wonder his words were edged with impatience now? As the van stopped near the lodge, Fannie stepped down from the porch.

"Hi, Eddie! Hello, Fannie," she called out as she approached them. "Is everything okay?"

It was a poor choice of words, considering the awkward situation she'd witnessed—but when Eddie saw her, the tender expression on his dear, handsome face was priceless.

"It is now," he replied softly.

Once again Eddie felt awash in relief and beholden to a member of the Kurtz family for coming to his rescue. Bless her, Fannie's kerchief and old dress were splotched with several colors of paint, yet she'd never looked prettier. Her dark eyes and lashes accentuated her patient, compassionate smile, and she was even more beautiful inside than he'd ever imagined. Despite the times he'd barely noticed her—not to mention the way he'd ignored her handwritten declarations of love—Fannie had shown up to support him.

He quickly stashed the duffel in the back of the van and opened the passenger-side door.

"Um, Fannie Lehman, I'd like you to meet Fannie Kurtz—"

"And I wish you all the best, Fannie," Preacher Marlin's daughter said as she held the other girl's gaze. "Have a safe trip home. You'll be in our prayers."

As comprehension dawned, Fannie Lehman blinked. "Eddie, are you telling me you've already found somebody else? And how does she know about—"

"I'm telling you *I* wish you all the best, too, Fannie. Take care of yourself," he put in quickly. "And, Dick, I appreciate you taking Miss Lehman back to Clearwater. Safe travels," he added as he passed the driver a thick white envelope.

As Eddie stepped over to stand with her, leaving the disheveled blonde gaping beside the van, Fannie's heart swelled. When she slipped her hand into his, his firm, gentle grasp held their *future*.

Lord, stand by Fannie just as You've always been present for me. I can't thank You enough for answering when I asked and opening this door to my happiness when I knocked.

When Fannie Lehman had finally gotten into the van and it was headed toward the road, Eddie sighed. "She's escaped a difficult situation, but I feel sorry for her. Minerva told me she's just about made herself ill with anxiety," he murmured. "The way you and your family have helped me is a sure sign God led me to Promise Lodge for a reason—and that He didn't intend for me to get tangled up in her manipulating ways."

Fannie's smile held an intriguing secret as she glanced away from him.

"What're you thinking?" Eddie whispered as he slung his arm around her slender shoulders. "We agreed to talk about things as we get better acquainted, *jah*?"

"We did." She turned to face him, thrilled to be standing so near him, and to know that her fondest dream stood a chance of coming true now. "God led you here as the answer to my prayer, Eddie. Is that an arrogant, overblown thing for me to say?"

His hazel eyes widened. "You are the opposite of arrogant," he whispered. "I'm learning that you have a lot to say, and that you've not been afraid to say it—no matter how shy you've claimed you are. And if you talked God into bringing me here, Fannie, I'd better pay close attention. You've got power, girl!"

Fannie laughed out loud. Who could've believed strong, capable Eddie Brubaker would ever say such a thing about *her*? "Maybe I have an edge because Dat's a preacher—"

"Nope. This is about you, Fannie. Only you."

His whispered words stirred something deep within her soul as he gazed into her eyes. There was no doubt that Eddie was seeing her now—that she was no longer invisible to him. And when Fannie caught her reflection in his tawny eyes, she sensed that their time together had truly begun. She couldn't wait to discover how the rest of their story would unfold.

"Considering all the times I've seen the letters S-W-A-K lately, maybe it's time we put them into action," Eddie murmured as he pulled Fannie closer. "Seems to me you're just the right girl to do that."

He didn't have to ask her twice. Fannie rose to her toes, closing her eyes as he settled his lips firmly over hers. She forgot about everything except the warm, steady pressure of his mouth and the way she fit so perfectly against him. It was far sweeter than any kiss she'd imagined in her fantasies over the years.

When at last he eased away, Eddie sensed a big shift had taken place. Fannie Kurtz wasn't the type to throw herself at a man or flirt outrageously or make demands. Her inner strength and steadfast devotion spoke volumes. He'd have to elevate himself to be worthy of the love she'd been secretly nurturing for so long.

"We've sealed our intentions with a kiss, Fannie," he said. "I feel *so happy* being with you."

Fannie's face glowed. "I predict we'll have a long, long time to find out just how happy we can be. We've knocked, and God's opened the door for us."

The Wrong Valentine

Rosalind Lauer

For Caroline and Alex,
You write the most heartwarming notes
So proud to be your mother

Chapter 1

Snow.

It danced in the air, the fat flakes flipping and glimmering as they floated down from the white sky.

Martha Lambright gripped her warm mug of coffee tighter as the cold white flurry overcame the earth, landing on the winter grass, the shop rooftops, the handrail that framed the porch of Madge's Country Diner. It was a cold February morning, and Martha had just stepped out of the diner for some fresh air. At breaktime she often popped out this side door for some peace and quiet away from the clamor of the kitchen and the chatter of the teenage girls who helped with the prep work and cleanup. Just a bit of escape.

Instead of escape, this coffee break alerted her to danger.

If the snow accumulated, if the roads froze over, the ride home could be treacherous. Dangerous. She couldn't risk it, not with her children to protect.

Was it sticking? White flakes were already clinging to the handrail. The sky above was white and opaque, though it hardly seemed cold enough. Her heartbeat quickened as she considered fleeing. She could contact her driver, Mose Troyer, and ask him to come immediately. They would fetch the children from Polly's place and then cautiously, ever so slowly, she would hold the children close to her in the buggy as they journeyed the last mile to home.

How would she reach Mose? Madge would let her use the restaurant's phone, of course. But what was Mose up to? She tried to recall their morning conversation, after they'd dropped the children off with Polly and headed down the main street of Joyful River. The hardware store. He'd said something about picking up feed for the Troyer horses. And then the bulk store. Madge had an order that needed to be delivered to the diner.

Frowning at the furious white snow, Martha tossed her last bit of coffee, now cold, onto the bushes below the porch. She would call the hardware store first and ask after Mose. If she couldn't reach him, she would find another driver or hire a car. Anything to get home safely.

As she turned toward the door, the clip-clop of a horse's hooves grew louder, signaling that a buggy had turned into the diner parking lot. She glanced over and saw that the gray buggy was being pulled by an amber mule that she recognized right away as Sunshine.

"Mose!" With a mixture of relief and anxiety, she waved to get the buggy driver's attention.

Not that she needed to, as he was pulling round to the back of the restaurant, fully intending to stop the buggy near her. Halting the mule just shy of the back fence, Mose jumped out of the buggy and went around to open its back door.

"Martha! I thought that was you when I turned in. Is it lunchtime already?"

"Just taking a coffee break," she said. "But look at this snow!"

"It's beautiful, isn't it? One of Gott's wonders, for sure."

She straightened, stiffening with cold and fear. For the past few months he'd been her steady driver, bringing her to work and delivering the children to a sitter five days each week. He knew that she stayed home from work whenever winter weather hit this part of Pennsylvania. How could he not understand the danger she was facing now?

"Two cans of cooking oil," he said, loading the heavy tins onto the back porch. "And you'll be happy to know I picked up six dozen chickens from the Kraybills' farm. That'll keep you busy in the kitchen for a good. . . ." His voice trailed off as he looked from his cargo to Martha's face. "Something's wrong. Are you feeling all right?"

"It's the snow. I was just about to track you down for a ride home. Can you take me as soon as you unload? I want to pick up the children and get home before the roads become slippery."

"The snow? But it's not going to stick. That's what everyone was saying at the hardware store. Mitch had the TV on, and the weatherman said there'd just be some short flurries."

The Englisch owner of the hardware store, Mitch McGill, kept a TV on in the back of the store, and it often attracted customers who were interested in weather forecasts or how-to videos for fixing things.

"They're expecting sunshine for most of the afternoon," added Mose.

"How do they know?" Martha hugged herself, rubbing her arms to ward off the cold. "They might be wrong. They've been wrong before."

That morning, when Ben had headed off to work, everyone expected mixed rain and snow. No problem on the roadways. Just a bit of slush. No one had expected the temperature to drop so suddenly. . . .

Mose left a sack of flour in the back of the buggy and moved quickly up the porch steps to stand beside Martha. "I can see you're worried." His dark eyes were earnest, warm with compassion. Wooing her trust. "I understand why. But this"—he held out his arms, as if he could collect the wispy snowflakes—"this is just a passing snow flurry."

As if to taunt them, the wind kicked up, tossing white snowflakes onto the shoulders of Mose's black coat. Martha shuddered.

"I can't take any chances," she said. "Can you please take me home?"

"Well, sure. I can do that. But I hate for you to miss the rest of the workday. And Madge would be sorry to lose her best fry cook just before the lunch rush."

Good, kind Madge. Martha's mother-in-law had provided Martha with this job after they'd lost Ben. Beloved husband, devoted son. But Madge would let her go for the day. Madge understood Martha's need to keep her family safe in bad weather.

"I just need to go home," Martha said firmly.

"Okay. As soon as I'm finished unloading the buggy, I'll come get you. If the snow is looking bad, I'll get you and the children home right away."

Martha nodded, reassured by his promise. "I'll be in the kitchen, all ready to go." A quick exit, a tense trip to pick up the children, and then she would hold April and Milo tight in the buggy as they made their way home.

Safe and sound, that's where they needed to be. Home. Soon.

Chapter 2

Just then, the door creaked open, and three Amish teens flew onto the porch amid a mixed chorus of giggles and squeals. The skirts of their dresses swished as they ran past Martha and Mose to find a clear view of Main Street.

"I told you it was snowing!" Bonnie Martin reached out to the railing and scooped up a handful of white flakes.

"I love snow!" declared Sara. "So white and puffy, like feathers in the air."

"Me too," agreed Nella. The youngest of the girls, Nella had been hired on last summer at the age of fifteen, after she'd finished her schooling. Amish youth attended school through the eighth grade and then helped out on the farm at home or worked in the community.

As Martha watched in dismay, the girls made a game of running and sliding on the snowy porch.

Teenagers.

At the ripe old age of twenty-two, Martha felt that she was decades apart from most of the girls who worked in Madge's kitchen. And in many ways, she did inhabit a different world.

She was a mother of two, a widow, a bit of a loner since her husband, Ben, had been killed in a tragic vehicle accident. Thankfully, Ben's mother, Madge Lambright, helped Martha stay connected to her Amish community and be able to care for her family with this job and a place to live. Martha was grateful for the Lambrights' support, and she liked her job. She found satisfaction in cooking tasty meals that could nourish and satisfy folks. The work wasn't a problem. She just disliked feeling like a fish out of water among the other young women.

Martha found Nella to be the most agreeable and eager to learn her way around the kitchen. Seventeen-year-old Bonnie was the most stubborn and the least interested in any sort of work, and sixteen-year-old Sara fell somewhere in between the other two girls.

"Enjoy the snow now, 'cause it won't last long," Mose told the girls. "It's just a flurry."

"Aw," the girls groaned in unison.

"I wanted to make a snowman," Bonnie said, a pouty expression on her face.

Though Bonnie was the oldest of the trio, she often didn't act her age. Or maybe her immaturity was just that temporary goofiness of rumspringa. Martha had seen some girls go wild during the teen years, when Amish parents loosened the reins. It was as if all sound reason flew out of a girl's head during rumspringa, only to return and roost, a happy lark, around the age of twenty.

"There's hardly enough time to make a snowman during your break," said Martha, lifting her face to the white sky. The fat bits of snow like popping corn on the fire belied Mose's prediction; she needed to get inside and prepare to make her exit.

"I'll see you girls in the kitchen in ten minutes." She wasn't their boss—not officially—but turning out the chicken was her responsibility, and the younger girls sometimes needed corralling to keep them on target. That day, they would need to rise to the occasion, as she was going to leave the frying of the chicken in their hands.

Back in the kitchen, the hot air of the ovens and the scent of baking bread immediately warmed Martha, who did a quick assessment of what needed to be done. She decided to write down detailed instructions so that the girls could prepare the chicken just the way Madge's customers liked it.

"How is it out there?" Beulah asked from her workstation, where wispy clouds of flour puffed in the air as she measured out ingredients for a batch of corn bread. "I hope we don't get snowed in again."

"It's really coming down." Martha picked up a notebook and pencil from Madge's desk and started making notes. "I'm getting a ride home as soon as Mose is finished unloading."

"That bad, eh?" Beulah swiped at one cheek with the back of her hand, making the smudge of flour more pronounced. "I wonder if Madge will have to close the restaurant."

"No, we're not closing," Madge said from the kitchen doorway. "The snow is gone, and the sun just came out, quick as you can say *one-two-three*."

"Really?" Martha lowered the notepad, feeling lighter already. "And I was just about to rush home."

"No need to go." As she spoke, Madge paced through the kitchen, inspecting the progress of her cooks and bakers. "But you sure do have everything under control here, Martha. I see that the first batch of chicken is ready for frying." She nodded at the trays of chicken pieces coated in seasoned crumbs, the special mix of spice, herbs, and breading that comprised Madge's secret Amish recipe.

"And we've got enough chicken for the dinner batch soaking in buttermilk in the walk-in," Martha added.

"Perfect." Madge smiled, patting Martha's shoulder. "You've

got our secret recipe down pat. That's the key to keeping our customers happy. And, Beulah, whatever's in the oven smells delicious."

"That's a batch of corn bread." Beulah tapped the measuring cup against the lip of the mixing bowl.

"On a cold winter's day, a warm kitchen is surely the place to be," Madge declared.

Just then, the three kitchen helpers returned, preceded by their merry voices.

"The snow is melting," Sara said.

"But I saved a snowball." Bonnie held up her cupped hands to reveal a dripping white orb. "I'm going to put it in the freezer and keep it forever as a reminder of this day."

"You'll do no such thing," Madge said. "Toss it back outside or into the sink, and hold on to the memory in your heart. You girls need to wash your hands and get back to work. Bonnie and Sara, you two can help me with vegetables and sides. Nella will help Martha. Off we go."

Madge's instructions set everyone in motion, washing up and then manning different workstations. A few minutes later, Martha supervised as Nella dropped two batches of chicken into the fryers.

"I love doing this!" Nella exclaimed.

"Mind you don't get burned. Always wear the oven mitts," Martha instructed. She set a timer for when the chicken was to come out and instructed Nella to listen for it as she tidied up the work area.

"I'll be back in two minutes," Martha said as she headed down the hall to the front of the restaurant.

Some early-lunch diners were seated at tables, and one of the servers, June Hostetler, stood by a four-top table, taking the customers' orders. Two of the regulars, Old Seth and Ezra Graber, manned their customary stools at the counter. Both men were widowers. Seth was a retired schoolteacher, and Ezra had earned his way as a blacksmith until he left the business to three of his sons. Though Ezra was Amish and Seth was Englisch, they'd become good friends through their patronage at the diner.

"Good morning," Martha said, passing the two men to peer out the window. Although she trusted Madge, she needed to see for herself that the snow was gone.

"It's as if it didn't snow at all," she said.

"It's still right cold out there," Ezra said. "But I have to say, it was a joy, walking in the snow. Made me think of my grand-children, how the young ones love to play in it. Young Ezra was hitting the barn with snowballs before he left for school this morning."

"I could have picked you up." Seth's gray eyes shone under his bushy brows. "You're getting too old to be walking on the roadside in the dead of winter."

"Seven miles a day," Ezra claimed, tapping his chest. "Keeps the heart healthy."

"Good for you," Martha said, moving behind the counter. She noticed that the two men didn't have their coffee yet, and June was nowhere in sight. "Can I get you fellows some coffee?"

"That'd be right kind of you," Ezra said.

"Appreciate it," Seth agreed. "June has a knack for disap-pearing."

Martha didn't comment on June as she poured two mugs of coffee. Her coworker had made it clear, more than once, that she was only doing this job because her parents insisted on it. "I'll be done with this, soon as I find the right fellow," June al-ways said. Martha silently wished her well with that. June was approaching twenty, and at that age, the pool of marriageable men had already dwindled significantly in a town the size of Joyful River.

Martha knew this well, as she herself was twenty-two, wid-owed, and resigned to a life raising her two children on her own. Not that folks didn't try to matchmake. But for Martha, love would not be found with the crusty old beekeeper who lived like a hermit in a river hut or the auctioneer who had a streak of cruelty beneath his charming facade. For her, the memory of Ben's love would be enough. It would have to be enough.

As Martha delivered mugs of coffee to the men, the kitchen door opened and Madge emerged with Mose. Madge was checking off things on her clipboard and giving Mose some instructions.

"You can bring the milk tomorrow if you're too busy today," she told Mose.

"This afternoon will be fine," he said. "I'll swing by the dairy, then bring the delivery here when I come to pick up Martha." His eyes were on Martha as he spoke, and she nodded in silent agreement. Though at this point it was clear that she didn't need to rush home anymore.

"Martha?" Madge's focus turned to the counter. "Denki for getting these fellas their coffee. Where's June?"

"She'll be back in a second," Martha said. What was the harm in covering for June Hostetler? Madge always said the staff here was one happy family, and Martha wasn't one to upset the apple cart. "But you'll need to wait to order your lunch," Martha told Seth and Ezra. "I've got a batch of chicken coming out of the fryers."

"Get to it!" Seth agreed. "Far be it for us to get in the way of mouthwatering fried chicken."

Chapter 3

Mose wheeled the hand truck out of the restaurant, nodding at everyone he passed. Since his return to Joyful River more than a year ago, he'd hustled to find work so that he could stay in his hometown. That had meant piecing together odd jobs like tending chickens, fixing fences, and filling in as a gofer on Doug Kraybill's construction crew. Mose rarely said no when someone needed a quick hire, but over the past few months he'd found the most satisfaction in his own business transporting Amish folk around town in his buggy and doing pickups and deliveries for local Amish businesses. The business had started as a series of favors for Amish folks who needed local transportation, and over time he had learned that he and his reliable mule could answer a need in Joyful River.

And so, Mose's Buggy Service had come to be. He had steady passengers who needed rides to and from work each day. In between hours, when he was looking to pick up a fare, he stopped by Junior Kraybill's Amish Grocery in town. Lots of folks walked there, then needed a ride home with their purchases. And he was good friends with Junior's son Dennis, who had also left town to explore the world during his rumspringa but returned within a year or two. Dennis Kraybill's experience had gone more smoothly than Mose's, as his parents weren't ashamed of his behavior. In fact, his mother, Birdie, announced with pleasure that once the "running wild" was done, Joyful River always brought a young man back home.

In the warmer months, Mose spent Fridays and Saturdays giving buggy rides to Englisch tourists who came to Pennsylvania Dutch Country in pursuit of quilts, fudge, jams, and other Amish novelties. All in all, he was happy with his growing business and glad to be settling in Joyful River.

One of the more interesting places Mose worked was the Country Diner, where he now stowed the dolly in the shed behind the restaurant and then headed back inside for a cup of coffee to go. There was no denying that Madge extended a warm welcome to everyone who came through the door, but for Mose, the diner was also a place to mingle with Amish folk in a more casual environment than the church meeting. This was a social setting without the rules of church. A mostly Amish crowd without the watching eyes of his father, Bishop Aaron Troyer, who led their Amish church and community.

"Mose." Ezra motioned to him from the counter, his long beard brushing his shirt as he nodded.

"How goes it?" asked Old Seth. "Do you think today's snow is the last of the winter weather for us?"

Time for a discussion of everyone's favorite subject: the weather. Mose leaned up against the counter and removed his broad-brimmed black hat.

"Hard to say. The skies are clear now, but the beginning of February is a little early to call it quits."

"Right you are," Seth agreed. "We did have that March blizzard a few years back."

"Well, I knew it was no blizzard today. Didn't feel the snow in my bones at all," Ezra replied.

"My friend, your bones have been forecasting the weather for years," Seth observed.

"Doing a better job than the *Farmer's Almanac*," Ezra said, and the three men chuckled.

"Hi, Mose." Suddenly June Hostetler was behind the counter, hands on her hips. She tilted her head, the arc of her long neck reminding him of a curious goose. "I thought you were long gone. You like me so much you just can't leave?"

Mose smiled down at his hat, not wanting to look her in the eye and encourage her. June had it all wrong—so wrong—but he couldn't think of a kind answer to her question.

"I'm just back for a last cup of coffee. To go, if you wouldn't mind."

"Sure thing."

While June filled a cup with hot brew, Ezra and Seth got back to talking about the weather. Mose held his breath, eager to be free of June's attention. After he paid her and she finally moved off to tend the tables, he let out a sigh.

"Looks like she's sweet on you," Seth said.

Mose didn't answer.

"Isn't your father good friends with her father?" asked Ezra.

"Yah. Longtime friends."

"Puts a little pressure on you." Ezra nodded "They probably want you married, eh? How old are you, anyway?"

"Twenty-two."

Seth clapped him on the back. "Ah, you've got time. Plenty of time."

"Not really," said Ezra. "Most Amish folk are married by their early twenties. Folks need to start a family. That's how it's done." He squinted up at Mose. "Are you baptized, son?"

"I'm preparing with the ministers for baptism in the spring." The meetings and classes took four months or so, but Mose was glad to be on his way. Years ago, when he'd left Joyful River, he'd been running from his father, his family, and the commitment to Amish life. He'd been a wild teen, and while most young folks got a pass during rumspringa, Bishop Aaron had expected better behavior from his son.

Angered by his father and feeling the loss of his mother, Mose had fled. He'd wanted to strike out on his own without a whole community watching his every move. But now, with the interlude of time and experience, he was ready to join the church, glad to be back in the town that was his home. Although they'd made their peace when Mose returned a few months ago, a strain still existed between father and son.

Which pushed Mose to work as much as possible, taking odd jobs and delivery chores that were sure to keep him out of his father's house for most hours of the day. Although it was the home of his youth, he didn't feel completely comfortable there under the watchful eye of his father. Not for lack of effort from Dat's wife, Collette, who worked cheerfully to bring the family together for meals, puzzles and games, and community events.

So Mose turned his attention to work, and plenty of it. He'd never cared much about money, but now he saw it as a step toward independence, the path to having a place of his own. It was time for him to stand on his own two feet.

"Baptism is good." Ezra patted his arm. "An important choice, and a good one. Though I reckon it's like staring into the sun for you, with your father being the bishop and all. Living with the leader of the church."

"Staring into the sun?" Mose smiled. "You've got that right, Ezra. I didn't know you were so wise."

"Comes with age," Ezra said. He nudged Seth. "Mose here is the son of Aaron Troyer. You've met him. Bishop Aaron."

"I have, indeed. How's that, being the son of a bishop?"

Mose picked up his coffee and took a sip, considering. "Awkward. I love my father, but his shoes are too large to fill."

Seth nodded. "Yep."

Ezra pointed at Mose. "You need to walk in your own shoes."

Mose looked down at his boots as Ezra's words sank in. He was walking in his own shoes, choosing his own path. He was making progress.

"It's an age-old conflict between father and son," Seth said, gesturing with his hands as if framing the horizon. "Every man struggles to step away from his father's shadow. Funny thing is, after you step away, you realize the sun was always shining right on you, after all."

Chapter 4

It was after three, the "staff lunch" period when there was a lull in the restaurant, but the kitchen girls had not made an appearance in the break room. Grateful for the quiet of the small, tidy space, Martha took another sip of tomato rice soup and savored the moment alone. Beulah had finished eating already and slipped out for some air. Across the table, two other workers sat eating in silence as they leafed through magazines.

After the commotion of the brief surprise snowfall, Martha had checked outside before she'd gathered her meal. Sunny and cold. Her day was back to normal.

Just then, the high-pitched trio of voices filled the hall.

"They're back," Edna said without looking up from her magazine.

Martha was chewing the last of her sandwich as Sara, Nella, and Bonnie swept in. Their cheeks were rosy from exertion, and their coats seemed to hold the cold air of the February afternoon.

"Guess what we got," Nella said, waving a brown paper bag happily. "Valentines!"

"Cards for Valentine's Day," Sara corrected. "It's coming up soon, you know. And every girl should have a special someone in her life." She placed her lunch box on the table and shrugged off her coat.

"I'm not sure who to give my card to," Bonnie said as she took a seat. "Such a hard choice."

Just then, June hurried into the room. "Did you get them? Did they have them? I wanted to go, but I still had tables to finish up."

"We got three cards, and the corner store has a good assortment." Bonnie handed June the flat paper bag, and June quickly went through the cards. "I'll go back with you at lunch tomorrow if you want."

"So you each got one?" asked June. "I'll need more than one. Four or five, I think, since I have a couple of fellows who seem interested."

"You'd send a valentine to more than one guy?" Nella asked. "But what if they all want to court you?"

June giggled, shrugging one shoulder. "I guess they'll have to take a place in line."

Martha noticed how the three girls seemed so enamored of June. Maybe they thought her confidence might be contagious. Or maybe they were happy to have a leader among them. Martha herself had always been a little put off by June, but the younger girls didn't realize that any nineteen-year-old woman who was as popular as June claimed would certainly be married by now.

June handed back the cards and started counting on her fingers. "I need one valentine for Jimmy Yutzy, and one for Don Schmucker. And two other fellas from church. And maybe one for Mose Troyer."

That caught Martha's interest, but she kept her face passive.

"Our Mose? Who does the deliveries?" asked Bonnie.

"He's good-looking, and of a mind to settle down. Or that's what I heard."

"Mose is a nice person," Nella said emphatically. "He always has something nice to say."

"He's a kind fella," Sara agreed, "but he's too old for us."

"Not for me," June crowed, as if her age were a good thing.

"But maybe he has a girl," Bonnie said. "How can we find out?"

The girls looked to June, who frowned, and then noticed Martha finishing her soup.

"Well," June said, "someone here sees Mose for at least an hour most every day." She nodded at Martha. "Mose drives Martha and her children each morning and afternoon. You two must talk, don't you?"

"We talk," Martha said, not willing to spill Mose's private information. "And he's a very kind man."

"Does he have a girl?" asked Nella.

Martha was softened by the young girl's earnestness. "I don't know, but I think not. He doesn't mention any girl in particular."

"Then I'm definitely giving him a card," Bonnie said.

"You never know what might open the window to love," Nella said fervently.

As the girls chatted on, Nella settled in next to Martha and set aside the cards to begin eating her lunch. "Do you want to see our cards?" Nella asked Martha.

"Sure." Martha wiped her hands on a napkin and turned toward the cards. Two of them were cheerful, covered with colorful hearts. One included a cartoon drawing of a fat cat that Martha knew her daughter would like. The third card was more serious—a photo of red roses with shiny gold-swirled writing. This card made Martha feel sad. It was so dark and dreary, not at all like the feeling of falling in love with someone.

"What's wrong?" asked Nella. "Don't you like them?"

"They're fine," Martha said, "if you like store-bought cards."

Bonnie looked up from her soup. "What other cards are there?"

Martha shrugged. "When I was courting, my sisters and I made valentines by hand. It was fun, and more personal."

"You made cards?" Nella seemed amazed. "Like with markers and paper?"

"And ribbons and felt. And a little bit of glitter sometimes. It made for hours of fun, and it allowed us to personalize each valentine."

All the girls were staring at Martha, as if she'd just discovered how to slice bread.

"Did the boys like your cards?" Nella asked.

"They did. Our parents liked them, too."

"Your parents?" Bonnie's brows rose. "Why would you give your mem and dat a valentine?"

"Because valentines are for everyone. They're a sweet way to show people you love them, and love comes in many different forms."

"But who has the time to make cards?" June pushed her lunch pail aside. "Especially when you need four or five. I'll be purchasing my cards this year."

"You can have the one I bought." Sara's eyes were bright with enthusiasm. "I want to make my own valentines by hand."

"Me too," Nella agreed. "It'll be fun, and if I have time, I'll make some for my sisters and brothers. That way, everyone in the house will get a valentine."

"I'll make one or two," Bonnie said. "It'll be special. And we can work on them together."

"I'll bring in some supplies," Sara offered. "My mother has plenty of glue and felt. And sewing notions, too."

"I'll buy some ribbon at the store," Bonnie said. "And some glitter."

"Are you girls sure you can pull this off?" asked June. "I mean, not everyone is an artist."

"But when something comes from the heart, it's full of love," Martha said quietly. "It may be a little rough at the edges, but it's far more special than a card purchased at the corner store."

"That just makes my heart melt," Sara said. "I'm so glad we're doing this."

"Sara," Bonnie said sternly, "hearts do not melt."

"You know what I mean."

"You'll need to squeeze your card creation in during your lunch break," Martha said, looking up at the clock. "And speaking of time, I need to get back to work." She stood up from the table, feeling lighter, more hopeful. She wasn't sure why, but the notion of the girls making their own valentines cheered her.

Maybe it was about the notion of spreading love. Maybe it was the very fact that most of the girls were willing to spend some time and effort to bring someone joy. Or maybe it was the memory of her own valentine preparations, sharing scissors with her sisters and recommending ways to cut or fold paper.

As she returned to the kitchen and tied on a cooking apron, the thought of the homemade cards gave way to memories of her husband, Ben. He had appreciated her cards; he'd insisted on saving them all, even after they'd wed. They had been childhood sweethearts, had married when she was eighteen, and had shared many joyous days and nights.

How she missed him!

Ben Lambright, her valentine, her one and only.

The calendar pages turned, days passed, and her life went on. She'd learned to move forward, to make big decisions and adjustments. And yet, one thing would never change: her heart still belonged to Ben.

Always and forever.

Chapter 5

With the satisfaction of a good day's work, Martha climbed into Mose's buggy at four thirty. Her shift brought her into the restaurant to start the prep for lunch and dinner, and allowed her to leave early enough that she could feed her children dinner at home.

"It feels good to sit after a full day," she told Mose.

"I bet. Are you warm enough? There's the lap blanket."

"It's fine, denki." She held up one hand to shield her eyes from the golden sunlight illuminating her side of the buggy. "The sun is keeping me warm."

"Quite a change from that snow this morning," he said.

"Indeed. I was relieved to see it stop. It allowed me to put in a full day of work."

He nodded, his eyes on the road as the mule took them to Polly's house. The steady clip-clop of Sunshine's hooves was soothing, and they settled into a contented silence for the journey.

As their buggy passed bare trees and pale fields, Martha thought back on her day in the kitchen. She could see that the excitement over Valentine's Day was going to grow more heated as the holiday approached. Martha wondered if the girls had heard her message about making the holiday about all kinds of love. It was her older sister, Hester, only seven years old at the time, who'd pointed out that February 14 became a sad day for a person who didn't have a true love—which was a lot of folks. Such wisdom from one so young. So much better to make Valentine's Day a time for people to thank their loved ones—mothers, daughters, friends. Not just couples.

Martha looked over at Mose, recalling the girls' questions about his personal life. Did he have a true love for Valentine's Day this year?

She truly didn't know, but she recognized that Mose Troyer was a complicated man. A bishop's son who had returned from a stint with the Englisch to walk the Amish path. A former rebel, troublemaker, drinker, and who knew what else. Mischief in his eyes but warmth in his words. There'd been a time during rumspringa when Martha had whispered about him with her girlfriends, wondering at the nerve of the bishop's son to break so many rules. Parents and church leaders were supposed to look the other way when youth misbehaved during the teen years, and yet there was a different expectation when it came to the bishop's family. Folks expected better behavior from the leader of the church and his family members.

Mose Troyer had left town for a few years, but since his return he'd moved back with his family and was juggling many jobs to make a living. For the past few months he'd been taking Martha to work and delivering her children, April and Milo, to their sitter, Martha's sister-in-law Polly Lambright. Martha didn't know Mose well, but the children adored him. He seemed amused when April babbled on; he captivated her boy. His buggy was one of the few places where Milo would sit still and content these days. In their short time together, April had become quite attached to the easygoing driver who seemed to sense the right time for quiet and the right time for conversation.

Seeing that they were turning onto the lane of Polly and J. R. Lambright's home, Martha smiled and tightened the scarf around her neck. The joy of fetching her children each day never waned. It was sometimes the highlight of her day.

"I'll just be a minute," she said as Mose stopped the mule in front of the modest two-story house.

"Take your time. I have my book to read," he said.

"Mem! Mem!" Milo ran to her as soon as she opened the side door. He had only begun walking recently, and was still a bit wobbly on his feet.

Martha swept him into her arms for a hug and then tousled his shiny blond hair. "And look at you with your coat on. Aunt Polly has you all ready to go."

"Milo here has an internal time clock," Polly said as she picked up a crying toddler from the floor. Little Ellie ceased crying the minute she landed on her mother's hip. "Your boy seems to know exactly when you're coming to pick him up, and he's raring to go."

Like Martha, Polly had married into the Lambright family, becoming part of Madge and Emery's extended brood. Ben had always been close to his older brother, J.R., and Martha felt right at home in J.R. and Polly's house. When Martha returned to work after Ben's death, it seemed natural that Polly would mind her children while she was at the diner. So here they came, five days a week, and the children certainly benefitted from their aunt's loving care and interactions with their cousins, young and old.

"April?" Martha called, moving through the main room. "Where are you, sweetie?" Martha found her daughter sitting at the kitchen table, her blond head bent over a picture she was coloring with crayons. "There you are. Are you ready to go home?"

"Not yet, Mem," she said, drawing intently with a yellow crayon. "I'm not finished making my valentine."

"A valentine?" Martha shook her head. "Just like the girls at the shop. They're all atwitter with Valentine's Day coming."

"My older ones were making cards for friends at school," Polly said. "They left the craft box out, and, of course, the younger ones want to follow their lead, every time."

Martha moved behind her daughter to take a closer look. April was coloring in yellow hair on the stick figure of a girl. "Who's that?"

"That's me," April said.

She moved her hand, revealing a larger girl beside the stick figure, probably a woman, also with yellow hair. *That's probably me*, Martha thought. She had pale gold hair, and so far the children shared her coloring. There was also a yellow-haired boy, and a dark-haired Amish man with a broad-brimmed hat.

Our family. Martha felt a stab of sadness at the thought of April drawing her dat.

"Tell your mem who you're making the card for," Polly prodded.

"It's for Mose," April said. "See? This is you, Mem. Here's me and Milo. And this is Mose. It's all of us, all together!"

Martha tapped her chin. "It's nice to be together, but Mose is not in our family."

"I know, Mem. But I want him to have a valentine."

"That's very nice of you," Polly said. "Is it finished?"

"Not yet."

"How about you bring it home and finish it later, so Mem can get you home for dinner."

April put the crayon down and sighed. "Okay."

"Off you go," Polly said. "Go get your coat on, so you don't keep Mose waiting."

As April climbed down and scampered off, Martha picked

up the drawing and frowned. "I wish my daughter didn't have a crush on the buggy driver."

"He's more than a driver, isn't he?" Polly rocked the child on her hip as she spoke. "Mose is a good and kind person. And April sees him nearly every day. It's normal to form an attachment."

"It's one thing to be friendly with him, but she made him a valentine."

Polly took April's drawing from Martha's hands and went to the desk in the main room. "You worry too much. Like all good mothers." She slipped the valentine into a large manila envelope and handed it to Martha. "Mose will be tickled to receive this. It'll be fine."

"I hope so."

As Martha corralled the children out to the buggy, she wondered why April's valentine for Mose bothered her so much. Maybe it seemed disrespectful to Ben. Martha had recently realized that April didn't remember her father. It was understandable, as April had been only three when Ben died, but Martha had prayed that some memory would stick with her. And Milo hadn't even been born when Ben died.

Such heartache.

But Martha had to trust in Gott and keep moving ahead.

The buggy door opened, and Mose jumped out with a wide, welcoming grin. "Come out of the wind! It's nice and warm in here."

"Mose!" Milo called as he toddled across the frozen lawn. The child had mastered only a dozen words, but, of course, *Mose* was one of them.

"Hey, buddy. Let me help you up." Mose lifted Milo into the buggy, and then watched cautiously as April climbed in on her own.

"I can do it," she insisted. "I'm a big girl now."

"I can see that," he said.

"They grow up so fast," Martha whispered to Mose before climbing into the front seat.

"She's learning responsibility from you," he said. "It's because you're a good mother."

Martha wasn't so sure, but she allowed herself to take the compliment and hoped it was true. Sometimes she worried that her fears would affect the children. Reality could be cruel. She had learned as much when Ben was killed. But now she needed to try her best to keep her children safe. With the support of family and good folk like Mose, life would go on.

As April launched a hundred and one questions at Mose, Martha let her mind wander. She spent much of the ride home trying not to let herself imagine how her days and nights would have been if Ben's life hadn't ended in that terrible accident.

As they finally turned onto their street, she pulled her thoughts away from what might have been. She had been blessed with two beautiful children, and she needed to shake off her regrets and sorrows to maintain a loving home for them.

Thy will be done, she prayed silently. If the words flowed in her prayers often enough, the heart would eventually learn to accept them.

Chapter 6

Mose had a smile on his face as Sunshine pulled the buggy away from Martha's small home on the back end of Madge and Emery Lambright's property. He drove plenty of Amish folk here and there, but those two children, Milo and April, had to be his favorites. April always had a hundred questions, and Milo could be a moody customer, but that made his smiles that much more rewarding.

After Mose dropped them off at home, he turned Sunshine onto the highway and rode out to the furniture factory to pick up a few men who were ending their shift. Four men were waiting for him when he arrived. Having grown up in Joyful River, Mose knew the back roads and neighborhoods well, and he enjoyed the conversation during the ride.

Next, he turned his mule toward Main Street, where he sought to pick up any stragglers who might need a lift home from the shops. That night, he was particularly eager to find a passenger or two. It would be an honest excuse for arriving late to his father's dinner hosting Linda and Len Hostetler and their daughters.

He checked in at Junior's store, but Dennis and his father were getting ready to close up for the day. No customers for Mose. Things were looking up when he spotted two girls with their scooters outside the pretzel shop. He helped them load their scooters into the back and told a few jokes to get them laughing along the way. But the girls lived just on the edge of town, and he had them home in no time at all.

He swung by Main Street one more time, but the town was quiet, half asleep already. He had no choice but to call it a day and head home.

As he rode up the lane to his father's house, he saw the Hostetlers' buggy tied up on a fence post. Of course they were still there. Len and Linda had no qualms about staying at least until nine o'clock.

Out by the barn, Mose took his time unhitching Sunshine. He checked the water in the trough and stroked the mule as he leaned into her. "I guess I'm out of excuses."

Sunshine nuzzled him.

"Yah, you're a good mule. Go on, now." He bid the mule good night and turned her out. In the distance, the house looked inviting, the lantern light of its windows glowed in the dark blue night.

Well, looks could be deceiving.

He came in through the kitchen door and was glad to see that the table had been cleared. His stepmother, Collette, stood at the sink, up to her elbows in suds. His sister Amy stood beside her, drying.

"There you are," Collette said. "We saved you a plate. It should still be warm in the oven. Pork chops and mashed potatoes."

"Denki." He glanced cautiously toward the voices out in the living room, then went into the closed porch off the kitchen. He washed his hands in the scrub sink. When he returned, Amy was using a kitchen towel to set the heated plate on the table with a fork and knife.

"Where are Tess and Suzie? I don't see them in the living room."

"They're off in the sewing room with Dottie," Collette answered. "They've got the paper and sewing kits out. Time to make valentines, I reckon."

A girl thing. He cut into the pork chop and swiped a piece of meat through the gravy.

"Someone's been asking about you, big brother."

"Len? Please, tell me it's Len."

Amy gave a laugh, then covered her mouth, as if she didn't want anyone to overhear. "You know who."

June. He sighed as his head lolled back. "And what's she been asking?"

Amy sat in the chair nearest him. "She wants to know if you have a gal. A valentine."

"And you told her that I do. I have a lovely valentine, and we're about to be engaged."

She swiped the hand towel at him, dusting his shoulder. "I couldn't say that. It's not the truth."

"As far as you know." Smiling, he cut off another piece of pork and placed it in his mouth. Delicious. Collette was a good cook. "Did you tell her I'm courting someone else?"

Her eyes opened wide with curiosity. "Are you?"

"Nay. But I'm not interested in June."

"She said she might like you if you maybe liked her."

He groaned. "Not that childish game. What did you tell her?"

"That I'd talk to you."

"Don't give her any hope."

Amy folded her arms. "Look, I'm just trying to do a favor. Don't blame the messenger."

"Okay. Tell her that I'm courting someone else."

"Is that true? Because I won't lie."

"I'll find another maidel to court if it lets me off the hook with her."

"Enough matchmaking," Collette said from the sink, "and lend me a hand."

"Oops. Sorry," Amy said, rising from her seat. "But we're not matchmaking. We're trying to stop a match. Unmatch. Or something like that."

"It's not my place to pry," Collette said. "But I do need your help so I can return to our guests."

Amy ran the dish towel over a plate. "I'm back on the job."

As Mose enjoyed his quiet dinner, he tried to think of a way to put off June without being rude. He'd tried dropping subtle hints, but June was not one to read a person well. Instead, she kept pushing, which was making these weekly dinners with the Hostetlers awkward for him.

His father's friend Len was easy enough to talk with, but Len's wife, Linda, bossed every conversation and meddled in other folks' matters. And Mose didn't like the way Linda trounced on his stepmother, Collette, who was kind and warm to everyone she met. Even now, when other Amish women would have congregated in the kitchen to help with the cleanup, Linda was out there, probably relaxing.

And then there were the daughters. The younger one, Dottie, was okay. She liked spending time with Suzie and Tess, and she got along with everyone. June was another story, just like her mother in many ways. She had a way of dropping bad news about other folk and pretending it was out of concern, when it was really just gossip. June loved to complain and hated to lift a finger. When she was in the room, Mose went out of his way to be included in conversation with the men, just to avoid talking to her.

Unfortunately, his father didn't seem to notice the way he tried to escape the girl. In fact, Dat had mentioned her recently after one of the dinners with the Hostetlers.

"I've noticed that June is around your age," Aaron had said. "You know, she doesn't have a beau. She'd probably go on a buggy ride with you if you asked."

Not if she were the last Amish girl in Joyful River. Or all of Lancaster County.

Of course Mose couldn't say that, and he could tell that his father was uncomfortable pushing him toward June. Though push he did. "You know, it's about time that you found a good Amish wife and made a home for yourself," Dat would say.

Situations like this were one of the things that had driven Mose to leave Joyful River years ago. Upon his return, Mose's father had accepted that he was his own man, his own person. He understood that Mose was now committed to living a good plain life, abiding by Amish law.

And yet, Dat still pushed. He couldn't seem to help himself. After every visit with the Hostetlers, Dat pushed again. Mose remained quiet but felt himself turning inward, peeved. Once or twice, Collette told him on the sly not to listen to anyone on matters of the heart.

"You know what's right for you," she said.

Gott bless her. The problem was, Mose had never met an Amish girl who was quite right for him.

With a sigh, Mose brought his empty plate to the sink and stepped back to watch as Collette took a tray of lemon bars from the oven. "I thought something smelled delicious," he said.

"I'll cut them in a few minutes," Collette said, untying her kitchen apron. "Come out and join us for dessert."

"I'd rather not," he said. "Maybe I can grab one later."

"Come, now. Are you going to hide here in the kitchen until our guests go?"

"I was planning to head out to the barn."

"You mean hide out in the barn," Amy teased.

Amy and Mose were chuckling when there was a flurry of movement at the door and, as if on cue, June appeared in the kitchen.

"What's so funny?" she said, coming over to join the group. "I want to hear the joke."

Amy cleared her throat as her eyes held Mose's.

He raked back his dark hair with a casual shrug. "We were just trying to make light of our problems."

"I see."

Collette and Amy dispersed, Collette to cut the dessert bars, and Amy back to the dishes.

June remained beside Mose. "We missed you at dinner."

"I had to work. Lots of folks need rides home at the end of the day."

"Well, you missed a good dinner." She tipped her head to one side, an odd habit that made her resemble a cackling goose sunning on the riverbank. "You work a lot of nights, I know, but you won't be working Sunday. Are you going to the singing at the Eshers' place?"

"Probably not." Definitely not. But it would be rude to be so blunt.

"Why not?" she asked.

Stalling, he turned around and tossed his napkin into the trash. He could hardly tell June that, since his return from his travels beyond Joyful River, he felt too old and wise to engage in the traditional matchmaking activities for Amish youth. Granted, he was only a few years older than June, but he felt like an old dawdi when he was around teens and women his age.

"I'm not sure I really belong there," he said, soft-soaping it. "Singings are really for the younger folk."

"You're young enough," June insisted. "You have to come. Sit beside me, and you'll be sure to have a good time."

"It's just not for me. I'm sure you understand."

"I don't think I do." Her voice grew stern, like an irate schoolteacher. "Why would you miss out on a social event meant to bring folks together? Have you grown shy in your old age, Mose?"

"Not shy. Just . . .thoughtful."

"Well, maybe you need to do a little less thinking and take some action."

Mose looked to Amy, who simply shook her head. She couldn't get him out of this one.

"If you don't socialize, you're going to end up all alone, Mose," June said. "Do you really want that?"

"Dessert's ready," Collette announced. "And I heated the kettle in case anyone wants tea or instant coffee. Lemon bar?" She extended a platter to June, and Mose was grateful to have a barrier between himself and the persistent young woman. Grateful for the distraction.

June shook her head, but Mose helped himself, thanking his stepmother.

"Let's go join the others in the living room," Collette said. "I've barely had a moment to visit with Linda."

Relieved, Mose led the way into the living room, pulling up a dining room chair next to Len, which would put him squarely in the path of the men's conversation. Not that he cared about the right time to plant alfalfa or the best way to chase moles out of the ground. But he'd choose farm talk over June talk any day.

June was right about one thing: he was going to end up alone.

Alone, but at peace. Certainly not with the likes of a pushy one like June Hostetler.

Chapter 7

Martha awoke with a copy of *Goodnight Moon* in her hands and her young son sleeping beside her. She must have dozed off reading to him. She leaned down to place a kiss on his smooth, pudgy cheek. How she loved him! There was something wonderful about a sleeping child, freshly bathed and diapered and snuggled up in winter pajamas for bed.

She slipped quietly out of his bed, tucked the covers around him, and added a second blanket on top. This time of year the heat from the woodburning stove didn't always make it into the bedrooms, but if she left the door open it would be warm enough.

Out in the main room, April was still perched at the kitchen table.

"You've been working very hard on your card." Martha opened the grate of the potbellied stove and stoked the fire.

"It's a lot of work, Mem," April said slowly. Her head drooped, and her crayon strokes were slower now.

"Finish up, sweetie." She added a log to keep the fire going. "It's past time for bed."

"Mmm, it's not done yet."

"Let me see." Martha smiled as she took in the bit of grass under the feet of the people and the sun in the sky. With April's coaching, Martha had carefully printed *Happy Valentine's Day* across the bottom of the page. "It's very nice."

"I want to add hearts in the sky. Lots of pink hearts. But I can't draw them."

"Hearts in the sky. I could probably draw them, and you can color them in. Want me to do it in pencil?"

April nodded.

"Okay, but after I do my part, you're going to bed."

"Aw, Mem . . ."

"You can finish tomorrow at Aunt Polly's."

"But I wanted to give it to Mose tomorrow, in the morning."

"Tomorrow evening is soon enough. Valentine's Day is still more than a week away."

April pursed her lips and then nodded. "Okay, Mem."

Following her daughter's instructions, Martha drew a dozen or so hearts in the sky—large and small. "It's raining hearts," she teased.

"Mem, you think Mose will like it?"

"I know he will. Now, off to bed with you. Let's go brush your teeth."

With April tucked in, Martha made short work of straightening the house and washing the dishes in the sink. Once the place was tidy, she pulled on her boots and a shawl and traipsed outside to the woodpile.

The wood supply had been getting low, but as she approached she noticed that it had doubled in size that day. Someone must have come by the house to replenish her supply, probably J.R. or another one of Ben's brothers.

They were so good to her. This little place made a fine home, but sometimes the chores of keeping a house were just too much for her. The Lambright family knew that, and so often they took care of a task before she could even make a request.

After Ben's death, Madge and Emery had insisted that Martha and April stay in the small house on their property. Both April and Milo had been born there, on the bed where Martha slept each night. For Martha, it was home.

Martha's mother, Babs Eicher, wanted her to come home to York and move the children into the house Martha had grown up in.

"Then you won't have to work," her mother had explained. "And you'll be free to start courting. You're a young woman. Too young not to marry again. But, Martha dear, you'll never find a husband while you're living in the pocket of the Lambrights. That's going to intimidate any good Amish man. Come home, and get out from under their shadow."

Martha had declined repeatedly. She told her mother that she didn't want to uproot her children, but in truth, there were many reasons to stay. She loved the Lambrights. Madge and Polly and J.R. made her feel like an important part of the family. And her job at the diner brought her a strong sense of connection to the community and daily satisfaction.

Gott had blessed her with a good life in Joyful River. With His grace, she would bloom where she was planted.

Inside the house, she added another log to the fire and set the fresh batch of wood in the corner. She washed her hands and quickly packed a sandwich for the next day's lunch. Then she went to the table, picked up April's valentine, and smiled. Her girl was a pretty stubborn customer when she set her sights on something. She slid the valentine back into the manila envelope and put it next to her lunch pail, ready to go in the morning.

As she changed into her nightgown, she thought about how valentines had been the big topic of the day. It was going to be interesting, watching the kitchen girls make their own cards. It made her remember the valentines she'd made for Ben. He'd kept them all. Where were they stored?

She hung her dress and prayer cap on the wall peg, then went over to the dresser to check the drawers Ben once used. Empty. Of course, his family had helped her go through his things after he'd passed away.

Maybe under the bed. She dropped to her knees and took a peek into the shadowed space. A flat, plastic bin was situated under the center of the bed, and she reached in to slide it out. Popping the top off, she was pleased to find that the valentines were right on top—half a dozen of them. She took them out and put them on the bed, allowing herself a quick look at the other contents of the bin. An odd collection of things. There was a package of thick men's socks. A fishing reel Ben had probably never used, as he'd found fishing to be too slow. There was a set of bedsheets that had probably been a wedding gift, and quite a few romance novels that she'd tossed in the bin after reading.

As soon as she got a chance, she was going to clear this thing out.

For now, she took a pair of thick blue socks from the package and pulled them on. Ben would be glad she had some use for them. A blend of cotton and wool, the socks would help to keep her feet warm on the cold winter nights.

She slid the bin back, then popped up onto the bed, where the cards seemed to sing out memories of love and joy.

The card with the big red heart and red ribbon woven through the border had been the first. Just looking at the card brought her back to the day she had made it. They were still teenagers, and they'd spent time together at quite a few frolics, playing volleyball and soccer, chatting, and roasting marshmallows over a bonfire. He'd begun giving her a ride home from Sunday singings, and every time they were together, she'd come to like him more and more.

The card made of red construction paper with a delicate white snowflake pasted on top came later. That year, she had just gotten her job working in Madge's restaurant, and it was hard to hide the fact that they were so much in love while they were at work!

There were the pink roses she'd created by rolling and gluing small pieces of satin ribbon. Just two months before she'd made that card, Ben had taken her on a sleigh ride. Afterward, as they sipped hot chocolate by a bonfire, he'd asked her to marry him.

'Twas such a wonderful, good night!

So they'd been engaged that Valentine's Day, but they'd kept it a secret until wedding season in the fall.

Martha tried to pick her favorite, but every card represented a memory. She'd put so much love into them, and dear Ben had cherished and kept them all. These cards might show the kitchen girls how a card that was handcrafted with care could be special.

With a happy sigh, she decided to share them. Eager to show these to the young girls at the restaurant, she tucked them into the envelope with April's valentine.

This year, Valentine's Day might be fun again.

Chapter 8

The next day, the girls in the break room were delighted when Martha opened the large envelope and gently spilled her homemade cards onto the table.

"You brought us some of your valentines!" Nella's eyes opened wide. "They're wonderful."

"Certainly inspiring," Bonnie agreed, picking up the card with the pink ribbon roses. "These are so much better than I expected. But I don't think I could ever do something this detailed."

"I could show you how," Martha said. "It's not as hard as you think."

Even June nodded in approval. "They're very sweet, Martha. I didn't know you were so creative."

"I just had a bit of fun with paper and ribbon," Martha said. "Anyone can make one. I think what makes them special is the loving care that went into them."

"I can feel the love," Nella insisted. "My heart is so happy right now! I want to make one with a wispy white snowflake, and I'd also love to learn how to curl the ribbon into tiny roses. My mem would be tickled to get a card like that."

The cards purchased at the corner store were pushed aside as the girls began to organize their crafts corner in the break room.

"We should buy some satin ribbon from the fabric store," Sara said, putting a small shopping bag on the table. She pulled out scissors, glue, some cloth, and glitter. "I brought these supplies from home, but Mem didn't have any ribbon."

Most Amish women had bags of worn clothing and blanket scraps that could be salvaged for quilt squares, but decorative notions like ribbon were not a staple, since they could not be used on clothing.

"Let's make a list of supplies we need," Sara went on. "Nella and I could pick up a few things after work, and we can get started tomorrow."

"We definitely need pink ribbon," Bonnie said.

"And more red paper," added Nella.

As Sara composed a list, the girls further examined Martha's creations, making plans for their own cards with different colors and altered designs.

"Your valentines have given us so many ideas," said Sara. "Could we, maybe, hold on to them for a few days, just to keep us on track? I promise we'll return everything when we're finished."

"Sure," Martha agreed, placing a card with pink and red felt hearts into the top of the bag that Sara had brought. "Just be sure to keep everything together." She stowed the large envelope in her cubby at the back of the break room, determined to return it to Polly at the end of the day. Waste not, want not.

That afternoon, as the kitchen girls moved through their tasks, Martha saw a new enthusiasm in their eyes. Funny how a little project could boost a person's spirits. With everyone around her drawn into the card-making tradition, Martha realized that she, too, needed to make a valentine or two. Maybe something for her children, a reminder that they were loved.

Ben would have liked that.

That evening, when Martha stopped into the Lambright house to pick up her children, she waved the empty envelope at Polly. "I'm returning this to you," she said. "Denki."

"No, Mem," April insisted, plucking the envelope from her hand. "It's mine! I need it for my valentine."

Martha leaned down to kiss her daughter's cheek. "You know, you could just hand your card to Mose."

April shook her head. "Cards need envelopes."

Martha sighed, as Polly shrugged. "This is a girl who knows her own mind."

"Write Mose's name on the envelope!" April insisted, holding up her finished valentine. "I can't wait to give it to him."

Martha obliged, then thanked Polly and ushered her children out into the cold. Mose jumped out and helped the children into the buggy.

"Mose, I have something to tell you," April said as she climbed inside.

Martha turned around from the front seat to watch.

Mose was at the rear, leaning into the back seat. "I'm all ears."

"I mean, show you. I have something to show you." She lifted the envelope and pushed it toward him. "This is for you."

"For me? What is it?"

"Open it and see!"

"Open, open!" Milo chimed.

Mose flipped the flap and cautiously peered inside. "What's this? A drawing." He slid the paper out slowly. "A very nice picture."

"It's a valentine!" April squealed in delight.

"I see. 'Happy Valentine's Day.' You mean, you made this for me?"

"It's for you! Do you like it?"

"Indeed, I do. Tell me, who's this in the picture? This is you, and Milo, right?"

"And Mem. And you."

"Very nice. I'm grateful to be included in such a fine family. Denki, April. I especially like that you did the drawing your-self. Good job."

April basked in the praise, and Milo mimicked: "Good job! Good job."

"I'm going to keep this close," Mose said, sliding it back into the envelope. "Maybe I'll hang it inside the buggy so all my passengers can see it."

"Hang it up?" April pressed a hand to her cheek. "Then everyone will want one!"

"They'll certainly admire it." Mose looked from April to Martha. "We best get going."

He closed the back, came around, and climbed into the front seat, placing the envelope on the bench seat between Martha and him. Funny, but the awkwardness Martha had felt over April's crush on Mose had faded, and she was glad he seemed pleased by the little valentine.

"I'll bet this is the first valentine you received this year," she teased.

He chuckled, his eyes on the roadway ahead. "The first in many years."

"Well, it's a step in the right direction."

"Indeed," he said. Their conversation was interrupted by April's new slew of questions: Did he really like it? Had he been surprised? Did he notice the sun shining in the sky? And all the hearts?

Listening to their exchange, Martha felt a tinge of sadness. Interactions with Mose were proving to be beneficial to the children. He was their daily dose of male influence—a very positive role model. But Mose's presence reminded her of the many things her children lacked without their father in their lives. Songs and lessons, holidays and hugs. Thoughts of the things they were missing chipped away at her heart.

A shiver went through her, and she turned away, her eyes blurring the shadows beyond the window.

"Are you okay?" he asked. "Do you want the lap blanket?"

"I'm fine," she said, wondering how long the ache would linger in her heart. "Just fine."

Chapter 9

That night, when Mose steered his mule toward home and rolled into the darkness, he wondered what went on in Martha Lambright's mind. That woman was a hard one to read. Kind, loving to her children, and pretty as a glowing sunset. But at times, she was cold and silent as a potbelly stove in summer.

At home he freed the mule from the buggy and made sure Sunshine had some oats and water to get her through the night. Before heading to the house, he reached into the buggy and retrieved the large envelope. He thought his sisters would enjoy seeing April's valentine.

Mose paused in the golden light coming from the front window of the house and reached into the envelope again. He planned to tease the girls that he was the first person in the house to receive a valentine. But as he reached in, he saw a second card inside, a smaller rectangle of stiff paper. What was this? Another card from April?

He pulled it out and found an elaborately decorated card with a heart in the center and red ribbon woven through the paper at the border. The red heart in the center was symmetrical, perfectly drawn. This was not the work of a four-year-old. It reminded him of the valentines his sisters had been making this year. Lately Tess and Suzie had set up the card table in the sewing room so they could have a place to cut and paste paper hearts and ribbons.

Leaning into the light, he turned it over and read:

"Valentine, I'm grateful that Gott brought us together." It was signed "Love, Martha."

Martha . . . Martha?

She believed Gott had brought them together? Well, Gott's wonders never ceased.

She cared for him. She'd even signed it with *love*. Hard to believe thoughts of love or even companionship were on her mind when she lapsed into that stiff demeanor at times. Moody. But then, she was coping with a lot, raising two children on her own. He'd suspected that there were secrets under the surface. But through her pain, she'd opened her heart to him.

Hope spread through his chest like warm honey.

Martha liked him.

And his reaction was very different from the tension he felt when June Hostetler fawned over him. Martha's interest was a good thing.

Now that her feelings were clear, he could admit he was drawn to her, too. She was easy to talk to, good company.

Unlike the other girls who seemed interested in courting him. After his return to Joyful River, he'd come to see that most of the Amish girls here were giddy and silly. Too young and caught up in frolics and quilting bees.

Martha was his age, but in a different place in her life. She'd been married. She'd known heartache, as he had. But she was hard to get close to; a tough nut to crack. Martha was mature and wise, quiet but outspoken at the right times. Having been married before, she didn't have pie-in-the-sky ideas about a big wedding, and she wasn't in a rush to be wed before folks called her an old maid. And he'd grown attached to her children. April and Milo showed a fine mix of innocence and curiosity that brought him joy every day.

Yah, he was happy to have a valentine from Martha, though Mose wasn't sure how to respond. Maybe he should send a note back?

Entering the house, he stopped in the kitchen to show Collette the valentine from April.

She laughed out loud. "Oh, Mose! Isn't that the sweetest thing?"

"Looks like I'm pretty popular with the four-year-old crowd," he said with a smirk.

"I'm sure you are." She returned to mashing the potatoes. "Dinner will be ready soon. You'll want to wash up. And can you send the girls down to set the table?"

"Will do." He went up to the sewing room and found Suzie with glue on her fingertips. Tess was sewing lace onto felt hearts.

"That's going to look like a frosted cake when you're done," he teased Tess.

"Is not." Tess glared up at him.

"I think it'll be pretty," Suzie declared.

"Not as wonderful as *this* valentine." Mose flashed the drawing from April, and the girls' faces lit up.

"How cute!" Tess said, nudging his arm. "Finally, you got a valentine, big brother."

"That's so adorable!" Suzie said. "Who gave it to you?"

"April Lambright. I drive her family each day."

"You're a lucky fella," Suzie said, using the glue on her hands to paste delicate tissue paper hearts onto a card.

"Collette wants you downstairs to set the table," he said, looking over the finished cards drying on the table. "There must be a dozen cards here. Are you giving a valentine to every Amish boy in Joyful River?"

"Just the handsome ones," Tess teased, sticking the needle into one corner and standing up. "And why are you snooping on our work?"

"I'm not snooping. Just observing."

Suzie wiped her fingers on a cloth and joined Tess at the doorway. "Some of the paste is still wet, so don't touch anything," she said.

"I wouldn't dream of it," he said, smiling as they looked back and then disappeared.

Hearing their footsteps in the hall, he looked over their supplies. Was he supposed to make a valentine for Martha? He couldn't imagine cutting and pasting and sewing like his sisters.

But he could draw. He'd been a doodler all his life, and his mem used to find his sketches amusing. He took one of the red felt pens and a few large index cards. As he was searching for supplies, he came across a list the girls had put together. As he scanned the list, he realized that these were sayings to be used in their cards.

Be mine!
Our two hearts beat as one.
We belong together, valentine!
Your love brings sunshine to my heart.
Happiness is a warm hug.

Hmm. Maybe the greetings worked for teenaged girls, but Mose found them to be too gooey and sweet, like the coating of a caramel apple. It always stuck to the teeth.

Mose didn't feel comfortable writing about love or beating hearts. Too sappy, and too soon. Although he'd gotten to know Martha over the past few months, he didn't want to rush a special relationship.

He needed something simple.

Taking a seat at the table, he uncapped the red felt pen and placed one large white index card in front of him. On the plain side, he drew some small hearts and then strung them together. Then he attached the string to posts and made it look as if the hearts were hanging from a backyard clothesline. He added grass clumps below, and then some puffs of wind and a few flying hearts, as if they were being blown away by the wind.

There. He looked at the card and grinned. Kind of goofy, but no one could accuse him of being too soupy.

He wrote Martha across the bottom, then added the sun to the top, with rays shining down on the little hearts. That would have to do for now. He took the card up to his room and left it on the nightstand, planning to write a message later.

How would he give it to Martha? It might be awkward to just hand it to her in the morning, considering how she'd subtly slipped her card in the envelope. He wasn't sure how to handle it, but now that he knew how she felt toward him, he was confident he'd figure things out. As his dat sometimes said, "When you find the path, you figure out a way to get around the obstacles."

Mose went down to dinner with a new lightness in his chest. An unfamiliar feeling.

Hope.

Chapter 10

Friday dawned sunny and cold. Mose grabbed a quick breakfast of cold cereal, and then went out to fetch his mule from the pasture. He felt a new eagerness to see Martha, and a slight nervousness over the inevitable shift in their relationship. Actually, he was plenty nervous. Tight in the gut, and his palms were sweating, despite the cold. But as he squinted into the sunlight casting a golden glow over the winter fields and bordering trees in the distance, he recognized the necessity of growing pains. Change could be a good thing, especially when it opened up a new path in life.

Steam puffs came from Sunshine's nostrils as he patted her neck. "Yah, I'm happy to see you, too." He brought her over toward the barn and prepared the buggy for another day.

As Martha and the children approached the buggy, April's big hello and Milo's smile calmed his nerves. These children liked him, and their mem did, too. Martha commented on the sunshine, and he caught a flash of merriment in her blue eyes when she talked about the valentine-making project at the restaurant.

"With all the fuss, you would think it's a real holiday," she said as the buggy rolled along.

"It's been crazy at our house, too," Mose said, explaining how his sisters had set up a special craft table where they worked on cards during their free time. "So far they've made half a dozen valentines. Not sure there are enough Amish boys in town for their creative cards."

"It's sweet that they're swept into the spirt of love," said Martha.

"There must be something to it when a child as young as April wants to make a valentine."

Martha looked to the seat in the back, where April pretended to read a book to her baby brother. "April knew there was someone in her life who deserved a thank-you," she said.

When Mose turned to face Martha, her eyes held the promise of a summer sky. In that moment he wanted to say something, thank her for the valentine, but he didn't want to bring it up in front of the children. Besides, it would make for a happy surprise for her to find his valentine later in the day.

When his morning transportation runs were completed, Mose returned to the diner to pick up some food for a luncheon Madge was catering.

"We'll have everything together for you in a few minutes," Madge told him. "Sandra's almost done slicing up the pot roast, and June here is going to help load the truck."

June gave a wave from behind the counter, where she was serving coffee to the two regular patrons, Seth and Ezra.

"You'll be delivering the food to Carol Miller's house. She's hosting a lunch. You know where they live, over in Cricket's Glen?"

When Mose nodded, she went on.

"While you're waiting, feel free to have a cup of coffee," Madge said, "and make yourself at home. We'll find you when it's ready."

Mose declined the coffee and tried to be low-key, waiting at the counter with the two old-timers now that June had ducked into the kitchen. He hoped that the company of men was the best way to avoid June and the other girls, too. Every time he came into Madge's place, there seemed to be a procession of young Amish women going out of their way to say hello to him, ask about the weather, smile, and giggle. He was kind to the girls, but he was so over it. Someone was always inviting him to a singing, an Amish activity for single youth. He was so over that, too. He wasn't interested in singings or giggly girls. The space in his heart needed a wise woman who was secure in her life.

A woman like Martha.

He wondered what she was doing at that moment. Maybe he could get a glimpse of her in the back. While Ezra rambled on about his daily exercise routine, Mose went down the hallway, as if heading to the restroom. On the way, he passed a small room without a door. The sign overhead read "Employees Only," but he dared a look inside. A large table with chairs filled most of the room. There was a corkboard on the wall beside a small sink with the weekly schedule and some cartoons tacked upon it. The opposite wall had built-in cubbies, probably for the employees. Probably the employee lunchroom. He stepped inside and saw that the cubbies were labeled. He identified Martha's by recognizing her orange lunch pail; it was one of the top cubbies, second from the right.

It would be the perfect spot to leave her valentine, if only he had it on him. Right now it was sitting in the back of the buggy, pressed between the pages of a Mark Twain book he read from time to time.

"Mose?"

He turned to find June in the doorway, her head tilted in that goosey manner. "The food's ready."

"All right, then. I've got the buggy by the back door. But I'm sure I can manage. I'll do a few trips."

"I'm happy to help you," June insisted, leading him to the back of the kitchen.

Sandra, an agreeable woman with broad shoulders and a round face, handed him oven mitts and instructed him to put them on. "The trays are hot now, and they'll keep the heat during the ride there. You can take the mitts and return them later."

Mose took the heaviest of the trays and led the way to his buggy. In two trips, the buggy was loaded, and Mose was relieved to be riding away from June's dripping goodbyes.

When he arrived at the Miller home, where the lunch was being held, he started unloading, When he shifted the trays in the back of the buggy, a red envelope dropped down from the trays.

It was addressed to him. Strange.

He opened it and found a valentine—a store-bought card. Was it another one from Martha? She could have slipped it into the order, knowing the food would be transported in his buggy.

It was the usual sweetheart message signed by June. No surprise, considering the way she tried to corner him. Not to mention the pressure Len Hostetler and Mose's own father put on the two of them.

But this valentine made him feel a little sad and guilty that he didn't return her feelings.

And what was he supposed to do, now that June had made her intention known? The last thing he wanted to do was egg on June and the giggly maidens at the Country Diner.

How could he let June down easy? Bad scenarios went through his head as he brought the trays into the kitchen, where Carol Miller and a handful of Amish women were setting the metal food trays over Sterno pots to keep the food warm. He made sure everything was just right for the meal before he wished the women a good day and headed off.

With an hour or so to spare before his next delivery, he turned Sunshine toward Main Street and stopped in at Junior's Amish Grocery, where he found his friend Dennis behind the counter.

"What can I get you, Mose?" asked Dennis. "Did Collette send you out for some dried apricots or sugar for those delicious cookies she makes?"

"Not today." Glancing behind him, Mose was glad to see a lull in the shop's activity. A few customers browsed. Dennis's mother, Birdie, was helping a woman measure out some spices in the bulk dry-goods section, but otherwise the place was quiet. "Actually, I've come for some advice."

"I'm happy to help."

"Thing is, I've gotten two valentines in the past two days."

"Is that so?"

"Actually, three. But one came from a four-year-old. The daughter of a customer."

Dennis grinned. "Yah, we won't count that one. But it sure sounds like the Amish girls of Joyful River are starting to look past your rebel reputation." Dennis understood how some of the townsfolk could be reluctant to embrace a young person who veered away from the community. He, too, had left town during his rumspringa, and when he'd come back, some of his former neighbors were a bit lukewarm. But it was nothing like the ban, when a baptized person broke a church rule. Shunning was a punitive, deliberate practice. By comparison, the cool reception Dennis and Mose sometimes got was a minor inconvenience.

"I'm glad to know one of these women is interested," Mose continued. "She's a good friend, maybe could be more. But the other gal will never be a woman for me, and I don't know how to tell her. Or should I tell her at all? Does a valentine need a reply?"

Dennis tucked his thumbs under the straps of his shop apron. "And you come to me with these questions?"

"You've courted plenty since you came back to town. I figured you'd know how to handle things."

"I'm terrible at that game," said Dennis. "Sure, I've taken plenty of girls home from singings, and some of them were steady dates for a while. But nothing ever lasted long. Honestly, I think I'm just a stepping-stone for the girls to get to Jed."

"Your brother."

Dennis nodded. "The handsome one."

"Someone call me?" asked an elderly man, who Mose recognized as John Horst. "Back in the day, I turned a lot of heads." He moved slowly to the register with a basket of groceries in one hand, a cane in the other. Without a word, Mose helped lift the basket onto the counter.

"We were just talking about Dennis's brother," Mose said. "Handsome enough to turn all the girls' heads."

"Everyone knows a fellow like that," John said. "It's hard to compete with that."

Dennis shrugged. "I'm holding out for a girl who isn't a sucker for blue eyes. Till then, I'm just a boring Amish grocer."

Heading out of the shop, Mose still didn't know how to react to June's valentine. He preferred to pretend he never received it, but he doubted June would be discouraged by that. This was a young woman who pushed until she got what she wanted, whether it was the last piece of pie or a new pair of figure skates.

Mose didn't like being one of her targets, but there was nothing he could do about that now. He was going to focus on what mattered. At the moment, that involved his plan to get his hand-drawn valentine into Martha Lambright's hands.

Chapter 11

Friday evening, after the children went to bed, Martha swept the kitchen and living room, wiped down the kitchen counters, and cleaned the kitchen window, where grime from the woodstove always settled. It was more work than her usual cleaning, but when she remembered her parents would be arriving the next day after work for a weekend visit, she added some muscle to her tasks.

It wouldn't do to have her parents arrive from York to find an untidy little house. On the best of days, her mother, Babs, observed a handful of household chores that Martha could have improved upon.

Sometimes their visits were strained, but there was always an element of comfort when they were around. The children enjoyed them, and Martha thought it important for April and Milo to know her family as well as Ben's.

With the kitchen and living room tidied up, Martha went outside to load the basket with wood and then built up the fire so it would last a good while. She hung her muffler on a peg and then picked up her lunch kit to give it a good cleaning.

That was when she found a note card stuck into the side pocket. "What's this?" A large index card, but it was decorated with red felt pen. When she saw her name at the bottom, she realized that it was meant for her.

The whimsical drawing made her chuckle. "Hearts on a clothesline," she said aloud. It was cute, too skilled to be the work of April or any child. On the back of the card, she saw the message:

Your smile brings sunshine to my heart.

She sucked in her breath, moved by the romantic notion. She hadn't heard or read words like these since Ben had courted her.

Tears filled her eyes as she examined the card again.

It was a valentine.

Someone had sent her a valentine. She didn't know who, but the idea that someone cared was thrilling and a bit scary. Of course, it was someone she knew, someone in the community. She longed to know his identity, but at the same time she found the mystery of it all so exciting.

She plopped down on the comfy chair and pressed the card to her heart and allowed herself a moment of quiet joy.

To be cared for, to be loved; it was such a wonderful thing!

She looked down at the card again and smiled. Of course, this wasn't a gesture of love. That was something that developed between two people over time.

It was simply a token of admiration.

A wonderful token.

Who might it be from?

Someone from the diner, of course. He must have tucked it into her lunch kit while it was in her cubby. But who?

Her first thought was Levi Martin. Bonnie's older brother was a bit older than Martha, and he could have asked Bonnie to deliver the valentine for him, as he wasn't in the diner often. He worked as a carpenter at the furniture factory.

There was also Dennis Kraybill. His father's store was just down the street from the diner, so he was always stopping by. And word had it that he was looking for a wife, always attending singings and events.

And then there were the young Amish men who stopped into the diner to get a hot lunch. Each day, there were tables of them. Work crews enjoying a hearty meal. Maybe Martha had caught the attention of one of those fellows.

Even as she fantasized and guessed at the valentine's identity, she found that she wanted to keep the game going. She knew it was silly and daring, but she wanted to answer!

This was no time to make a new mess, but she couldn't resist. She dug through the children's box of craft supplies and opened her sewing kit and quickly concocted a heart-shaped card. She layered smaller hearts in the center of the heart, and then wrote *VALENTINE* in swirly letters on the front. On the flip side, she wrote, *You made my day!*

There. She tucked it into the side pocket of her lunch kit, the same spot where he'd left his note. She hoped he'd find it the next day. But would he be around on a Saturday?

Would she ever meet him?

Was he someone she knew?

Or could he be a man from another church community who was a customer in the diner?

For now, his identity almost didn't matter, as she was adrift on a puffy cloud of romance. Maybe nothing would come of this aside from some sweet moments of joy. That would be all right. But in the meantime, she was realizing that June had been right about one thing: the game was so much fun.

Saturday afternoon was a pure pleasure for Martha. When she climbed into Mose's buggy at the end of her shift, it was with the sweet knowledge that the card she'd made for her secret valentine was no longer in her lunch box.

He'd found it!

The correspondence had begun.

Feeling as chipper as a morning bird, she chatted amiably with Mose all the way to Polly's, where she learned that Milo had a slight fever and was feeling sour. Martha didn't mind letting April sit up front while she cuddled her boy in the back seat. She was glad when Milo drifted off while Mose answered April's endless questions about everything, from the wrinkles in raisins to the color of the sky.

At the house, Martha's parents were already settled in and had spent the afternoon tackling some housekeeping chores. Jacob had put on a watch cap and tackled the wood pile, where he spent hours chopping and splitting wood. His work produced a supply that was sure to last Martha through the rest of the winter.

Babs had done two loads of laundry, tediously pinning Milo's and April's small bits of clothing onto the lines strung from the back of the house. "We had some good sunshine, so I think they should be dry by now," Babs predicted.

"Denki for your help," Martha said as they brought in the laundry together. Most Amish women took care of laundry in the middle of the week, but when Martha worked, she couldn't squeeze the big task into her day.

"I'm happy to help," Mem said, picking up the full laundry basket. "And now, let's find something to do in the kitchen. These bones need a bit of thawing."

"Sugar cookies," said Martha. "I've been wanting to bake all week."

"Did you say cookies?" April asked, looking up from the swing Ben had hung from the big oak tree.

"Perfect. I'm about due for tea and something sweet," Babs said.

In the warmth of the kitchen, as Martha creamed butter and added sugar to the bowl, she wondered about her parents' new surge of support. This was a refreshing trend, a relief from their usual stance of telling her how to fix her life. Whatever the cause, she was happy for the final result.

Martha rolled out the cookie dough, and April had the idea of using only the heart-shaped cookie cutter for this batch. "For Valentine's Day, Mammi," April told her grandmother. "You know, it's coming soon."

"It is, indeed." Babs touched the girl's cheek affectionately. "Hearts it is. And I'll make a red and pink icing to frost them with."

Overjoyed, April joined the cookie making, showing great patience as she pressed the cookie cutter into the sheet of dough. Milo slept through the entire activity, though Martha was relieved to find that his fever had eased when she crept into the room to check him.

We'll have to set some cookies aside for Milo. And for my valentine, thought Martha. A ridiculous notion, as she didn't know his identity or how to get the cookies to him. But the thought gave her a renewed sense of fun and giddiness. The simple illustration and message of that card had filled her with a lasting sense of well-being and joy.

She was loved.

Someone cared about her. Maybe he was thinking of her right now, on this cold February Saturday afternoon. She found great comfort in knowing that a special man was out there, thinking warm thoughts for her. Love was a light inside her, glowing in the darkness and warming the cold spaces that had stalled her life since she'd lost Ben.

How could she have forgotten the power of love?

Chapter 12

When Sunday dawned, Martha made sure the children were properly dressed in their church clothes long before the gathering began. She wanted to have plenty of time to make it to Rose and Ray Graber's house, where church was being held in the barn. The Grabers were close by, but half a mile away, so it wasn't a bad walk. Still, Martha made sure everyone was bundled up against the cold before they set off down the road.

April walked ahead of Martha, holding her grandfather's hand. With Milo in her arms, Martha walked alongside her mother.

"You're getting to be such a big boy," Martha told her son, who rested on one hip. In truth, he was a bit heavy, but it would tucker him out to walk such a distance. She pressed her lips to his forehead, relieved that there was no fever. Whatever had bothered him the day before had been gone when he awoke this morning.

"Milo walk, Mem," he said.

"No, honey. You can walk when we get there." Martha turned to her mother, reminding her "It's not too far."

"The fresh air will do us all good," Babs said. "Besides, I wanted a chance to talk with you before church. There's going to be another guest from York there. Someone we're happy for you to meet."

"That's nice, Mem," she said, hugging Milo close to her chest. "A friend of yours?"

"His name is Friedrich Zercher, but everyone calls him Fritz, and he's a widower. He lost his spouse, just like you. He's a member of our church, a friend, and he's very much in need of a wife. So right away, when he let his needs be known, I thought of you."

"Oh, Mem." Her heart fell as realization dawned. "You're matching me up with a man from your church?"

"A good Amish man. He's an established butcher with a successful business."

"I don't need a matchmaker, Mem. When I'm ready to marry again, I'll find a husband, same way most Amish women do. And I won't choose a husband just because he's successful."

"Don't you know that many folks get fixed up? And you do need a husband, more than you know. I see that it's a struggle, working and minding the children, and then keeping your household going. You need help, and Fritz needs a wife. He's got children of his own. I can't imagine what it's like for them, in a house without a woman in charge."

Martha hitched Milo a bit higher on her hip and stared down the road at the sparse landscape. The trees were gray, bony and bare against the winter wheat fields, chopped and stubby during these cold months. The bleak winterscape reflected her reaction to this news Mem had sprung on her. A match from York? More pressure to leave Joyful River and agree to a marriage of convenience?

It was the last thing she'd expected that day.

She felt for Fritz's children, their hearts aching over the loss of their mother.

But she was tending to a broken heart of her own. Single-handedly caring for her own children, who'd lost their father. She couldn't push their needs aside to take on someone else's family now.

"So this man, your friend Fritz, he's going to be at church today?" Martha asked.

"Yah. Your dat will make sure you two get a chance to talk sometime during the church supper." Babs touched her shoulder, trying to encourage her. "I know it's a lot for me to spring on you, but the situation seemed so perfect, your father and I knew Fritz would be right for you."

"You can't know that, Mem." Martha knew her own voice sounded weak, but suddenly it was hard to breathe. "You can't know what's in another person's heart."

"Sometimes marriage isn't guided by the heart; it can be a matter of practicality," Babs said. "But we're putting the cart before the horse here. Just meet him. Talk with him. He's a very kind man."

Kindness? Most of the single men in Martha's church community were "kind," but that did not make them good marriage prospects.

"And Fritz sent you a letter of introduction. We all thought it best to prepare you. Didn't you receive his note?"

Note? Martha's heart froze in her chest for a second. She couldn't be talking about the valentine, the illustration that had made her smile. "How did he send it?" she asked.

"I don't know. Through the mail would be my guess."

"I haven't checked my mailbox for a week or so," Martha admitted, feeling oddly relieved. In rural areas like this, residents were assigned boxes that needed to be checked at the post office in town.

"Well, that explains that. We'll stop at the post office later. But just so you know, no one wanted to take you by surprise," Mem said.

But no one asked me what I wanted, she thought. It hurt that her parents didn't trust her to take care of her little family, but that was the Amish way. A household needed a man, a husband, a father. In her head, she understood that. In her heart, she wanted to be the person choosing that man.

Chapter 13

During the preaching and songs, Mose had to force himself to keep still, his eyes straight ahead. Otherwise, he'd be staring at her throughout church, his head swiveled so that he could get a peek of her over in the section where the married women sat.

The second valentine had reinforced his joy and hope. The first card hadn't been a fluke! Martha was glad for his affections.

He made her day.

During one of the hymns he broke discipline and glanced over at her. Her pale cheek seemed so smooth, and the gold of her hair reminded him of summer wheat. And though Milo was fussing, trying to climb out of her arms, she remained calm and steady, her temperament smooth as the surface of a pond. There was none of the drama or giddiness of the other young Amish women he knew.

Her inner strength, her forbearance, made her so attractive to Mose. She was a woman who would be more than someone to court. Martha was a true friend, someone who was interested in talking about matters deeper than the weather and the price of butter.

Before he looked away, he saw Milo try to climb over her shoulder, and he had to hide a smile. He wished he could give her a break and take the tyke for a walk, get some fresh air outside this heated barn. He would gladly take the boy off her hands, but he knew that action would set tongues a-wagging.

Mose's mind drifted to a story he'd heard that morning. He'd risen before dawn to hitch up his buggy and head out to give elderly folk rides to the Graber house. The buggy rides on church day were Mose's idea, his way of demonstrating to the community that the "bishop's son" had returned to the flock and was ready to become a baptized member of the church. Of course, there was no charge for Sunday rides. Sunday was a day of rest, and Amish folks were forbidden to transact business on Gott's day.

Still, some folks needed help getting to church, and Mose had the means and the energy to ease their burdens. For him, Sunday rides had become an act of joy.

Two of his passengers, an elderly couple who lived on the other side of town, had kept him amused with tales of their youth. The old man, Kermit Smucker, teased his wife lovingly and told everyone that his Bess was the love of his life.

"Always has been, ever since I saw her serve a volleyball at a frolic when we were kids. Bess had a strong serve, all right. And she made apple pie that would melt in your mouth. Such a buttery crust."

"You use butter instead of lard," Bess said, and Mose nodded as if he had a notion of baking someday.

"Delicious pie. But when I was courting Bess, her mother didn't like me so much. Didn't want her to marry me. Told us we had to wait. I told her folks, your Bessie is worth waiting for, and I'll wait forever. If I live to be a hundred and two, you just tap my shoulder and I'll marry her on the spot. Well, that changed her mother's mind." Kermit leaned forward to add: "Mostly, I don't think her mem wanted to wait a hundred years to marry off her daughter!"

The laughter of the morning lingered in Mose's heart as the church service went on through songs, sermons from three preachers, and prayers. The format was rigid, but when Mose had lived among the Englisch, Amish church was one of the things he missed most. The biweekly service provided the blessing of drawing everyone in the community together.

The preaching and songs ended, and folks filed out of the barn to get fresh air and give men the space to reset the church benches into tables and chairs for the meal. Mose remained in the barn, scanning the crowd of departing folks for Martha, but there was no sign of her. She must have left by the opposite door. He stuck around to help move the benches and set up tables for the food. It would be a simple spread—mostly sandwich fixings and salads—as it would be wrong to have Amish folk cooking up a storm on the one day meant to be free of work.

As the men finished their task in the barn, Mose's father walked past with a group of preachers leaving the ceremony. Church day was a big day for his father, the bishop. "Denki for helping," Aaron told the men as he passed. He paused a moment beside Mose to place a hand on his shoulder and nod.

A nod of approval.

It was a rare gesture from his father, a gesture that bolstered Mose's sense of self. At last, his father was beginning to see him as the man he had become.

With the task nearly completed, most of the men dispersed and headed outside, while churchgoers started trickling back inside. Mose went out, chatting and walking alongside his friend Dennis. At a table loaded with thermoses they got cups of coffee and kept walking until they found a spot near the post and beam fence to hang out.

As he leaned against the fence, Mose took a sip of coffee and searched the crowd for Martha. He alerted to June Hostetler, who stood with a group of teenaged girls over by the greenhouse. He'd be sure to stay away from there.

And only a few yards away, near the outdoor pump, he spotted Martha. Although most folks spent the church social time with friends, Martha was with her parents, Jacob and Babs, whom he'd met briefly the day before. She seemed to be introducing them to some older folks. The children weren't with her; they were probably being minded by one of the other young mothers in the group.

Babs was talking up a storm, but Martha stood back, quiet and small. She had the look of a turtle about to retreat into her shell.

What was upsetting her?

A man beside Jacob lowered his head and spoke to Martha intently. A married man, from the looks of him, a streak of white running through his beard. He seemed to be lecturing Martha on something, as she listened, she nodded sternly. Occasionally, Babs joined in, waving her hands as she spoke.

"Who's that man over there?" Mose asked Dennis. "The older man talking to Martha Lambright and her parents?"

Dennis cocked his head as he looked over. "The one with the skunk beard? Not sure that I know him. I'd say he's a visitor, not from these parts."

"What makes you say that?"

"Look at his shoes. Fancy boots. Not anything you'd wear around here. More of a city man."

"Good observation," Mose teased Dennis. "You know, you're smarter than you look."

Dennis grinned. "Yah, and more handsome, too."

Mose started to smile, but the humor was lost as he sensed Martha's increasing dismay. The conversation with the visitor was upsetting her. It was as if all joy had drained from her, leaving her sparse frame to juggle fear and dread.

Something was wrong. And Mose felt powerless to help her here, under the watchful eyes of his father's church congregation.

Chapter 14

The man her parents planned for her to marry was old.

How old? Of course Martha couldn't ask his age, but from the white streak in his beard and the wrinkles under his eyes, she knew he was a generation or two ahead of her. Looking into his face was like confronting a stern grandfather. He made her so uncomfortable that she was having trouble getting any words out.

When Babs asked about his family, Fritz proudly announced that he had five children at home in York.

Five? Five. Martha felt tired just thinking about feeding all their laundry through the wringer, hanging countless shirts and socks and aprons on the line. All those meals to cook, dishes to wash. All that cleaning and mending.

Her mem asked him the ages of the children, and he stroked his beard, trying to remember. The youngest was a boy, five years old now, and the oldest daughter, Mary, had just turned sixteen.

Sixteen. The same age as the kitchen girls at the Country Diner. Not much younger than her.

Martha nodded as the weight of doom fell over her.

He was an old man, indeed. Her parents wanted to marry her off to an old man.

Mem asked about his business, and he went on about how he and his wife had opened a shop outside York many years ago. But he helped out local farmers and ranchers, too, when they needed it. Dat asked if it was a reliable business to support his family, and he said that Gott had blessed him with a house and more than enough to feed his children.

And enough money to buy leather boots, Martha thought, noticing the shine on the fine leather that she'd been staring down upon, mostly to avoid Fritz's stern eyes. Maybe the man was just nervous, but something about his crinkled eyes and stark gaze scared her. She wanted to turn away and run off as fast as her legs would carry her. If she weren't here, surrounded by church folk, she might have tried to escape.

"Well, you're a quiet one," Fritz told Martha. "Are you shy?"

"Mostly surprised," Babs answered for her. "Martha didn't know you were coming today."

"But I wrote you a letter introducing myself. Mailed it near two weeks ago. You should've gotten it by now."

"She hasn't checked her mail this week," Babs explained.

"Well, you should get on that," Fritz said.

"I will." Martha was eager to check the mail, itching to tear open the envelope and look at his writing and confirm that he was definitely not her valentine.

No, Fritz wasn't the man behind the funny, sweet illustration in red ink. She refused to believe her card was from him. Her special valentine was someone vital and bright, a fella who enjoyed her for who she was, not some older man who wanted a live-in nanny.

As Fritz continued to chat with her parents, Martha felt her knees go weak. She staggered back, looking for something to lean on, something to help her keep her head up and at least see the conversation through. She expected to lean against the fence but instead bumped into a person.

"Oops! I got you, there."

"Sorry!" Martha gasped, glad to have someone hold her upright as she stumbled. She turned and saw that it was Mose who'd caught her. "Mose, denki. I lost my balance there for a second."

"Martha! Are you all right?" Babs asked, rushing to her.

Martha touched her brow with one hand. "I think so. My head . . ." Her mind was swimming with thoughts, and she still felt the strong instinct to escape.

"Do you have a headache?" her mother asked. "Maybe you have the bug that Milo got."

"Maybe." Although Martha had felt perfectly fine until her parents had sprung this suitor on her. "I just don't feel quite myself."

"Maybe you should sit down," Mem said.

"There's a place over here." Mose guided her to some bales of hay, where a few teens sat, chatting.

Mem sat her down, then went back to Dat and Fritz.

"You look pale," Mose said. "Do you want water?"

She shook her head. "What I really want is to go home."

He nodded. "I can give you a ride."

"Would you?" Tears came to her eyes at the kindness of his gesture. "I hate to make you go to the trouble."

"No trouble for me. Sunshine is hitched and ready to go." He extended a hand to her, helping her to her feet. "We'll tell your mem, and then find Milo and April on our way to the buggy park."

"Denki, Mose. I appreciate your help."

Somehow, Mose helped her escape quickly. He made excuses for her to her parents and Fritz. He found her children and corralled them toward the exit. And he guided her along the gravel drive with a gentle but firm arm at her back until they reached the hostlers, who located Mose's buggy.

As soon as she sat in the buggy, relief flooded through her. She was free, safe with Mose.

"I'll have you home in two shakes of a lamb's tail," he said.

"Denki." She sighed as he called to Sunshine and the mule moved forward. "I feel better already."

Chapter 15

As Mose guided the buggy along the road, he sensed that a bad situation had been averted. The pink hue had returned to Martha's cheeks by the time he halted the buggy in front of her small house. He was glad she'd begun feeling better, but he'd kept quiet during the ride, letting her rest.

"Here we are," he said, hopping out to help the children climb down.

"Denki for the ride." Martha climbed out of the buggy, smoothed down the apron of her church dress, and adjusted her shawl over her shoulders. She looked better, her old self again. "Do you need to head back, or can I offer you a snack? You probably didn't get to eat anything after church. I could make some coffee, or hot cocoa."

"I want hot cocoa," April piped up.

"Cocoa!" Milo echoed.

Mose grinned down at them. "I guess I could come in for a quick nip of something warm."

"And a cookie shaped like a heart," April said. "We baked them yesterday. I helped."

"I bet they're delicious," he told her.

Inside the house, Martha flung off her shawl, lit the stove, and put the kettle on to boil. "Coffee, tea, or cocoa?" she asked Mose.

He chose tea, and she sent the children into the other room to play while they waited for the milk to warm.

Mose saw April drag out a bin of wooden blocks.

"Come on, Milo. Let's build a barn for the horses so they don't get cold."

"Horses," he said, dropping to the floor beside her.

Turning back to the kitchen, Mose took a seat at the table. "If you don't mind my asking, what happened back there by the Grabers' pump?"

"I confess, I was truly feeling ill, but there was no medical cause," she said. "That older man you saw there? My parents invited him here from York. He's a member of their church, and apparently, they think he'd be a fitting husband for me."

Mose removed his hat and stared up at her. "That man?"

"Fritz Zercher is his name. He's a butcher. With five children."

"Ooh, that's a handful, for sure." Mose could barely believe what he was hearing. That man was a suitor?

Martha pressed her palms to the kitchen counter, as if needing support for a second. "I was blindsided. And a little scared to be pushed into such a situation. I didn't know my parents were doing some matchmaking on the sly."

"That explains the shocked look on your face back in the yard," he said. "I was afraid you were going to faint."

"My legs were unsteady," she said, taking the chair beside him. "The pressure to go along with my parents' wishes weighed on me in that moment. I had to be polite. I couldn't just tell them that the man is all wrong for me."

He nodded. "That must have been awful. I have to say, your

mem could use a few tips in the matchmaking department. How could your folks expect you to marry someone who's years apart from you?"

"Apparently, an Amish widow is supposed to jump at any chance she gets."

"And your parents don't realize you have your fair share of chances here in Joyful River?" *That you have a man sitting right here who wants to know you better? Your new valentine?* Mose wanted to say the words, but he didn't want to push too hard, especially after Martha had been pressured by her parents.

"My parents think it's time for me to stop living off the generosity of the Lambrights and come home to York."

Move to York? That would be terrible.

"Is that what you want?"

"Heavens, no. This is the life Ben and I wanted for ourselves, for our children." She rose and went to the stove to stir the chocolate milk. "Joyful River is our home now."

"I'm glad to hear that," he said. "But it seems your parents have put you in a pickle. How did they leave the situation with Fritz? Are you supposed to be courting him now?"

She pressed one hand to her cheek. "I sure hope not. Fritz said he sent me a letter, but it's been a while since I checked my mail. I need to take a walk to the post office later and fetch it." She turned off the gas burner and put down the spoon. "That's how I'll handle it. I'll read his letter and then respond with a letter of my own. A very polite but firm 'No, denki.'"

"And your parents? They're sure to be disappointed."

"I'll have to weather that storm when it comes. It wouldn't be the first time I did something that Mem didn't approve of, and it probably won't be the last." She looked toward the living room. "And one day, I'm sure my children will go against my wishes. But I do hope that, when they're grown up, I'll know to give them the space to make their own choices."

A chance to make their own choices . . . Her comment hit home with Mose. He knew how a person could feel shut down by a parent who tried to control him. It was precisely the issue he'd had with his father that had forced him to leave. "A person needs to choose their own path in life," he said. "You're a good mother to recognize that one day your children will need to be making their own choices."

"I just do my best." She smiled as she placed two mugs of cocoa and a plate of pink and red iced heart cookies on the table. "Have a cookie. We made them for Valentine's Day."

When he looked up at her, the sparkle in her blue eyes lifted his heart. The trust between them seemed to grow stronger by the day, and he'd come to cherish their time together. "Fantastic," he said, picking up a cookie as the children came rushing in. "A very sweet valentine."

"Ooh, I want a pink one," April said.

"Just one," Martha warned. "Supper's not far off."

"Milo, too," the little boy said, climbing up onto a chair.

As the four of them enjoyed a snack around the table, Mose felt that he was a part of their little family. Had Gott brought him here to be a father to these children and a husband to Martha? He lived to help them. And in turn, they had helped him reconnect to his home town, to his Amish upbringing.

This was where he wanted to be. He hoped and prayed that his dreams of life with Martha and her children would become a reality.

Before Mose left to return to the church meeting and ferry some folks home, he got the mailbox key from Martha. "I'll check the box for you and deliver your mail when I'm done with my runs."

She was most grateful, as she hoped to clear up the Fritz situation with her parents before they returned home in the morning.

What Mose didn't say was that he was also eager for her to dispense with the other suitor. A man didn't need competition when trying to court a young woman. Even if that competition was an old man with five children.

Chapter 16

Sunday night when Mose got home, he moved through the empty house. Everyone was off at the singing, the gathering that capped off a church day. In the sewing room, he took a handful of index cards from the stack. His sisters wouldn't mind, and they certainly wouldn't miss these amid the supply of ribbons, satin, and colored papers.

In his room he changed out of his church clothes, stretched out on the bed, and started to draw.

He sketched a man under a tree bearing hearts instead of apples. The man was scratching his head in wonder and reaching up as if to pick a heart. On the back of the card he wrote:

> *Valentine, sometimes you have to reach for a miracle.*

On another card he drew a young Amish maid sitting on a giant heart.

He sketched a giant heart with wings. And then he drew a garden where all the flowers had heart-shaped centers.

As he sketched, he couldn't help but smile. Sometimes he cracked himself up with these drawings. But mostly he hoped that Martha liked them. He would give her one a day all week, leading up to Valentine's Day, when he hoped to give her a bouquet of flowers.

When he finished the cards, he tucked them into the box under his bed. Before closing it, he removed the two valentines that Martha had made for him and propped them on the quilt. He thanked Gott that she had started the card exchange. Otherwise, he might never had known.

He stared at the cards a minute, feeling like a fool.

A fool in love.

It was the only good kind.

On Monday afternoon when he went into the break room at the diner to leave Martha a valentine, he found a new card addressed to "Valentine" waiting for him in her cubby. He took a quick look inside the envelope and saw a small heart-shaped snowflake cut from white paper and then glued to a lavender sheet of paper. How she'd found the time to make this with her parents visiting and her children needing care, he couldn't imagine. On the back, she had written:

Valentine, the thought of you warms my heart.

It was so personal. His whimsical little drawing seemed silly by comparison, and yet, that was his style. He slid the card into the side pocket of her lunch pail and slid the lavender beauty inside his coat before he turned to go. He didn't want the giggle girls to see. They asked too many questions.

He left another card on Tuesday, and another on Wednesday. But when he went to leave the break room that day, June appeared in the doorway.

"There you are! I've been looking around for you."

"I was just about to grab a coffee before my last delivery," he said, moving toward the door. He'd need to grab a cup to make good on his story. "Did Madge ask you to find me?"

"Nay. I have something to give you." She removed an envelope from the pocket of her kitchen apron. "A valentine. I gave you one last week, but I reckon it lost its way to you."

"A valentine," he stated the obvious, trying to stall.

"Here!" She handed it to him, and he couldn't avoid taking it. "Valentine's Day is next week, you know."

"I've seen you girls working on your cards in here." He pressed his thumb over the edge of the envelope. "But I wasn't expecting anything from you, June. Thing is, I've been exchanging notes with someone else."

"You have?" She seemed more surprised than disappointed. "Who?"

"I can't really say." He pressed a palm to his chest and was reminded of Martha's card tucked inside his coat. "Don't want to start gossip."

"So you have a secret love?" June gasped. "I had no idea. You could've told me. Most of the girls who work here are intending to give you a valentine."

The giggle girls. Mose didn't want them to waste their time. "I hope they don't."

"Look at you! The former rebel who now has girls at his heels."

"Not really."

"But it's true. Girls like you. I don't understand it, when I was never in trouble. I've always done the right thing, and where did it get me?" Her voice cracked. "No fella wants to be my beau."

"That's not true."

"I'll never find someone."

"June, don't be that way. You can't let a minor twist in the road get you down."

"This is a terrible twist in the road." Distress was evident in the high pitch of her voice. "A dead-end road! Folks are beginning to notice that I don't have a steady guy. I'm already too old."

"You're only my age."

"It's different for girls." Her face began to turn a vivid pink, and she looked away as a sob slipped out. "So much pressure to marry."

Oh no . . . not tears. He'd never seen her cry before, and the burst of emotion made him nervous. He couldn't hug her or pat her back as he'd do with one of his sisters. "I know how hard that is, getting pressure from your parents and all."

She sniffed, turned toward him, and took the card from his hands. "I'm back to square one. That's what happens when you're unlovable."

"You're not . . . who told you that?"

"I won't say his name, but I'm thinking maybe he's right. I push folks too hard and always say the wrong thing. I'll never find a husband."

"Don't let this get you down. I'm sure you'll find someone."

She shook her head. "There's no one left. I'll die an old maidel."

"Come on, now." He didn't want to be in this position, comforting June Hostetler, but there he was. "You've got a lot going for you. I reckon lots of fellows just don't know you're interested in courting."

"Well, who isn't? How could they not know that?" She sniffed again and stared at him hard. "Do you have any single friends? You must know some fella who's longing for a wife. . . ."

For Mose, the rest of the conversation was like a game of dodgeball. He had to move quickly to evade the probing questions she threw at him. When he finally escaped to get back to work, June had somehow extracted a promise. If she couldn't find a valentine by the big day, Mose would find her a single fellow who'd agree to a date.

Who might that be? Mose was no matchmaker, but he couldn't think about that now. He truly hoped June would find her own fella. But something she'd said had got him thinking that evening. Maybe it was time for Martha and him to go public, tell their families. It would feel good to have the truth out, and then June and the giggle girls at the diner would leave him alone.

He wanted to ask Martha, but it was still awkward to discuss his feelings. He liked being with her, but he sure didn't want to talk about what was happening between them. That kind of talk was not his strong suit.

It would be much easier to write about it.

Chapter 17

On Thursday night Martha washed dinner plates and tidied the little house, leaving the unpacking of her lunch pail—and the search for a dear valentine—for last. She tucked away April's mittens and noticed that Mem had left her scarf in the bin under the window. Mem had probably been distracted, scheming over the "surprise visitor."

What a shock that had been! A desperate push from her parents into the arms of an elderly man. She'd nearly fainted from panic at the church lunch. Afterward, with a little time to think things over and Fritz Zercher's letter in hand, she'd found the composure to deal with the situation. She'd written a kind but firm no-thank-you to Fritz. And then she'd explained to her parents that if and when she married again, it would not be a marriage of convenience but a marriage blessed by Gott's love.

Mem had started trying to convince Martha to give old Fritz a second chance, but then Dat had intervened, telling Mem not to interfere when their daughter was "trusting in Gott."

That had closed Mem's mouth on the spot. And just like that, the matter had been resolved.

By Thursday night, the week that had begun disastrously for Martha with a surprise elderly suitor had eased to lighter, merrier times. How she enjoyed the daily card from her mystery man! She'd begun to look forward to the new illustration each day, and she tried to brace herself for the time when the little cards stopped.

Would the cards stop coming after Valentine's Day? Or was this little correspondence something that could go on? Although she was curious about her valentine, she sometimes felt that she didn't want to know his identity. There was a good chance she would be disappointed to learn it was a stranger—just one of the older men who frequented the diner, or an Amish farmer who came in for Madge's fried chicken.

But in the meantime, Martha was happy.

Her valentine had opened her heart once again. After Ben's death, she had been sure she would never love again, but this humorous, dear man had reawakened sweet feelings of longing that lifted her mood.

The idea of love made her heart feel light and joyful once again, and that sweet feeling bubbled through her days and nights. Thoughts of him made her smile as she dipped drumsticks in the breading at work. She was reminded of his drawing—the clothesline of swaying hearts—as she hung laundry to dry. When she settled into the big chair to read to the children, she thought of the giant heart he'd drawn, and the way it seemed so comfy and soft under the woman sitting on it. It was as if he had studied different moments in her life and portrayed them in his cards.

She couldn't stop thinking of her mystery valentine.

Someone loved her! Someone cared.

The knowledge that she was loved had given her confidence and hope to engage the folks around her. She'd begun spending her lunch breaks with the kitchen girls, showing them techniques to use on their cards and encouraging them. Of course, she didn't dare make her own valentines in front of them. Then she would have to explain about her secret valentine, and it would become the talk of the restaurant.

It wouldn't be her secret anymore.

So she had crafted the new cards at night, working at the kitchen table after the children were in bed. While she'd had her supplies out, she'd made cards for the children, one for her parents, and one for Madge. Her instructions to the girls at the diner had reminded her that love came in many forms.

That night she planned to start a bigger project. The card she would give *him* on Valentine's Day. At lunch earlier that day she had purchased some pink satin ribbon from Needle 'n' Thread. It would make lovely rolled roses for the valentine on the big day.

But first . . . there was the matter of her daily valentine. She put her lunch box on the table and dipped her hand into the plastic pocket on the side. Her fingers found the card.

There was an Amish farmer reaching up to the tree of hearts, and a message about reaching for a miracle.

Martha wanted to laugh and cry at the same time, amused by the funny man and awed at the prospect of their love being a miracle. It was breathtaking! Wondrous! Sweeping!

And ridiculous, all at the same time.

This couldn't be love, could it? In love with a stranger? The women at the monthly sewing bee would roll their eyes at such a notion. And they knew best.

But still, she couldn't help but smile over the card. He had such a good heart.

She was about to fetch her bag of ribbon, paper, and craft

supplies when she noticed a sliver of white poking out from the pocket of her lunch pail.

"What's this?" She plucked out the folded piece of paper and saw that it was a note. A note signed by Mose.

> *Dear Valentine,*
>
> *Our secret exchange of cards has brightened my days. I'm grateful you brought us together by giving me that first valentine last week. When I saw the red ribbon woven around the border, I knew you'd crafted it with care.*
>
> *Now I'm wondering if it's time we let our friends and family know that we're sweethearts. The secrecy has been fun, but I'd be happy for folks to know about us.*
>
> *Looking forward to courting you for all to see.*
> *Your Valentine,*
> *Mose*

Mose. Mose! So, the bishop's son, Mose Troyer, was the one—her secret valentine.

Of course. She should have guessed. He was the one young man she spent time with, almost every day. She trusted him like a brother and shared so many of her concerns and worries with him. They were close, in their way, though she'd never thought of them courting.

She should have realized it. She knew Mose was good at sketching. And Mose was probably the only man she saw nearly every day. They shared their thoughts and ideas. They had come to know each other well. Sitting on a chair near the fire, she tucked her cold feet under her and considered the life of Mose Troyer.

She had to admit, his charms were not lost on her. Those blue eyes ... if she were a younger woman, in her courtship time, she might easily have fallen for the likes of Mose Troyer. Bad-boy reputation and all. For wasn't the joy of winning the love of such a man the notion that he could be tamed and soothed by the right woman?

But back in her teen years, Martha had chosen a young man with a very different approach to life. Ben had always walked the straight and narrow, following the rules of the church and respecting his elders. Ben had been solid and steady—not a hint of rebellion in his path. That was the sort of man Martha belonged with—if she ever married again. Someone solid and respectful like Ben. A good Amish man who would never think of leaving his hometown.

Not a man like Mose.

The realization hit her hard, as if she'd suddenly stumbled to the ground into a mucky pit of disappointment.

Her mystery valentine would not offer the companionship she'd longed for. She'd been fooling herself, dreaming of a love that was not meant to be.

And all along, he'd thought she'd known it was him. His note mentioned "that first valentine." How had he received a valentine from her? That was a curious notion, one that she couldn't explain. Looking back at his note, she realized he must have gotten one of the valentines she'd made for Ben—the one with the red ribbon around the border.

How had that happened? Had one of the girls given it to him? No ... it was some sort of mistake. A mishap that had let the wrong valentine land in Mose's hands.

Martha took one last look at the heart tree in his drawing. It had been a cheery, bright week with Mose's cards to light up each day. Her heart ached at the thought of it all ending, but end it must.

The secret valentine exchange had brought her joy and excitement, but it was just a temporary game. She hoped that Mose would understand that.

She penned a careful note to Mose, tucked it into her lunch pail, and went to bed. Tired though she was, she struggled to find sleep in the shadow of disappointment. She didn't want to let him go. Although she'd known all along that the secret exchange was merely a game, it was hard to give up the notion of being loved. So hard to let that bit of joy go.

Chapter 18

Friday morning, as Martha and her children rode in Mose's buggy under a chalky gray sky, Martha shivered and hugged herself.

"Are you cold?" Mose asked. "There's another blanket under the seat."

"I'm fine," she said, though that wasn't entirely truthful. Yah, she was cold, but it was the dread that made her quiver. It would be a terrible day. The temperature had dipped below freezing, and the floors at home had been cold as ice when she'd awoken that morning. And if that weren't burden enough, today was going to be especially difficult with the weight of the note she had to pass to the man sitting beside her.

How she hated to hurt him! And she worried that her somber answer would cast a shadow over their easy conversations. She had planned to hand him the note before she got into the buggy, but she'd lost her nerve, deciding that it was best to delay bad news. The note still sat in the pocket of her lunch pail, taunting her.

As Martha turned to look out the side window, a series of

soft clicks began to patter, as if someone were tossing pebbles against the windshield. "What's that sound?" she asked.

"Freezing rain." Mose stared straight ahead, focusing on the road.

"There's ice on the road?" The breath seemed trapped inside her as she stared out at the gray, driving rain. This was the weather that had killed Ben—a winter storm that had coated the roads with a slick layer of ice. Since then she had tried not to panic over white skies and snowflakes. Her mother and friends had convinced her it was important to stay rational when winter weather came along. But there, in that moment, she couldn't stop the mounting feeling of dread. "Maybe you should stop the buggy. Pull to the side of the road and—"

"The hail might pass. For now, it's best to keep moving," he said. "In a storm, slow progress is still progress. And we don't want to risk getting stranded."

"That's for sure, but poor Sunny is getting pelted out there, and . . . you know I can't . . ." Martha pressed a hand to her mouth, as if that might tamp down her fear. She needed to stay calm. Calm and rational. "We need to go back, Mose. Can you turn us around?"

"That wouldn't be safe, right now. I reckon the hill up to your place is getting icy and slippery at this point."

They couldn't make it home? Martha looked to the back seat, where the children huddled close together, hugging a hot-water bottle Mose had placed between them. How she longed to gather her children to her and hold them close! She had to keep them safe, protect them. That was what mothers did. "Can we make it to J.R. and Polly's?"

"We're going to try," he said.

"I can't believe it. The storm came on so fast." She tried to keep from panicking, but her fingers were digging into the upholstered edge of the seat as she watched the white pebbles dart through the air. She could see it accumulating on the ground now—white chips bounced and then filled in the spaces around rocks and grass.

"We're going to be okay. I'm taking it slow," Mose said. "It's a might slippery, but Sunshine is a steady mule, and she's got her winter shoes on."

"Mem?" April piped up from the back. "What's wrong?"

"It's going to be all right," Mose said, his voice smooth and calm. "There's some icy snow falling, but we're still moving along okay, and you know that Gott is watching over us."

"I know He is." Martha tried to take comfort in his words.

She knew that Gott made the sun and moon, the sky and clouds. The rain and snow.

And there was no stopping the weather. She took a deep breath and prayed for Gott's help in letting go of the panic in her heart. This was a time to trust in Him.

Thy will be done.

As she and Mose stared out at the falling sleet, they became aware of something moving along the side of the road ahead.

"Is that a stray heifer?" Martha squinted. "A goat?"

Mose shook his head. "It's a person."

"It is!" A man, it seemed. His dark coat and hat were sticky with clumps of white. "He's waving for us to stop. Mose, I think he needs help!"

"Out in this storm . . . it's Ezra Graber."

"Old Ezra. He must be frozen through to the bone," Martha said.

"He's always walking along this road, to and from the Country Diner. Seven miles a day, he says. But he's going to be cutting his walk short today." As they came up alongside the man, Mose called to the mule to stop and carefully applied the brakes. The buggy meandered to the side of the road, halting safely a few yards from the sparkling white rise in the embankment.

"If you'll sit tight here, I'll go reel in our friend Ezra."

"It's bound to be slippery out there," Martha warned.

"I'll be careful." He pulled a watch cap over his dark head. "I've got ice clamps on my boots, just in case." He opened the door and climbed down from the buggy, leaving Martha and the children in the odd quiet punctuated by the relentless tapping noise of ice crystals against the buggy windows.

April stirred in the back seat. "Where did Mose go, Mem?"

"Gone to bring a man in out of the cold."

Ice crystals were settling on the edge of the windshield, but Martha could see them a few yards ahead, Ezra stiff and slow-moving as Mose approached.

"Is that snowman coming with us?" April seemed concerned.

"He is covered with snow, but don't you worry. A few minutes inside and he'll thaw out and warm up."

"Snowman?" Milo climbed up on the seat and perched on his knees for a better look through the frosty window.

"Not a snowman," Martha said. "Just a regular man."

"He's coming!" April cried. "Mose is bringing the snowman!"

Martha swung her gaze to the front window and saw that the two men were at the buggy, Mose guiding the older man to the back door, which opened to a tinkling shower of ice.

When Mose leaned in, his hat was dusted with ice. "Why don't you slide on over, Milo, and make room for Ezra Graber here."

The children were silent, their eyes wide open as they scurried across to the far side of the bench seat and watched Mose help the older man into the buggy. Ezra landed with a thump and a sigh. His eyes closed wearily, and from the coating of ice chips on his coat, hat, and beard, Martha worried that he was, indeed, a frozen man.

"Are you a snowman?" April asked.

The frosted man turned to her. "I might as well be, cold as ice from head to toe."

"Children, give Ezra the hot-water bottle. He needs to warm up," Martha said as Mose climbed back in and took the reins. "We were so concerned when we saw you on the side of the road. It's no weather to be out and about! How long have you been out here?"

"Half an hour, maybe more. It's a good thing you came along when you did." Ezra took the hot-water bottle from April. "Denki." He placed it on his lap and pressed his mittened hands over it with a sigh. "Nice and warm. The hands are the first thing to go."

"Are you all right? I'm sorry we don't have a warm drink for you." Martha worried that the man was in a daze. "Here, take the lap blanket." She turned around on the front bench and leaned into the back to hand him the blanket. "I wish we had some hot tea or coffee for you."

"Denki." He pulled the wool blanket over his thin body and leaned back into the seat. "I'll be okay. It was foolish pride that got me here. Always pushing to walk my miles every day. Too hardheaded to take a day off."

"Your five miles a day?" Mose asked. "Or is it seven?"

"Something like that. Anyway, I started out today fine, and then when the ice storm came, the road became too slippery to walk. I moved to the grass on the side, but then there's that slope and the rocks. Went down twice before I realized I was in a pickle."

"That's awful, Ezra. It could have been so much worse. These roads can be so deserted," Martha said. "It scares me to think of what might have happened if we hadn't come along."

"You can look at it that way," Ezra said. "But the way I see it, something wondrous happened. Gott sent you along to save me. I'm one fortunate man."

Now Martha was sure he was in a daze. "It's good that you're counting your blessings," she said.

"You folks are good Samaritans, and I'm grateful for your help."

"Mem, what's a good smoritan?" asked April.

"It's from a Bible story, honey," Martha said, sensing that her daughter's thoughts had shifted to s'mores. "It's a person who helps someone in distress."

"I'm just glad we came along when we did," Mose said as Martha turned back to him and checked the road.

Sleet was still falling like crazy.

As she watched, Mose called to the mule to slow as he applied the brake. The buggy slid along at an alarming angle.

Martha braced herself against the front panel of the buggy as they slithered to a halt before the stop sign. "Are we all right?" she asked.

"We're fine, but the storm is getting worse. There's no turning back up that hill, and I don't trust the ridge road that takes us up to the Lambrights or back to Ezra's place. We need to stay on the flat road to town. We'll go to my father's place. There's room for everyone there."

"I'd appreciate anyplace I can sit inside and get warm," Ezra said.

"It'll be good to be safe until the storm passes," Martha agreed. She hated to impose on Bishop Troyer and his wife, but she knew it was close. Having been there a few times for church, Martha knew the house was just down the road.

"Good. We'll take it slow and easy." Then Mose leaned closer, and added in a hushed voice: "You just keep talking with Ezra, keep him awake for now."

She nodded, realizing that Mose was worried that the old

man had suffered from being out in the cold. "So, Ezra..." Trying not to reveal her trembling hands, she scooted around to focus all her attention on the back seat. "Tell us about your exercise program. Joyful River is a beautiful place to walk, when the weather isn't so dangerous."

The man gave a small smile that was somehow reassuring as the ice rained down upon them. "It is, indeed."

Chapter 19

"We're here," Mose said. "Our trusty mule brought us home."

Turning toward the windshield, Martha saw that ice was still pelting their buggy, but the fury of the storm had eased once they pulled off the open road. They now bumped along a lane bordered by a post-and-beam fence.

Martha's panic eased as the farmhouse came into view. They had made it. Her body sank against the seat in relief.

"Mose?" April piped up from the back seat. "Do you think Sunshine knew the way?"

"She did, indeed. It's good to know your way home."

"She's a good mule," April said.

Mose bypassed the front door. "That porch'll be too slippery. Dat will have spread gravel on the back patio," he said, guiding the buggy around to a little path that cut through the side yard. Halting the mule, he came around to help Martha, Ezra, and April out of the buggy, testing out the gravel path and finding it safe. He carried Milo in his arms and hustled them all into the back door of the house.

"Collette?" he called, holding the door open for them. "We're here to weather the storm."

A dark-haired woman who'd been sweeping under the table straightened up and gave them a smile. Martha recognized the bishop's wife from the peaceful smile that graced her broad lips. Her recent marriage to Bishop Troyer had softened Collette's formerly stern demeanor.

Touched by happiness, thought Martha.

"Come in and get warm," Collette said. "You're all welcome. Martha Lambright, isn't it? And Ezra, too. Come in, come in."

"We're grateful to be here," Ezra said. "Your Mose got me in from the cold. I was trying to do my walk, but the ice storm had another idea."

"It's terrible out there," said Martha. She wiped her feet on the rug by the door as she faced the warm kitchen. It seemed bright against the gray day, ever so welcoming. The air smelled of coffee and cinnamon.

"We'll get you all warmed up in no time. We could see it was getting bad," Collette said. Her wide eyes showed her concern as she faced Martha. "Come, dear.

"Denki." Martha instructed the children to remove their boots, and there was a bit of commotion as they flopped to the floor and shed their outer clothing. It was such a relief to be welcomed there. Such a joy to watch April tug off her boots and help Milo with his coat. They were safe. Gott was good.

Ezra removed his wet jacket and hat and handed them over to Collette. "Sure do appreciate your help."

"We were too far to turn back," Mose explained. "I figured this would be the safest place to ride out the storm."

"You figured right," came the low voice of Bishop Aaron. He stood in the doorway leading to the main room, his reading glasses propped on his head and a copy of an Amish newspaper in his hands. "Ezra, did I hear that you were out walking in this?"

"Poor judgment," Ezra admitted, smoothing down his beard with one hand.

"We'll find you some dry clothes to borrow. In the meantime, make yourselves comfortable. I'm glad you're off the road."

"I'll make us all a cup of tea," Collette offered.

"Let me get the girls to mind the children." The bishop stepped into the main room and called up the stairs. "Suzie. Tess. Come. We have guests." He turned back to the kitchen. "They were about to head out to the pretzel factory, but when we saw the ice, we called off the day's work. I reckon Smitty might close up, anyway."

"And if this gets worse, Madge will close the diner, too," said Mose. "Send everyone home."

"I need to get word to Madge and Polly," Martha said. "They'll be worrying about me."

"I'll call from the phone shanty. Ease their minds," the bishop said.

"I can make the calls, Dat," Mose offered. "It's bound to be a might slippery on the lane out to the shanty."

"I already put the ice clamps on my boots, and I've got a few other calls to make. You tend to the mule. And mind the door to the buggy barn. It was frozen shut this morning."

Just then, Suzie and Tess came bounding into the kitchen, pausing only when they saw the children.

"This is a wonderful good surprise. We have little ones here," said Suzie.

"Not that little," said April. "I'm four."

"So cute." Tess squatted down in front of the children. "Do you like puzzles?"

"Maybe they're too little for puzzles," Suzie said.

"They can learn," Martha said, seeing the longing in April's eyes. Her daughter loved the attention of older children.

"Come on," said Tess. "We've got a puzzle you'll love."

The teenaged girls shepherded the children into the main room, and Ezra followed the bishop upstairs to find dry clothes. Seeing her children settled in the main room, Martha returned to the kitchen.

"I'm going to tend to Sunshine and get the buggy into the barn," Mose said, adjusting the knit cap over his head.

"Denki," Martha told him. "Thank you for taking such good care of us."

He paused and fixed his gaze on her with a look that warmed her and seemed to remind her of what they'd just endured together. "Gott was watching over us," he said, then ducked out into the cold.

"He's a good man," Martha said, as if that were some sort of new discovery. Of course he was. She'd seen nothing but kindness and dedication in the months he'd driven her family.

"Mose is working hard to find his place here in Joyful River," Collette said, taking the whistling kettle off the stove. "Now, have a seat.

"Can I help with something?" Martha asked, touching the back of a wooden chair.

"Nothing to be done," Collette said. "I've got some corn bread left over from this morning, so here we go." She delivered a mug of tea and a golden cube of corn bread to the table. "Do you take milk? Sugar?"

"A little milk, denki." As Martha dipped the teabag a few more times, the bishop passed through, bundled in winter gear. With a few words for his wife, he headed out to the phone shanty.

Martha cupped the warm mug and relaxed as the events of

the morning flashed through her mind, unbidden. The falling ice and slippery roads. The way the buggy had slid along on the frozen pavement. Frightening events, but she didn't experience the usual terror. With Mose by her side, she'd made it through with measured control.

In fact, she felt bolstered by the experience. Strengthened.

When she looked up, Collette was beside her with a container of milk. "You seem to be a thousand miles away."

Martha shook her head. "I was just thinking of how well Mose handled the buggy today. You know, my husband, Ben, died in a roadway crash during an ice storm. Since then, I've been riddled with fear whenever winter weather comes around."

"Of course you're scared. It was a terrible tragedy."

Martha felt Collette move away from the table.

"That road accident rippled through our church and touched us all. My son, Harlan, was friends with Ben, and he still speaks fondly of him."

"That's good to know. Ben deserves to be remembered." The memory of her love for Ben shone like a lantern inside her, a constant flame. But that day was one of the first times that the memory of his death didn't cripple her with fear. "When the ice storm came upon us today, I felt the old panic returning. But Mose told me it would be all right. He had a plan and a determination that made me feel hope. And then, when we came upon Ezra, there was no time for me to worry, with Ezra and the children to tend to."

Collette sat opposite Martha with her own mug of tea. "You were put to the test, and Gott gave you the strength to carry on."

Martha let out the breath she'd been holding and faced Collette. "It's a blessing I never expected. And during such a trying moment."

"Even in our darkest nights, our fiercest trials, Gott is there." Collette spoke with such authority, Martha felt sure she'd suffered many a trial herself. In that moment, Martha took comfort from Gott's support. It was good to know she was not alone.

She'd never been alone.

Even in her deepest moment of sorrow, Gott's love had never wavered.

Chapter 20

"Play cheesy," Milo said as Martha handed him a quarter of a grilled cheese sandwich.

"It's grilled cheese," Martha said. "Don't play with it. Eat it." When it was clear that the storm was going to endure for a while, Martha and Collette had made a lunch of grilled cheese sandwiches and tomato soup for the houseful of family and guests.

"I think he's talking about Parcheesi," Tess said, stirring her soup with a spoon. "We played a few rounds earlier, and afterward, we let Milo play with the pieces. He really likes the yellow ones."

"Cheesy," Milo said with a smile.

"Yah, I played him in a few rounds of cheesy," Mose said, taking a sandwich from the platter. "He beat me, twice."

"You're all so good with children," Martha said, looking around the table at the Troyer family, plus Ezra, who smiled from the end of the table. "We're blessed to be housebound with you."

"It's a day off for us, so we might as well have fun," said Tess.

"We should do some baking this afternoon," Suzie suggested. "Mem, do we have chocolate chips?"

"Mem made heart-shaped cookies," April said. "Hearts show love."

"Heart-shaped cookies! And tomorrow is Valentine's Day." Tess's mouth opened in a round O-shape. "Do we have a heart-shaped cookie cutter? Do you know, Collette?"

"I believe we do."

"That's what we're doing this afternoon." Tess nodded. She was quite the instigator. "Great idea, April."

April smiled, basking in the praise and attention of the older girls.

As talk of other afternoon activities went on, Martha surveyed the lunch table with a wonderful feeling of lightness and warmth. This home, these people brought her such a feeling of joy. Who could have imagined that it could be so much fun to be stuck inside with a family she barely knew?

And stuck they were. After his walk to the phone shanty, Aaron had announced that everything in Joyful River seemed to be shut down for the storm. Madge had been glad to hear that Martha and the children were safe, and she'd promised to get a message to J.R. and Polly Ezra's daughter Heidi had been relieved to learn that her father had been plucked from the roadside.

The bishop had asked Collette to rearrange sleeping arrangements so that the guests could have rooms. "For the next day or so, there's nothing to do but stay warm and enjoy the white landscape Gott has wrought."

The afternoon cookie baking gave Martha a better understanding of the friendship between Suzie and Tess.

"We weren't always sisters," Suzie explained as she carefully pressed a heart-shaped cookie cutter into the smooth dough. "I grew up with my brother, Harlan, and then Mem married Bishop Aaron. Now I have Mose as a second brother, and Tess and Amy as sisters."

"And we do everything together," said Tess. "I don't know how I ever made it through the day without my sister Suzie."

"I went from having two children to having a houseful, with grandchildren nearby," Collette said. "'Twas a wondrous blessing."

Martha smiled. From the light in her eyes to the glow of her skin, Collette shone with happiness. "And where is Amy now?" Martha asked.

"Off with her grandmother," Collette said. "Aaron's mother is in her eighties. Slowing down a bit, but she's not ready to give up her house."

"I hope they're all right in the storm," Martha said.

"They're fine. Dinah doesn't venture out much. A bad hip. But Mose will go and check on them when the roads clear a bit." Collette looked down at the cookie tray. "Are these ready for baking?"

"One more!" April added a wobbly little heart she had shaped by hand, and Collette popped the tray in the oven.

With the last batch baking, Martha headed out to the main room, where Mose was helping Milo build something out of two small blankets and a few books.

"Mem, look! Look!" Milo led her over by the hand and then crawled under one suspended blanket.

"We made a tent," Mose said. "Perfect for hiding and napping."

"I think he's about due for a nap," Martha said.

"I'll take him up." Without hesitation, Mose lifted Milo into his arms and took him up the stairs.

Watching them ascend, Martha sat down on the love seat and contemplated a nap herself. It was so cozy by the potbelly stove. Ezra and the bishop were tending to the animals in the barn, and the girls were in the kitchen, beginning to ice the first batch of cookies.

When Mose returned, he took a seat beside her, and for once, they were alone together. She knew it wouldn't last long, but for now, it was a sweet moment.

"He was asleep before we reached the top of the stairs," he said.

"Denki. For everything."

"No need for thanks. I'm happy you're here." When she looked over at his gentle smile, she felt her resolve melting. This was the perfect time to talk to him, come clean about the mistaken valentine. The small mistake that had led to a lovely exchange of drawings and cards. The romantic interlude that had lifted her spirits. A sweet time that had to end.

But she couldn't. Not here, not now. When this storm was over, when she had to return to her solitary life, she would set things straight.

For now, she kept the bad news at bay as he shuffled the deck of cards in preparation for playing Go Fish.

Dinner was a savory beef stew that simmered in a Dutch pot and filled the air with a hearty aroma. Martha baked hand-dropped biscuits—better to lap up the gravy!—and everyone left the table feeling well-fed and content.

After the children were put to bed, the board game Trouble was set up at the kitchen table. Ezra and Aaron declined and went in by the potbelly stove to chat and read, while Collette sat in the kitchen with her knitting and laughed as Tess and Mose revealed their competitive streaks. A few rounds of Trouble were followed by Monopoly, which Martha hadn't played in months.

In truth, she hadn't had time for much laughter or game

playing since she'd lost Ben. It made the day at the Troyer house that much more special.

It was late when the girls headed upstairs and Collette turned down the big kerosene lamp in the kitchen. Martha was carefully stacking Monopoly dollars and binding them in rubber bands, while Mose collected markers and Chance cards.

"I put your sleeping bag and pillow in your father's office," Collette said. Mose had lost his room to Ezra for the night, while Martha and the children were staying in Amy's room. "But Ezra said you won't disturb him if you need to go in the room. Says he's a heavy sleeper."

"I'm all set," Mose assured her.

"Then I'll say good night." Collette put her knitting in the basket and paused a moment, as if she had something to say. Was she leery of leaving them alone together? It wasn't quite the accepted thing to leave a man and a woman alone—unless they were youth in their rumspringa. Martha didn't want to cause Collette any discomfort, but the moment passed quickly. Collette put her knitting basket on her arm and headed into the shadows and up the stairs.

And then they were alone.

Mose replaced the Monopoly box on the shelf and dropped onto the sofa. "It's late. I should be tired, but my head is still swollen from my big win in Monopoly."

"All those hotels!" She sat on the couch beside him, glad to have this moment alone. "But the girls played well, too. You're lucky to have so many sisters at home. You have all the players you need for cards and games! I don't think I've had this much fun since I was a teen in rumspringa."

"Rumspringa?" He made a sour face. "Now there's a time I'd rather forget. My teen years were full of pursuits far more reckless than board games. I got myself a motorbike and a cell phone."

"I remember seeing you on the motorbike," Martha admitted.

"There were wild weekend parties at Englisch farms and plenty of drinking. I let my chores go, and I spent a lot of time with the Englisch. I was a wild one."

"I remember. I had an eye on you during those years. Of course, I was in love with Ben, but all the girls had little crushes on you. We found you so intriguing, being the bishop's son, and yet, such a reckless one."

Mose raked his hair back and groaned. "Reckless and stupid."

"We were fascinated," she said. "And then you went away." Martha let her head rest back on the couch. "You left Joyful River, disappeared from sight."

"It seemed like the only choice at the time."

"Really?"

"My father and I couldn't see eye to eye, so I left. Ended up in Philadelphia. But you don't want to hear all that."

"Tell me," she insisted. "Please. I've always been curious about how it would be to live with the Englisch."

He told her of his time in Philadelphia. He was an outsider there, though over time he blended in, working hard and making enough to get by. He met some nice people, some not so nice. Overall, he learned that he was a good person, a person worthy of Gott's love. He had never felt that way under the high standards his father had set as a church bishop. In the end, Mose had realized that his integrity and worth as a man would be judged by Gott.

"Which is a complicated way of saying that I settled my mind and came home," Mose admitted.

Martha was awed by his adventure, both physical and emotional. Her life had been a simple one. She'd lived in two Pennsylvania towns, two Amish communities. She'd married a plain man and spent her days cooking and caring for her children. She picked up a heart-shaped cookie. "I'm a simple sugar cookie. Just a few ingredients. But you're much more complicated. A Dutch apple pie."

"Or whoopie pies," he suggested. "Those are my favorites. I love the cream filling."

"My specialty," she admitted. Though she hadn't made them in some time. "Next day off, I'm going to make a batch for you and your family."

"See that?" he said. "I like whoopie pies, and you like to make them. It shows that we belong together."

Her heart sang as he leaned in to kiss her. The contact was fleeting at first, then deeper, warmer. Comforting and promising so much more. Martha's doubts and worries melted away in the heat of their kiss.

Right now, tonight, this is where I am meant to be.

Closing her eyes, she leaned against him and relaxed in the warmth of his arms. Safe and sound and oh so loved.

Chapter 21

The next morning, Mose sensed the change as he stirred in the sleeping bag on the office floor. Things had shifted. His bond with Martha had solidified through their shared experience the day before. The crisis on the road, and then the day of fun and conversation, board games and good food. Had it been only one day? The previous night, when he'd carried Milo up to bed, it had seemed that Martha and the children had been a part of this family for years.

And something else was different. The weather had changed. The cold draft that usually leaked around the living room window shade wasn't bothering him anymore.

He wrestled free of the sleeping bag and raised the shade. It was still dark, but the air was definitely warmer. The thermometer outside the window showed that the temperatures had moved above the freezing mark during the night. The ice that had formed along the top of the fence and bushes was gone. Melted. In an hour or so, the rising sun would finish the job.

Soon they'd no longer be homebound. With mixed feelings, he went into the bathroom to get dressed and then headed out to the barn. As he ventured down the gravel path, the chunks of ice gave way beneath his feet, crumbling to mush. The sky over the distant hills appeared golden as the sun appeared; a sign of a clear day.

"Sunshine!" he called to his mule. "Looks like we're back in business today."

"Happy Valentine's Day!" Suzie and Tess chimed in unison as Mose peeked in the door, pausing at the doorjamb to step out of his muck boots and leave them outside the door.

"Same to you," Mose said casually, pretending the day didn't matter when in truth he was more focused on it this year than ever before. With the commotion from the day before, he hadn't had a moment to finish Martha's final valentine, but he figured there'd be time toward the end of the day.

It warmed his heart to step inside and see Martha and her children seated at the kitchen table along with Collette and his sisters. He longed for a time when they would be part of his family, a part of his home.

"The ice is crumbling fast," he told them. "Dat and Ezra have already hitched Sampson to a buggy. Ezra seemed eager to get going."

"He was up long before dawn," Collette said. "We were hoping you'd give the girls a ride in so that your dat could check on some folks after the storm."

"I can do that."

Over a breakfast of pancakes and bacon, they made a plan for the morning. Mose would drop the children off at Polly's, then continue on into town to take Martha to the restaurant and Suzie and Tess to the pretzel factory. That meant he wouldn't be able to talk openly with Martha in the buggy, but that could wait.

He'd waited this long. But he was determined to have that important talk before the end of the day—Valentine's Day.

* * *

The roads were fine for the morning trip, and the mood in the buggy was lively as Tess and Suzie told stories and taught the children a few songs along the way. Sitting in the front beside Mose, Martha remained quiet but cheerful. As the mule's hooves clip-clopped on the wet road, Mose silently thanked Gott for the chance to get to know her better over the past few days and months.

The children were dropped off at the Lambright home, and then they headed into town. When Mose pulled the buggy into the diner parking lot, he thought of the day when he might be able to kiss Martha goodbye in the morning.

Gott willing, that day was coming soon.

The girls called out their goodbyes to Martha, and then it was a short ride to Smitty's Pretzel Factory.

As Tess reached into the back for her lunch pail, she called out to Mose. "Someone left their lunch back here," she said. "I saw it when we loaded our things in." She came around the side of the buggy and handed him Martha's orange lunch pail.

"It's Martha's," he said. "I'll take it over to her."

He put the lunch box beside him on the seat and then turned the buggy back toward the diner. As Sunny trotted down Main Street, he realized Martha might not want her lunch, as the food had been sitting in the back of his buggy overnight. Well, at least it would be frozen and well-preserved.

When he pulled into the parking lot at the diner, he brought the buggy to a halt and considered the orange lunch box. In all the commotion, he'd completely forgotten to look for a valentine from her. He slid his fingers into the side pocket and found a slender piece of paper. Not a homemade card but a note. A note for him.

> *Dear Mose,*
> *You've been ever so kind, and you are a good*
> *man. Of that I'm sure, and I do appreciate the*

transportation you provide my family most every day. But I must be honest with you and tell the truth. The valentine that you received from me was not intended for you. It's one I made many years ago for my husband, Ben, when we were dating.

The truth is you received the wrong valentine. I'm sorry for the mix-up and I wish you well! I understand that June Hostetler is working on a valentine for you, and I imagine you're on the list for a few Amish maidels!

Best wishes,
Martha

All the air left his body as the message hit him like a physical blow.

So, it had been a mistake.

The wrong valentine?

And what of their exchange of valentines? Their time together? Their conversations? Their kiss? Was he really nothing more to Martha than a hired driver?

Wounded to the core, Mose folded up the note and stuffed it into a pocket. So much for his Amish love. Martha was putting an end to their relationship.

He tipped his head forward and rested his forehead on his fist.

This couldn't be happening. How could she be giving up on the love between them. She was closing the door and wishing him well. Why?

He needed answers. Perhaps the truth would cause him more pain, but it couldn't be worse than the broken heart that was weighing his body down at the moment. There were questions he needed to ask.

Chapter 22

In the diner's kitchen, Martha couldn't help but smile. Although she was going through the usual motions of her day, washing her hands, tying on her apron, and heating up the fryer and the ovens, she felt the difference in her life. It seemed like a normal morning, and yet, in her heart, everything had changed. Out of the blue, she had found this man who cared for her, and she cherished the moments with him. After so many lonely days and nights, she felt . . . loved. Truly loved. The thought of spending more time with Mose filled her with joy.

Having arrived a bit earlier than usual, she was alone in this part of the kitchen, but she didn't mind getting started on her own. Humming one of the silly songs the children had been learning, she took out a large stainless-steel bowl and turned to fetch her seasoning ingredients from the shelves when he entered the kitchen.

"Mose . . ." She was happy and surprised to see him, but her delight faded when she saw the strain on his face.

"The wrong valentine?" He shook his head, a wounded look in his eyes. "So you never really cared for me?"

Confusion swirled, and then she saw him put her lunch pail on the counter. There was a folded paper in his hand. The letter she had written to him. "Oh no. You found the note?"

He nodded.

"No, Mose, I didn't mean that. I—"

"When you got my drawings, you didn't know who they were from?"

"I didn't, but they were wonderful. I looked forward to them each day."

"Drawings from a stranger?"

"Valentines from a mystery man. It was so charming." She bit her bottom lip. "Your drawings got me through a hard spell."

"Until you found out they were from me and that ended the charm."

"Mose . . . no." She covered her eyes with her hands, needing a way to explain herself clearly. "When I wrote that note, things were . . ." She lowered her hands and felt breathless at his stern gaze. "Well, different."

"It was only days ago."

"I know, I'm sorry. I wish I could explain what was going through my head then, but it's complicated. I mean, when I got your first drawing—the first valentine I'd gotten in forever—my spirits soared. And then, day after day, your drawings won me over, and the sentiments were so sweet and caring. Maybe I was foolish, but it felt so wonderful to be loved again. I mean, I knew it wasn't real love, but your notes made me feel happy and cared for. I felt like you saw me for who I was, and you appreciated me."

He looked down. "I did. I do." He looked at the note and refolded it. "But you responded. You made valentines for me, not knowing that I was the person receiving them."

"It was sort of a game. A secret valentine. I was making

valentines for the person illustrating the drawings. I felt such a connection."

"Until you learned it was me."

"Oh, Mose . . ." Martha frowned, not sure how to explain herself. She had to be truthful with him; lying was wrong, and a good relationship had to be based on truth. But she didn't want to admit that she had dismissed him when she learned his identity. Part of her had thought he was still the daring rebel who'd left town years ago, and she'd thought of herself as being an obedient, prudent Amish woman.

A boring Amish widow. Old before her time. Too experienced and wise to befriend the younger girls she worked with. In a way, she'd thought herself better than Mose. Better than the giggle girls, who ran through the kitchen and delighted in new-fallen snow.

"I made a terrible mistake." She drew in a steadying breath. She needed to tell him everything, own up to being a prideful person. And then, maybe, he would forgive her and they could start anew. "I'm so sorry, but—"

"Martha?" Madge Lambright popped into the kitchen with her usual bustle of energy. "I'm so glad you're early. I don't know if you realize it, but it's Valentine's Day, and we always get an extra-large dinner crowd. Folks like to eat out. We'll need to prep a few extra trays of chicken."

Martha drew in a shaky breath and nodded. "I'll take care of it."

"Denki." Madge turned and nodded at Mose. "And I've got a task for you, if you have time later. We need to pick up an order of milk from the Lapp Dairy Farm. Their truck driver couldn't get through in the ice storm yesterday."

"I can handle that for you," he said.

There was an awkward moment, during which Martha waited for Madge to go. This was her work time, yes, but she was in the middle of an important conversation. Couldn't Madge sense that?

"Okay, then," Madge said, drawing in a breath.

"I've got to go," Mose said, looking up at the wall clock. "My grandmother needs help."

"Mose, wait," Martha said. "I need to explain."

"No need," he said coldly. "I got the message."

"But . . ." Hope drained from her as he walked stiffly from the kitchen. "Mose!" she called after him, but he didn't stop. He was gone before she could close the terrible gap between them.

Chapter 23

Mose had hoped to clear his head during the ride to his grandmother's house, but by the time he arrived there, he was more confused than ever.

The wrong valentine. Martha's cards hadn't been meant for him. She'd fallen for some mystery person—not him.

He parked the buggy, removed a bag of groceries, and took a deep breath. He would need to stay steady, or else his grandmother would know something was up. She always knew.

He rapped on the side door, then pushed it open. "It's me, Mose," he said, wiping his boots on the bristle rug.

"Come in!" His mammi sat at the kitchen table, her walker nearby. "Do you want some breakfast? A cup of tea?" Although Dinah Troyer had seemed to diminish in size over the past few years, there was no mistaking the quick intelligence in her eyes.

"I'm good. I brought you eggs and milk," he said, putting the items into the refrigerator.

"Perfect timing, 'cause we're out of eggs," Amy said from

the sink. "I just finished the dishes. Soon as I sweep up, can you give me a ride to work?"

"Sure." He was heading back to town, anyway. He needed to get his friend Dennis to come to the diner to fulfill that promise to June. Mose went to take a seat at the kitchen table, but his grandmother waved a hand, stopping him. "While your sister is sweeping, I have a few tasks for you."

He forced a smile. A bad day was quickly getting worse.

After he cleared a clog in the bathroom sink, tightened the railing along the stairs, and moved some serving dishes down from the high cupboards, Dinah beckoned him to the table.

"Come. Sit. Tell me what's eating at you."

He sighed and took a seat. "It's a confusing situation, Mammi, and there's nothing you can do to fix it."

She shrugged. "But I give very good advice."

This much was true. And Mose liked that she didn't pressure him to work harder or find an Amish wife. Instead, she told him stories that usually had a moral. Other tales were simply amusing. "The problem is, I've fallen for someone, but she doesn't feel the same way."

"That's a shame. But maybe she doesn't know you. Give it time."

"She knows me, all right," he said. "That's the problem."

"Time cures all, you know that. If it weren't for patience, I wouldn't have been able to marry your grandfather, the love of my life." Her hand shook slightly as she smoothed over the vinyl tablecloth. "I wish you'd had a chance to know him better."

"I have some memories of Dawdi. How he'd come in from the outside smelling of fresh-mowed hay and the oil used on the harvester. How he loved to smoke a pipe and tell all of us grandchildren stories. He loved to tell the one about how his grandparents came to America on a big boat."

"Across the Atlantic Ocean." She nodded. "He loved that

old nugget. I'm glad you remember him, Mose. My Bud was a good man, and I thank Gott that he was a patient man, too. You see, he had to wait out my parents. They assumed I would marry the son of their good friends. What was the boy's name, now? Floyd? No, Lloyd. Lloyd Herschberger, and he was nice enough. But when we were together, there was no bubble and fizz. No joy between us." She shook her head. "Like flat soda pop."

Mose smiled. "And with Dawdi?"

"Plenty of bubbles," she admits. "Like a roiling boil. My point is, I've seen the way that June Hostetler is being pushed on you. A nice enough girl, but don't settle. Wait until you meet the girl who makes your heart bubble over."

"And what if I've met her but she doesn't feel the same way?"

"Well, then, you must court her. Don't be a pest but do be persistent. Let her know the way true love feels; remind her that you'll climb the highest mountain for her. And have patience. Good things come to those who wait."

"Ach, Mammi." He tipped his head back and stared at the ceiling. "There are so many obstacles. It's a complicated situation."

"And that's going to stop you?" She shooed the notion away. "No one ever said love was easy."

Chapter 24

A frantic sense of loss had chilled Martha ever since Mose had walked out. She felt doomed, seeing the end of her hopes, her happiness, her chance at love.

The only consolation was this familiar place, the diner kitchen, where her movements were familiar and easy, like a song that she knew by heart.

A very sad song, she thought as she pushed herself to press on, trimming the chicken pieces, filling vats with the buttermilk marinade, rolling drumsticks and thighs in Madge's special seasoned crumbs.

As Martha worked, the giggle girls came through with tales of excitement about their finished valentines. June also had an exciting prospect to report: she was going to have a Valentine's Day date. A fella had made that promise to her, and she was holding him to it.

In response, Martha hugged her belly, hoping that this day would end soon.

Sometime after the lunch rush, Madge wheeled in a small cart loaded with a few crates. "Mose brought the milk delivery.

Just so you know, there're two cases of buttermilk here. It wouldn't do to run out!"

Martha simply nodded and left her station to help Madge load the buttermilk into the walk-in cooler—a task that Mose usually handled.

"He's avoiding me," Martha said.

"What? Who?"

"Mose."

Madge nodded. "I sensed that something was going on." She sighed. "Men can be so hard to read. You should go talk to him. He's in the restaurant, sitting at the lunch counter."

"Maybe later," she said, mostly to get Madge off her back. She couldn't bear to see him now. She just couldn't . . .

But as the minutes wore on, she couldn't stay away. She had to see him. She needed another chance to explain. She popped a tray of chicken into the oven and headed down the hall.

The hallway seemed to be a mile long. She quickly passed the laughing girls in the lunchroom and then paused at the entrance to the dining area.

There he was, talking with June. His eyes seemed soulful and sympathetic as he looked across the counter at the waitress. It was clear that he really cared for June.

June, who was setting up her Valentine's Day date. Obviously, with Mose.

It was too late for Martha. He'd already moved on.

Not that she blamed him.

There'd been so many times in the past few months when she should have seen what was going on. The way he cajoled the children, showing them how to look at the positive side. The tender love he showed when they were tired or sad. His patient and dutiful service of their little family, greeting them each morning and evening with an encouraging smile and constant support.

Mose had shown his love in many ways, and she'd been

blind to it. She'd clung so hard to the husband and memories of the past that she'd been unable to open her arms to the future. And now that her eyes had finally been opened, it was too late.

Her face hot with sorrow, she stepped out of the main dining room and ducked behind the wall before Mose could see her.

She was so crushed. So disappointed with herself. Her throat was thick, and she was on the verge of tears. She had to get away.

Moving quickly, she bolted down the center hallway. Flying past the break room and kitchen, she raced to the back door and flung it open and stepped out into the cold.

"What have I done?" she whispered, pressing her face to her hands and leaning over the railing. She'd been a selfish, proud fool . . . such a fool. And now she'd lost a chance at love, the love of a very good Amish man.

Crossing her arms against the cold, she tried not to think of him, not at that moment, when she needed to go back to work soon. But when she closed her eyes, she saw his face . . . eyes that warmed her with kindness and patience, and a smile that could make her melt clear down to her toes. She'd be happy for the chance to look into his face morning, noon, and night. To see the love-light in his eyes and laugh along with his jokes.

But it was not to be.

Martha opened her eyes as a small sob escaped her throat. Here she was, her heart aching and breaking from a surprising new love on this Valentine's Day. It hurt, but she would have to deal with that later. She had work to do—chickens to fry and mouths to feed. And she couldn't face her coworkers in an emotional state.

As she took a deep breath and swiped at her eyes, she heard the door being shoved open behind her.

"There you are!" Nella's voice was squeaky as a chipmunk behind her. "You're needed in the lunchroom."

Martha swallowed hard before turning to the younger girl. "The lunchroom? What's that about?"

"It's a surprise and I can't tell you, but . . ." Nella's brows hardened as she got a glimpse of Martha's face. "You've been crying? Oh, Martha, what's wrong?"

"It's my own fault, my own doing. I had a secret valentine, a wonderful fella, but now I've ruined it all."

"A secret valentine? That's so romantic!"

"It was. Before I hurt him."

"What did you do?" Nella's eyes shone with concern. "Maybe he'll forgive you?"

Fresh tears filled Martha's eyes. "It's too late."

"Aw! I'm so sorry! I wish I could help." Nella rubbed her arm like a consoling parent.

Martha took a calming breath. "You are helping."

"I wish I could help more. But actually, the surprise might make you feel better. At least, I think it will. Come. You'll see."

Pushing through her reluctance, Martha followed Nella down the hall to the break room, where Bonnie and Sara stood with big smiles lighting their faces, their hands hidden behind their backs.

"Surprise!" they chimed in unison, flashing colorful papers at her.

"Happy Valentine's Day!" Nella picked up a handmade card from the table and held it under her chin. "We made valentines for you!"

"It was the least we could do, after all you taught us," Sara added.

"And you taught us that everyone deserves to get a valentine," Bonnie said. "Especially a friend like you."

Martha's hand moved to her chest as emotion swelled there. A friend? She had always seen herself as being beyond friendship with these girls, too old and wise, but was that true? She'd been wrong about so many things.

"This is so sweet of you all," Martha said, looking from one girl to the other. "So kind."

"Aw, you deserve it more than anyone here." Sara stepped forward to rub Martha's arm. "You work so hard, but still, you found time to teach us how to make valentines."

"And when we heard you talking to Madge about all the stuff you have to do at home, the wood chopping and taking care of your children. And how Milo had a fever and how you had to prepare meals for your parents' visit and all . . ." Nella was babbling on, but Martha was stunned by the information she'd soaked up. "We just never realized how full your plate is. All the things you have to do. And we want to help."

"We can help with your children," Bonnie said. "We have brothers and sisters of our own, so we all know how to mind them."

"And anything else," Nella insisted. "Cooking, cleaning . . ." She shrugged. "The boring stuff can be fun if we do it together."

"Denki." Martha felt on the verge of crying again, but this time, they were happy tears. "You girls have made this a wonderful Valentine's Day." She went around the group to give them each a hug, then everyone talked at once as the girls shared their valentines with her. The large pink satin rose on Nella's valentine was beautiful. The delicate snowflake cut from white paper overlaid Sara's creation. And Bonnie's card revealed colorful hearts, cut in various sizes and layered upon each other.

"They're all so beautiful." Martha couldn't help but smile. "You girls are so creative! But they're truly special because they come from you."

"From the heart," Nella said. "And made with love."

Chapter 25

Back in the kitchen, Martha returned to her cooking with a new resolve. The sweet kindness and support of the girls had helped her see that she was surrounded by folks who loved her on this Valentine's Day. She was so fortunate! She had to thank Gott for all the love in her life.

She felt bolstered but also resigned to a loss for now. It had hurt, seeing Mose with June. But from what she knew of Mose, she didn't think that relationship would last—not if he stayed true to himself. Valentine's Day would be over at midnight, but love was a powerful thing any time of year. She would try to continue their relationship, earn his trust again. As she slid a tray of chicken into the oven, she was dreaming up new valentines to make for Mose. Quaint little sayings that might touch him, or jokes to make him laugh. Who said that little cards and notes had to end on Valentine's Day?

With a bit of time before she needed to prepare the next batch, she wanted a cup of tea. But she wasn't sure she was ready to head out to the dining room to fetch it, considering the risk of seeing Mose with June again. She took off her apron and peered down the hallway toward the dining room, nodding as Sara passed her.

"Mose is looking for you," Sara said, carrying a bus pan into the kitchen.

Martha's heart ached at the prospects of what he might say, but she knew she needed to face him. She set her shoulders back and proceeded to the dining room, where she immediately noticed June still lingering at the counter and flirting. Oh, that June. But the young man talking with her wasn't Mose. It was Dennis, the Amish grocer's son.

That surprised her. And from the way Dennis's gaze was fixed on June, the attraction was clear.

Nella came by with a pitcher of water and leaned in to whisper: "Do you see that? Mose fixed them up for Valentine's Day." She shot a look at Dennis and June. "I hope this one sticks. June so wants a beau!"

Martha took in a breath, letting it soak in. So Mose wasn't interested in June. Of course not. Martha's jealousy had been unfounded. She turned toward the tables and saw Mose seated at a window, beckoning her. Her heart swelled at the sight of him as she approached.

"Have a seat," he said.

When she shook her head, he explained, "I cleared it with Madge. She said the table is ours for fifteen minutes, and I'd like you to hear me out."

She nodded and sat down, feeling awkward around him. She had to clear the air. "Mose, I'm sorry you found that letter. When I wrote it, my head was in a different place, and I was holding myself back. Not just from you, but from everyone. Even the kitchen girls here, Sara, Nella, and Bonnie."

"The giggle girls?"

"They made valentines for me, Mose. They want to be my friend, and I've always pushed them away, thinking I was too old and wise for them." She stared down at the table. "Turns out I'm not wise at all. And it only took one ice storm, one night in your home in the midst of your loving family to see what a fool I've been. I was so stuck on your wild reputation I didn't see that you are a responsible man. You got us through that ice storm. You saved Ezra, too. Your care for us has never wavered. Over the weeks and months, I've fallen for you, Mose. I was too stuck in my widow's mindset to let you in."

"You were busy being a mother of two children, trying to make your way. I understand that. And I want to be a part of it."

"Still?" She looked up. "Even after the letter? After everything I did to push you away?"

He opened his hands on the table and smiled. "I'm still here. Here to stay."

She reached out to him, and her hands felt small and safe in his hearty grip. "I'm sorry that I've kept you waiting this long."

"True love is worth waiting for."

True love! Her heart soared with the knowledge that it was all real. Not just a secret, imaginary valentine who had won her heart. She and Mose had fallen for each other day by day, one heartbeat at a time. She simply hadn't recognized it until the valentine mishap.

"I know you have to get back to work," he said. "But I wanted to ask if you'd let me bring you dinner on your next night off? A sort of belated Valentine's celebration. We can include the children."

"I would love that!" She smiled, her heart full of joy. "And can you bring one of your drawings? I think the children will love them."

He nodded. "I'll make valentine drawings for everyone. The *right* valentines."

Please read on for an excerpt
from Shelley Shepard Gray's next Amish romance,
A Is for Amish.

He renews my strength. He guides me along the right paths, bringing honor to His name.
—Psalm 23:3

A happy home is not merely having a roof over your head but having a foundation under your feet.
—Amish proverb

Chapter 1

It had been a while since they'd all been in one car together. Since each of his siblings lived in different suburbs and hamlets around the Cleveland area, whenever the four of them did get together, it was easiest to simply meet at a restaurant for a quick bite to eat.

This day was different, though.

Even though Martin was the oldest boy and the one driving, he felt just as nervous as his younger brother, Jonny. He held the steering wheel in a death grip, and worst-case scenarios kept running through his head.

What in the world were they thinking about doing? Had they lost their ever-loving minds?

"You okay up there, Martin?" Kelsey asked.

"Yeah, why?"

"Oh, I don't know. Maybe because you've been wearing a permanent frown for the last ten miles."

338 / Shelley Shepard Gray

Kelsey, all curly blond hair and blue eyes, was the closest to him in age. She was twenty-two to his twenty-three—except for two months during the year. Then they were the same age. Beth was the oldest at twenty-five, and Jonny the youngest at twenty.

"Have I been frowning? I didn't realize it."

"You sure are," Jonny said. "And the reason I noticed is because I've been frowning just as much. Guys, I can't believe we're actually thinking about doing this."

Even though he'd been just thinking the very thing, Martin felt obligated to calm his brother's worries. "Remember, all we're doing is thinking about this. Don't forget, if we change our minds this afternoon, no one will even know. Especially not Mommi and Dawdi."

"They know something's up with us," Beth chimed in from the passenger seat next to him. "Mommi sounded pretty skeptical when I told her that the four of us want to pay them a visit because we haven't seen them in a while."

"Has it really been that long since any of us went to visit?" Kelsey asked.

"I saw them around Easter," Beth said. "None of you could make it." Just as it did when they were all in elementary school, her voice carried a hint of criticism.

Martin groaned. "Don't act like I blew you off. I told you that I was stuck going to Cara's parents' house with her."

"I didn't say you blew me off, Martin." Her voice softened. "I am sorry that you two broke up."

"I thought she broke up with you, Martin," Jonny said.

She had. He hadn't tried to change her mind, though. He'd met Cara at work and had thought the snarky comments she made behind their customers' backs meant that she was fun. He'd soon found out that she was simply mean.